T0068056

DANCING

IN THE

DESERT

DANCING
— IN THE —
DESERT

NEDRA J. BURCH

ARCHWAY
PUBLISHING

Copyright © 2016 Nedra J. Burch.

All rights reserved. No part of this book may be used or reproduced by any means,
graphic, electronic, or mechanical, including photocopying, recording, taping or by
any information storage retrieval system without the written permission of the author
except in the case of brief quotations embodied in critical articles and reviews.

Archway Publishing books may be ordered through booksellers or by contacting:

Archway Publishing
1663 Liberty Drive
Bloomington, IN 47403
www.archwaypublishing.com
1 (888) 242-5904

Because of the dynamic nature of the Internet, any web addresses or links contained in
this book may have changed since publication and may no longer be valid. The views
expressed in this work are solely those of the author and do not necessarily reflect the
views of the publisher, and the publisher hereby disclaims any responsibility for them.

Any people depicted in stock imagery provided by Thinkstock are models,
and such images are being used for illustrative purposes only.
Certain stock imagery © Thinkstock.

ISBN: 978-1-4808-2693-9 (sc)
ISBN: 978-1-4808-2694-6 (e)

Library of Congress Control Number: 2016900901

Print information available on the last page.

Archway Publishing rev. date: 2/22/2016

A special thanks to special friends:

Twila, you are one in a million and I thank you from my heart. May God continue to bless you and yours.

Sylvia and Alvaro, thanks you for sharing your expertise with me. Blessings on you and yours too.

This book is dedicated to all who have Dreamed and lost. May you find your Rainbow.

Desert Dancing

Across the dry and dusty lands
They swirl and skim – turbulent sands.
Sometimes one, sometimes two or three
Like unleashed spirits – wild and free.
Joining forces at a whim
Across the ground they quickly skim.
Devils of Dust in the desert abound
Dancing along without a sound.
Suddenly, they disappear
Leaving no sign that they were here!

PROLOG

Clare watched the sun sink behind the distant mountains. The colors were breathtaking! Her mother used to call them, "sky-blue pink." She could never see a sunset where the clouds turned an iridescent orange/pink without remembering her mother's description of the colors. She shook her head in disgust as she thought about the absurdity of that color, *sky-blue pink*. It didn't exist.

She picked up her teacup as she got up from the small dining table, carried it to the stainless-steel sink, rinsed it, and carefully placed it in the dish drainer perched inside the companion sink. She looked around the small mobile home and smiled a sad forlorn smile.

"A big difference in living arrangements here," she said to herself. She thought for a minute of the up-to-date designer apartment she'd left in Portland. There she had all the most modern kitchen appliances, stylish and comfortable furniture and once a week maid service.

Considering the age of the 14 x 60 foot mobile home, it was in exceptional condition; a small screened-in back porch, a massive front porch leading to an additional bedroom with a private entrance. A new tin roof and carpeting made a cozy comfortable dwelling. She considered herself fortunate to have found a place that was nicely furnished, clean and up-to-date in the outback of New Mexico. It made her decision to move much easier. She'd only had to buy household items to settle comfortably into her small hideaway home.

She strolled into the bedroom where the queen-sized bed took up over half of the available space. Slipping off her Birkenstocks, she sat on the bed and looked around at the clutter on the dresser and chest of drawers as she snuggled down onto the well-worn rose-covered comforter she'd shipped from Portland to her new home. The old comforter was faded and worn but it was a link with her old life. Ever since the *accident* she had been trying to regain the feeling of safety and security she'd know those months before the 2006 Portland Rose Festival. As she settled herself on top of the worn comforter, she realized how tired she was. It was naptime. Some days the heat and dryness of the desert just seemed to drain her. Of course, staying up until the wee small hours might have something to do with her afternoon sleepiness too. She had forsaken the use of sleeping aids when she first arrived at her new home. After what had seemed forever, she was ready to return to life without crutches both figuratively and literally!

The residents of the small community of Animas wondered who their neighbor really was; she drove a new SUV and, although she made almost daily trips to the post office and frequent stops at the single convenience store and small café, she was none too friendly. The only way they even knew her name was that it was imprinted on the debit card she used to pay for her purchases: Clare Smith.

CHAPTER 1

Clare heard the clang of food carts coming down the hallway, their rubber wheels making squeaking noises on tile floors. It was an irritating noise. The cart stopped just outside her door but she knew there would be no food tray delivered to her room. She had tubes to provide any nourishment she needed.

The door to her room was cracked and if her eyes had been open, she would have seen the nurse and the orderly stop, exchange brief words, look toward her room and sadly shake their heads. But her eyes weren't open and she didn't seem to be able to make them open.

She heard the nurse come into the room, her rubber-soled shoes made a squeaky sound just like the wheels on the carts that they pushed up and down the hallways all day. It seemed that the only sounds that penetrated her head were squeaking shoes and rubber balloon tires.

The nurse dutifully walked to the myriad of monitors parked next to her bed and made notes of the appropriate readings, she checked the IV bags and adjusted the drip then she checked the tubes and needles to be sure they were flowing properly, and that the needles hadn't slipped. She looked down at the body in the bed.

"Oh, girl, why don't you wake up? Doc says you should be waking up."

Clare heard what the nurse said clearly. She fought to open her eyes. She wanted to speak but words wouldn't come.

The nurse finished her routine charting and turned to leave; she didn't see her patient's eyes flicker to life. She didn't see the pleading look emanating from them, begging to be noticed as the she walked through the partially open door. She didn't see the tear.

Clare closed her eyes again. She was tired. Her head felt numb. She could feel the tubes in her nose helping her breathe; could sense the needles in her arm where the glucose dripped, and even the sensation of the stomach tube where life-sustaining fluids were pumped into her body. She didn't actually *know* how many tubes and needles were attached but she knew they were there.

It seemed like no time had passed when Clare woke again. In actuality, it had been hours, but there was no concept of time in her foggy mind. The IVs were still dripping, the blood pressure cuff regularly inflating and measuring, and the "beep-beep" of the heart monitors steadily recording her rate and rhythm. Again, she managed to force her eyes open. This time the light wasn't as painful as it had been earlier; she managed to focus on some of the images in the semi-dark room.

It was a hospital room to be sure. The sanitary look was as apparent as the odor of antiseptic. She was more acutely aware of the tubes invading her nose, neck and stomach. She could make out the bank of windows covering most of the outside wall; could see the mini-blind covered windows allowing just a few thin strips of sunlight to sneak through. There were flowers, many with their wilted heads hanging, spaced neatly along the wide marble window sill. The green potted plants brightened the scene but made the dying flowers look even more pitiful in comparison.

She turned her head slightly to look at the bedside table. It was empty. She forced her eyes upward, saw the pole holding plastic bags of what she knew must be glucose and saw the tubing snaking toward her immobile arm. She moved her hand. The IV was inserted in a vein on the top of the hand. It stung as she wiggled her fingers. She tried to see the monitor registering her blood pressure and heartbeats, but turning her head to the left seemed impossible. She breathed a heavy sigh. At least she had her eyes open. She forced herself to look around the room again, taking in the tile floor and the partially open door this time. Then she closed her eyes again. A smile played about her lips.

The sound of voices brought her around again. She had no idea what the period was between her short bursts of wakefulness but she knew she was awake and aware of her surroundings. She listened to the voices. They were still in the hallway but just outside of the door.

"I know it is a miracle that she has survived at all but how much longer till she wakes up?"

"That is entirely up to her. We've done all we can for now. Her brain seems undamaged according to the EEG. We have repaired the damages to her jaw and it is healing exceptionally fast. Thank God, that bullet didn't go into her head at any other angle! She is indeed a miracle. She should be waking up any time now. Just be patient a little longer."

The door slowly opened and just as slowly, as though linked to the door, her eyes opened.

"CLARE! You're awake! Oh, thank God. Doctor, she's awake."

From the bed, she saw the tall exhausted man react joyously as she turned her eyes toward him. She recognized her father as he turned and shouted down the hallway. Turning from the door, he came quickly toward her bed. He had tears in his eyes.

The next thing she knew her room was filled with hospital personnel. A heavyset, balding man who was obviously her doctor, two nurses who hovered over her as he shined his little light into her eyes and listened to her heart.

"Clare," he asked, "do you hear me?"

She tried to nod her head but wasn't sure if it moved. It felt like it was huge. It hurt to try to move it. She moved her lips and sound came out but her mouth refused to respond to the mental demand to move and speak and she felt a sharp pain in her jaw area. She persisted in the attempt to speak and was at last rewarded as a squeaky noise was forced through her barely open mouth.

"Yes." Her voice was barely discernible but everyone in the room had seemed to hear it. Every face in the room was immediately plastered with a smile and tears crept out of eyes. A unanimous sigh of relief could be heard.

"Okay, everyone out. We don't want to tire her. Get lab in here to take some blood samples and bring me some liquid. We'll see if she can swallow; this is a milestone, move now, ASAP!"

The doctor turned to the man as he issued his order. "Well, Alex, looks like our prayers have been answered. We have your girl back. It'll take a couple days to see how impaired she might be, but she's on the road to recovery. It is such a miracle she is alive at all!"

"Thanks, Guy," said her father as he came nearer to her and took her free hand. "Clare, thank God. We've been so worried."

Clare smiled at him and nodded her head slightly. It hurt to move it, but not as badly as it had earlier. She looked from him to the doctor. "Could I have a drink," she mumbled. Her voice was soft and weak, but both men heard her.

"You can try to sip from this straw. Your jaw is still wired so it won't be possible to open your mouth very wide. Just sip slowly and try to swallow, take it slowly now. There is also a feeding tube. Just take it slowly. Sip." The doctor lowered a straw to her lips and she sipped from a plastic cup. It was the first liquid to pass her lips in several days but Clare didn't know that.

During the next two days, activity in the room was continuous. Various technicians were in and out. Physical therapists came and went. The feeding tube was removed and liquid feeding commenced. As soon as she was able to swallow liquids more easily and open her mouth enough to allow her to be spoon fed, her diet was upgraded to "soft;" she enjoyed tasting the normally undesirable hospital food. Circulation boots were removed from her legs; she was allowed, urged, to sit up on the bed, to walk around the room, with an orderly on each side of her. She recognized her visitors, Alex, Tina, Margaret and Aaron, Markie and Steve and spoke to each one of them. They didn't talk about the "accident." They just marveled in her recovery.

Days began to blur in her mind. It was routine; blood tests, breakfast, shower, a trip to physical therapy where she walked on a tread mill, lunch, a nap, visitors, the daily doctor's visit and pep talk, dinner and evening visiting hours. Clare began to feel like she was a caged animal.

A week after her she regained consciousness; she was transferred to the hospital's rehabilitation wing. Here she began the long and tedious task of restoring mental abilities and physical control of her body.

Clare Smith's recovery was definitely one for the records. Few people survived a bullet wound to the head and those who did usually had significant and long-lasting injuries; both mental and physical. While Clare did have minor paralysis in her right leg, it did not greatly impair her ability to ambulate. She walked a little slowly and at times her foot seemed to drag and caused a slight limp which became more obvious when she walked for longer periods of time.

Her speech patterns were not affected at all, although learning to talk again was a usual task confronting those with head injuries similar to hers. Had the damage to her head been greater, caused by a larger caliber bullet or the entry deeper into her skull, Clare's recovery would have been much harder and her treatments more difficult. There were times when she found herself searching for a word but on the whole she had no problems with speech or memory. She continually amazed the doctors and therapists

"I'm ready to get out of here," she confided to Steve, her fiancée, several weeks after being transferred to the rehab center. "I can walk on a tread mill at home and get much better food, even if it is frozen dinners!"

"That is the best thing I've heard in weeks. I'll talk to Alex and see what he can do. He seems to have Dr. Gruyere tied around his little finger."

"As well he should," Clare commented. "I think he donated enough money to the hospital to fund almost the entire neurosurgical suite."

"Well, it was something he felt was necessary. He really delved into the neurosurgical thing while studying about your type of injury."

"I'm sure" was Clare's noncommittal reply. She had been thoroughly schooled as to how fortunate she had been that the bullet Myra, her step-mother, shot at her had only done minor damage to her skull and shattered her jawbone. By rights, according to Dr. Gruyere, she should have died. Instead, she just had the slight limp, and some weakness in her hands and legs. They had been able to reconstruct the damaged jaw and her only reminder of the incident would be a small scar where the bullet skimmed her head. Any residual motor damage he believed would improve with time and continued exercise. There had been no actual entry into the head by the small caliber shell.

As for the excruciating headaches, which came on suddenly and left as fast, he also thought they'd diminish and disappear eventually. Alternatively, they'd get much worse and lead to seizures, but he didn't tell her that. He only told her the positive things, the worrisome things he saved for her father's ears only.

Alex Goforth, multi-millionaire, was so relieved at his daughter's recovery that he would have built an entire hospital if Guy, Dr. Gruyere, had asked for it. He harbored guilt that Clare had been the victim of his wife's jealousy and vowed that he would do everything and anything to see that for the rest of her life she lived in comfort, safety and security.

His wife, Myra, was securely tucked away at a posh convalescent home. It really didn't matter to her if it was luxurious or not. She lived in her own semi-catatonic state paying no attention to her surroundings. She ate little, talked not at all, and her health declined daily. Her once luminous beauty had faded and she was only a shell of the bubbling beauty that had once captured Alex's heart and given him two wonderful children. It tore his heart out to think of her condition now. But he still had Clare and that made up for the loss of Myra.

Sometimes it was hard for Alex to overpower the depression that lived on the brink of his mind. Why, he wondered had he been so unlucky in love?

★ ★ ★ ★ ★

Myra had seemingly been every man's dream girl. She had beauty, culture and talent; she was fun, generous and wealthy in her own right. It wasn't until after their marriage that signs of serious mental illness became apparent.

He had met Rose, Clare's mother, on a trip to Portland. His marriage was over as far as he was concerned. He had left Myra in the care of a psychiatrist who saw more of her than he did. Rose was assigned to help with restoration work on the Goforth Mansion and they began to work long hours together selecting colors and fabrics needed to bring the long-neglected estate back to its once glamorous state. Alex held a professional respect for Rose and slowly it developed into more than just respect and more than professional! It seemed they were made for each other.

Rose had been raised in Portland by an aunt, who they learned a generation later, was not the person she purported to be. Rose was kind, honest and beautiful. It was easy for them to fall in love and their one wonderful night together had resulted in Clare.

Alex didn't regret the time that he had spent with Rose. What he did regret, to some point, was his decision to give Myra one more chance in his life when, after his return to Boston, she seemed to have finally overcome her illness with the help of counseling and medication.

He broke off his short-lived relationship with Rose, not knowing that their one night of unleashed passion had resulted in her pregnancy. By the time he learned about that, Myra was also expecting a child. He was torn between the two women, but Myra held the ace in the hole.

The key to keeping him in their marriage was his son Aaron and, of course, the newly conceived child. She refused to give Alex a divorce unless he gave full custody of their son and the new baby to her! Alex couldn't sacrifice his children for Rose even though it meant giving up the child Rose was carrying. Should he have made a different choice? He'd struggled for twenty years over that question.

When Myra traveled back to Portland with Alex and became lady of the house they did have a good life; except for frequent barbs that Myra threw at Alex reminding him of his "indiscretion" with Rose which she had figured out via "woman's intuition." Alex was pleased at the thought of another child and prayed that it was a sign that Myra's mental problems were, indeed, a thing of the past so he ignored her barbed remarks about Rose and never actually told her the full story of their relationship.

When he had first learned about Rose's pregnancy, he offered financial help but she refused his offers. When she could no longer continue to work and had exhausted all other resources, she was forced to accept his help. Eventually he bought a cozy house for her and the child with the understanding that the house was not hers but the baby's. She refused to allow Alex to put his name on the birth certificate but she couldn't keep him from the hospital when the baby was born; couldn't deny him the experience of holding his first daughter.

Three years later when Rose met and married David Smith, Alex stayed in the background but always maintained contact with Rose and followed Clare's progress as she grew up. He knew about David's death, and made sure that Rose and his daughter never wanted for anything by arranging for a monthly check supposedly as a payment from an insurance policy David held. Rose never knew that the policy was backed by the Goforth Estate. Rose's health was precarious and Alex wanted to be available to step in if the need ever arose. It did when Rose suddenly died shortly after Clare graduated from high school.

As previously agreed when Clare was born, Alex's attorney contacted Clare after her mother's death and gave her the letter written years before that revealed her father's identity. A meeting was arranged, and after that, Clare became a member of the Alexander Goforth family.

Clare got along well with her siblings and began living on the edge of Portland elite society. All her dreams were coming true, family, money, education and love. It was indeed a Cinderella story - Myra was the evil stepmother.

Mentally unbalanced Myra had seemed to accept Clare, but a resurgence of her psychotic mental illness resulted in a night of terror with tragic results for the entire Goforth family.

Now, miraculously, Clare was recovering but had lost enthusiasm for life. Alex's family was scattered, each one attempting to pick up the pieces of their own lives. Alex, who had aged overnight, lost interest in everything except his hobby – roses.

CHAPTER 2

Thanks to Steve and Alex, Dr. Gruyere reluctantly allowed Clare to leave rehab only two months after her "awakening." The two most important men in Clare's life, her fiancé and her father, had cajoled and promised that Clare would have the best of care, nothing but the truth.

It was the first Saturday Clare was home, a bright August day, when Steve again broached the subject of their wedding.

"It doesn't have to be the elaborate affair like we were planning. We can have a simple ceremony with just family, like Aaron and Margaret had. You can wear the dress just as you planned, and we'll just wait until later for a honeymoon. We can live here in your apartment and Markie can watch out for you while I'm at work and school. She just lives next door. She isn't that busy being a housemother for those students who live in your house. Or, if you want, we can just go to the JP" he said hopefully.

"No, Steve, it won't work. Not right now. I don't need a babysitter all the time. I'm not going to start living like an invalid. I need time to gain my mobility, my independence, and to decide what I want to do."

"You don't love me anymore? You don't want to get married?"

Clare could hear the hurt in his words and hastily tried to reassure him. "It isn't that I don't love you or want to get married, it's just…Well, I'm not sure. I just need time. I can't explain it. I feel like the rug has been pulled from under me. Think of it this way…" she paused trying to think of how to express her deepest feelings and fears. "You know things have changed. I actually missed my brother's wedding! I can't believe he and Margaret have married and moved away. I miss them so much. Margaret was almost my constant companion for months after I started the University last year. She was my best friend and now she's gone. I am stuck here all day while Tina is in school, and I can't even think seriously about going back to classes until next semester at the earliest. The only time I really get out of here is when I'm at rehab and believe me that is not fun! My visitors, other than family and the residents of the house are therapists. You don't know how thankful I am that we decided to allow students to rent rooms in the house where Mom and I lived, and found Markie to manage things there. She's been invaluable to me. She helps me remember. There are things about the accident that I'm never going to understand, events I can't recapture without straining and I'm never sure if I have memories right or not. I am responsible for the destruction of the entire Goforth family! How do you think that makes me feel?"

"No! You are not. It was Myra….."

"Myra was only trying to protect her family, Steve. She saw me as a threat, and I was…am. I represented destruction to Myra, not only because I cut into her children inheritance, but also took their father's love. At least that is how she saw it. I reminded her of Alex's infidelity and made her insecure. My presence in the house caused her to regress mentally and led to her total breakdown. I was just as responsible for what happened as if I'd pulled the trigger."

"No, no, no! You're wrong. It was a terrible tragedy. That's all it was. Nobody blames you. Not Alex, not Aaron, and not Tina. Why do you blame yourself?

"Tina is lucky to be alive. Whoever took her was after me. Myra made that clear to me when we were in the garden. It was an accident that her hired thugs mistook Tina for me. Oh, Steve, don't you see, Tina might have died or worse! She could have been sold into white slavery or - or… who knows what the kidnappers and Myra had planned. Planned for me! *Not Tina, me.* It was all because of me! I can't just act as if everything is as it was before. I have to figure out where I want to go from here. And I have to do it alone; without anybody else helping me."

"And when you find out, what then?" Clare heard the anger in his voice and it scared her.

"Then I'll be ready to go on with my life."

"Just like that. Will you be ready to get married? Have our family?"

"I really don't know. In all honesty, I can't say and I won't hold you to any plans we might have made. You're free to do whatever you choose to do. I'm going to go away from here as soon as I can make arrangements. I don't know how long it'll take for me to find out what I need but till I do, you'd better keep this." She removed the diamond solitaire Steve had placed on her finger at the Valentine's Day dance months before.

Steve looked at her unbelievingly. "You mean to call our engagement off?"

"For now, yes. I have been thinking a lot. I don't know exactly what I want to do or go but I won't tie you to me when I don't know what the future holds. I may do fine physically. I may recover completely, or I may develop seizures or other problems, I don't know. But I do know I have to rid myself of this uncertainty and find some peace. Please understand and help me. I do love you, Steve, but I've got to be sure about myself before I do anything that involves other people. I'm not ever going to cause pain to others again."

"Oh, you don't think giving me this ring and calling off our marriage causes pain"? The shock and pain was evident in Steve's eyes and even as she spoke the hurtful words, Clare wished deep inside that she could take them back. "Maybe you're right. Maybe you do need time. I don't know. But you are hurting me now. I thought we had something special, thought our plans were strong and true. Now… now I don't know what to think."

Steve's eyes glistened with unshed tears. Clare felt her heart break. It was a sad time for her too. She'd seen all her dreams dashed in one swift moment and now she was destroying the one seemingly stable link to her once bright future. She couldn't help it. She wanted to make a total break, a clean start some place where nobody knew the Goforth name or the story of the tragic events leading up to the horror in the garden.

"Steve, please understand and forgive me."

"Ok, Clare, I'll give you time. But don't cut me out of your life completely. I love you, I'll always love you."

He stood and looked down at her on the sofa. "Let me know where you are, I want to know. I deserve the right to rekindle the fire we knew before Myra and her insanity doused it. Promise me that?"

"Yes, I do promise that." Clare watched with tears streaming down her cheeks as Steve turned and walked toward the door. There had been bitterness in his voice that she'd never before heard; she wanted to cry out to him, but she knew she couldn't. She didn't want to cling; she had to learn to stand on her own two feet, to face life unafraid.

Her first challenge was to decide on a plan, but not right now. She was tired, drained. The confrontation with Steve had been harder than she'd expected. Not that she expected it would be easy. She sat back on the sofa and turned on the TV. It was still tuned to the Travel Channel. A show about finding treasure in America was coming on. She decided to watch it. That was just what she needed to do, find treasure somewhere.

Unfortunately, the show only lasted thirty minutes but it gave her just enough information to whet her interests. New Mexico? She'd never been there and from what she'd seen on the screen, it looked lonely and desolate enough to hide from everyone and everything. Making herself a glass of iced tea, she turned to the computer to do more research.

New Mexico, the Land of Enchantment, was a cultural center for artists, had a glamorous history and miles of uninhabited or sparsely settled areas. Santa Fe, Taos, Albuquerque, Las Cruces, Deming, Lordsburg, Silver City, the names sounded musical and mystical to her ears. Stories of Billy the Kid, Geronimo, the Conquistadors, ancient Indian tribes dwelling in cliffs dating back centuries enthralled her imagination. It was all exciting and interesting.

As Clare shut down her computer, she decided to go to the university library and get more books on the desert southwest. That seemed like a good area for her escape.

* * * * * *

"Tina, would you like to take a trip with me?" Clare broke the rather uncomfortable silence between the two girls. Since getting out of the hospital, Tina had made an extra effort to spend time with her half-sister. Sometimes it was very difficult as Clare quizzed Tina about what had happened to her during the brief captivity a few months before. Tina had made it clear; she hoped that the incident was off limits for future discussion. Once again the two girls were sitting in Clare's living room finishing a DiGiorno pizza and drinking a beer. Not really a beer – it was a glass of O'Doul's - a rather good imitation substitute for the alcoholic brew. It went good enough with their pizza. Markie Markland, housekeeper for the sorority house next door and a long-time family friend usually managed to keep a 6-pack of regular beer in the frig, ostensibly for Steve or Aaron. She knew the girls had taken occasional cans of Miller Lite to drink with their pizza. She no longer kept alcoholic beer in the frig as she worried it might have adverse effects on Clare since her injury. Even though she didn't live in the apartment with Clare, she had taken full responsibility for her safe-keeping since she'd been released from rehab.

"A trip? What kind of trip?" Tina couldn't help but sound excited about this new turn of events. Anything to take Clare's mind off the past was worth listening to.

"Well, as you know, I've called off my engagement. I feel a need to get away and obviously I can't go alone," Clare motioned to her stiff leg with her impaired arm. I need someone to go with me; someone who can drive and be with me just in case something unexpected happens. You know what I mean."

"Yes, I know what you mean. But where and when?"

"Actually I've been watching the Travel Channel and some of the History Channel. I've been seeing quite a few shows on the Southwest, Arizona and New Mexico. I think I'd like to go there. I thought we could fly into Phoenix and rent a car, go through Globe, Safford, Silver City, New Mexico and then down to Deming, New Mexico. There they have a lot of what they call thunder rocks. I'd like to look around there, drive back up Interstate 10 toward Tucson and fly back from there. Spend maybe two weeks. I don't know. Just thought it might be different. We could visit some of the New Mexico wineries, some Indian pueblos, cliff dwellings, and there are some caverns in Arizona we could visit. The Desert Museum, Old Tucson, I don't know what all. Just take it as it comes. What do you say?'

"Well, I don't know. I can't take two weeks off right now with school in session. It would be Christmas before I'd have enough time for a two week trip, and I'm not too sure Dad would want me … want US to take off on an excursion like that alone. Especially over the holidays. You know how he is now days."

"I know. Maybe it wouldn't be a good idea for you to go with me. I'd ask Margaret but I'm sure Aaron wouldn't let her go. Besides, they are getting ready to move to Chicago in a week. Maybe if Markie went. What do you think about that?"

"Well, it might work"

"We'd be back in time for your classes. You have almost four weeks off at Christmas before the new semester begins. We could leave right after Christmas, and still have two weeks easily. Let me run it by Markie and see if she's willing to chaperone us.

"What about your therapy? How would you do that?"

"Actually, I can do it at any gym. By December, I probably won't need to go to clinic anyway. The things I'm doing I can do on my own. Most motels have some kind of exercise room and a pool, that's all I need. I know the routine. The main thing is to stretch and exercise. Markie could help with rub down stuff. I don't think I'd miss anything there. My only worry is that I might get one of those excruciating headaches. They seem to be less intense lately and I've not had as many, but I never know what to expect. If Markie was along and something did happen, it would be easier if there were two of you to take care of me. Oh, I hate this! This feeling like an invalid, I have to get away and learn to be independent again. You don't understand, do you?"

"Yes, Clare, I do but your recovery has been nothing short of miraculous. The simple fact that you have no speech or memory loss alone makes you a one in a billion!"

"That's true but you really don't understand, you... You can't."

"I do. During the time I was locked in that room, I felt so hopeless. Most of the time I wasn't even awake, but when I started to come around, before they shot me up again and knocked me out, I knew hopelessness. I think I understand."

"Oh, Tina, I'm so sorry that I caused you that trouble. It was me they wanted, not you. How can I ever make it up to you?" Clare hugged her sister close. Both girls had tears streaming down their young, unlined faces. Their faces were so similar in appearance that the hired kidnappers had gotten the wrong girl. They had held Tina prisoner in a cell underneath Portland's Pearl District for three days while they waited instructions from their boss, or bosses, as to her fate. Only when the newspapers printed the story of the tragic shooting at the Goforth Mansion did they get scared and release their hostage. The police had found Tina wandering the streets. At first thought they'd found another kid who had OD'd on street drugs.

Once Tina came out of her stupor enough to talk, she was able to tell authorities who she was but could give them very little information about her abductors. She had been kept pretty much knocked out from the time she'd been grabbed near one of the Benson Bubblers that was one of the attractions along busy Portland streets, until waking up in the local hospital. Fortunately, the drugs she had been administered were not the kind that caused immediate dependence. Her abductors had evidently figured they would get more money if they delivered their charge relatively unscathed to the next stop on her journey; wherever that was. Nobody knew what the actual plan had been. The kidnappers were unidentifiable and Myra Goforth wasn't talking. It was considered an open case still, but with no leads, it was inactive as far as the detectives on the Portland force were concerned. They had never even considered that anyone other than Myra Goforth might have been involved in the plot, a thought that had haunted Clare continuously.

"It's behind us now, Clare. You didn't cause it. Mother's messed up mind caused our problems. We both have to overcome what happened to us. To *ALL* of us, not only the physical injuries, but also the emotional ones. Clare, please don't blame yourself. It will eat you up and destroy you. You are too important to us all. Please don't do this to yourself. Remember we promised no further discussion about it?"

Clare looked at her sister and nodded. "You're right. We do need to get over it. That's why I'd like to get away for a while. Tell me you'll come along."

A smile played around Tina's rosebud shaped mouth as she nodded her head yes. Truth be told, she'd follow Clare anywhere just to be sure she was safe and didn't do any harm to herself. She knew that Clare felt responsible for the troubles the family had endured over the past few weeks, but Tina also knew that Clare wasn't responsible for any of them, and she feared that in her present state of mind, Clare might do something drastic. She couldn't survive any more tragedy. Yes, she'd go with Clare and she was sure Mrs. Markland would accompany them both.

★ ★ ★ ★ ★ ★

"No! Don't be silly. You can't go traipsing around the country in your condition. You need to stay here and get yourself well. Go ahead and go back to school if you want to get out and do something. But traveling all over the place just isn't going to happen! Besides it'll be winter and the weather is too unpredictable."

They were sitting in the library of the *Mansion,* as Clare called the Goforth home. The room was cozy but Clare felt uncomfortable. She didn't like to come to her father's home. Not only did it hold a bad memory of the night of the shooting, but also, always in her mind, was the fact that it was Myra's home.

"You don't understand I've got to get away. I think a short trip; two weeks at the most, will do me good. Tina and Markie will be with me, so I won't be in danger. It will give me time to think. You know a change of atmosphere and all that stuff…."

Alex looked at his love child. He knew she was unhappy, who wouldn't be after what she'd been through. Not only the shooting, but also her delayed recovery, although it was miraculous no doubt. Then breaking the engagement with Steve; he still didn't understand that.

"Clare, why not wait a little longer, until you're stronger?"

"I want to go as soon as I can. Semester break is the only time Tina will be out of class long enough to go with me, and I do want her to come too. She needs a break almost as much as I do. Besides, if we go over break, I can come back and start some classes myself when the new semester starts up. I *need* to go. If you won't let Tina go that is between you and her. I know Markie will go with me. I'm going, Alex, I'm going."

Alex recognized the same independent tone in her voice that he'd heard in Rose's voice when he tried to force her into accepting his help before Clare's birth. He knew he was licked. He didn't like it. Alexander Goforth hadn't made himself into one of the most successful shipping magnates in the Northwest by giving into whims. But he knew when to surrender and when to fight. This wasn't a time to fight.

"Alright, I'll let you three go. But I want a complete itinerary, daily reports of where you are, where you're going and what you are doing. If there are any medical problems, I want your promise you'll get right back here. We'll get with Dr. Gruyere so he can give you all three some tips as to what you should watch for, and you need to take Markie and Tina both to the PT clinic with you so they can see what has to be done there. I don't want any regression of your improvement."

Clare gave a big inner sigh. She really didn't need Alex's permission to go off on a trip, but she didn't want to go without his approval either. Besides, he would have to agree to allow Tina to go with her, so she had sought his approval and found herself agreeing to his stipulations.

The next two months were a drag. Clare read everything she could get her hands on about the Southwest, history, culture, food, mining, even jewelry making. She dutifully had Markie and Tina accompany her to PT sessions, which, as far as she was concerned, was a waste of time, but they would know what she did and how it was to be done.

"I can do all this stuff at home. I'll could take some weights with me but probably won't. Don't need the added luggage plus I'll probably be able to find access to a gym in the towns along the way if I need one. Motels have heated indoor pools so I can swim and that's about the best therapy for my leg now. I don't think PT will be a problem." Tina and Markie secretly agreed with her.

The meeting with Dr. Gruyere the first week in December didn't reveal anything they didn't know already. He wrote a prescription of pain medication to take care of the headaches and something to help her sleep should she need it. The nurse gave them telephone numbers and a copy of Clare's clinical records in the event something unexpected happened and she had to go to a doctor. "That way they'll know what has happened and can contact us if they need to," said the perky nurse.

Clare made a trip to her attorney's office alone. She needed to have some changes made to the will she had signed just before her *accident*. Steve had been named executor as well as conservator of her estate in the first will. Now that she'd broken with him, she needed to have Alex put in charge of her sizeable portfolio and appoint him as executor. She had also added a reasonable bequest for Steve. Mr. Sheldon, her attorney, assured he'd have the changes written and ready for her signature before the departure date for her trip. He wouldn't reveal any changes to anyone but would notify Steve by registered letter that he'd been relieved of any responsibilities regarding Clare's estate. If there were any questions, he could contact the attorney.

Tina and Markie made shopping trips for some attire more suitable to the desert climate and picked Clare up a few items as well. Clare didn't want to drag herself around shopping. She was overly conscious of her limp, which was barely noticeable, but she didn't want to meet up with anyone she knew. As the time for their trip drew nearer, she took care of airline reservations from Portland to Phoenix, car rental arrangements and return from Tucson to Portland at the end of the two-week trip via her Internet. Since they would be traveling during the holiday season, she didn't want any last minute flaps to spoil things. She left the daily schedules open but did make a list of some of the sights she hoped to see. High on the list were Indian ruins, ghost towns and small local museums. Of course, a trip to Arizona would require stops at Bisbee, Tombstone and tourist attractions around Tucson, the Desert Museum, old missions and Old Tucson where many of her favorite movies had been filmed. She hoped she was up to all the touristy things she penciled into her itinerary.

Clare couldn't get into the mood to shop for Christmas gifts. She kept recalling how excited she'd been only a year before while buying gifts for everyone and the excitement of her first Christmas at the Goforth Mansion and with Steve.

Myra had arranged the events at the mansion – a semi-formal dinner, complete with a roving photographer to record the event. Myra insisted on having family portraits taken of the family for her "history" book. Clare recalled how Myra had insisted Steve take his place next to her in the photograph although they were just dating at the time. Margaret was seated in front of Aaron that night, she remembered. Later, after the dinner guests had departed, the opening of gifts under the professionally decorated tree took place.

Gifts had been handed out by Aaron, who was still infatuated with Margaret but not yet engaged. They were, for the most part, useful items. Not too expensive, but not cheap either; except for the beautiful ring Alex and Myra had given her; diamonds and a marquis-cut emerald. She'd never had such an expensive gift and she still wore it on her right hand. Looking at the ring, she was overcome with sadness over what she'd lost.

Gathering her wits and drying her tears, she continued her reminiscing about the best Christmas she could remember. Christmas day, with glistening snow on the ground had been spent with Steve's family. They were warm and friendly and she remembered how comfortable she'd felt for most of the day. The only shadow cast on the holiday was the near accident Steve and she had experienced as a car skidded to a stop in front of them on the icy streets. Only Steve's skillful defensive driving had saved them from a terrible accident. Clare remembered how she'd gotten an ominous feeling when she saw a blue sports car in a parking lot and watched as the car that had nearly hit them turned into the same lot and the drivers began a conversation. Shaking her head, she tried to drive the still disturbing memories from her head and concentrate on her shopping list.

After much Internet searching, Clare had finally gotten gifts for the immediate family and Markie. She's sent her aunts and cousin in Florida gifts that really weren't much when she thought about it, but she'd make it up to her dear aunts the next time she visited them. She didn't really care if her cousin liked the book on flying history or not. She still had uncomfortable feelings towards her only cousin, James Miller.

There was no Christmas Eve dinner at the mansion this year but Clare, Tina, Aaron and Margaret and Alex did attend the mid-night service at the same church they'd gone to the year before. Clare was glad when it was over and she could return to her cozy apartment.

There was no glistening snow on Christmas Day this year; only a dreary gloomy icy rain. Everybody gathered at the mansion shortly before noon, exchanged gifts and made attempts at holiday joy but the cheerfulness was forced and false. The dinner was simple and served by Mr. and Mrs. Burns, Alexander's long-time butler and housekeeper. Plans were in place for the departure of Aaron and Margaret back to Chicago on the 26th and Clare, Tina and Markie would also begin their adventure on the same day.

CHAPTER 3

December 26th dawned cool and rainy; not unusual for December in Oregon. Clare prayed that the stormy weather wouldn't cause a delay in their 3:10 p.m. departure. As planned, Mr. Burns, Alex's butler/chauffer/man-around-the-Mansion, arrived with Tina and her luggage. He and Markie quickly loaded the baggage into the vehicle and they started on the first leg of their journey. They had to get to the airport early so they could make it through baggage checks in plenty of time for their flight. Airport security had hit a new high due to recent events on the world scene.

"Why didn't Alex come?" Clare asked Tina as they climbed into the still new smelling SUV.

"He said he didn't feel well; told to me tell you good-bye and then launched into a list of things to remember. He didn't see Aaron and Margaret off either. I really think he was afraid to come."

"Afraid of what?" Clare couldn't imagine the man she'd met a year and half before as being afraid of anything. Not only was he a physically imposing man, but with all his wealth and political influence, he was a major contender on every front.

"Maybe 'afraid' isn't the right word. Maybe I should have said 'scared'. He really doesn't like the idea of us going off on our own. I don't think he'll ever get over his fear of losing us. Clare, this has been such an ordeal for him; I'm not really sure we should leave him right now myself."

"You may be right now that you mention it. He sure isn't the same man he used to be. I know this has been hard for him, maybe harder for him than for any of us. I…I mean, he carries so much guilt. Feels he's responsible for it all. You know, he was aware that Myra had some problems but tried to go on as though things were normal. Oh, I don't know. Maybe our trip is just the thing he needs. Once were out of sight for a bit and return unhurt, he may be able to relax and start healing."

"Yes, that could work…. "An awkward silence filled the vehicle as Mr. Burns guided it through the city traffic, which had thinned slightly due to the holidays. Each girl was tussling with her own memories of the summer's events that had led to the current situation.

Arrival at the airport kept all three of the women busy for the next hour and a half. The new measures mandated by Homeland Security were aggravating and slow, but fortunately, they managed to pass through with no difficulty.

"I wonder what it would have been like if we'd been going overseas," Markie exclaimed. "I've never felt so violated going through a gate before in my life! If this is what happens every time you travel by plane, I'll just keep my feet on the ground!"

The girls laughed at her angry outburst and settled down with sodas and magazines while awaiting the call to board. Mercifully, the rain had spent itself and the sky was clearing so there would be no delay.

After a smooth flight, the plane landed safely at Sky Harbor Airport in Phoenix. Before they went in search of their luggage and the car rental booth, Tina made the first of many mandatory phone calls to Alex to let him know that the first leg of their journey had been successfully completed.

For someone who protested that she'd never traveled much, Markie was remarkably efficient when it came to finding luggage, porters and handling the business with car rental people. It was amusing to watch the five-foot dynamo as she did business with men who looked like giants next to her. She didn't let anyone intimidate her, yet she maintained herself in a poised purposeful manner that impressed everyone with whom she dealt. She left Tina and Clare at a snack bar while she conducted all things necessary to get them to their next stop. In no time at all she was back, keys in hand, escorting them to a vehicle and following the rental agent's directions to the nearby hotel.

The plan was to stay two nights in Phoenix with their headquarters at the Holiday Inn Express on University Drive, about one and a half miles from the airport. After a good meal and a little sightseeing in the area, they would get a good night's rest and spend the next day taking in a few of the typical tourist attractions of the city. Clare wanted to go to the Pueblo Grande Museum and Archeological Park where she could see the homes of Indians who had lived in the region 1500 years ago. She thought it would take about two hours for their visit so suggested they go there in the morning. She was grateful that the winter temperatures in the area weren't anywhere near as hot as the summer months. She had to admit, to herself at least, that she would never had suggested a trip to the Southwest during the hot summer months

After lunch and a rest, she planned to go to the Desert Botanical Gardens at Papago Park. Her interest in desert plants had been heightened as she had researched the Southwest. She was excited and eager to see the living plants of the desert.

Knowing she would have physical limitations due to the lack of inactivity in the past few months, she kept things light while they were in Phoenix but even the little she had planned might be more than she could handle in her somewhat weakened state. She vowed to herself not to let Tina or Markie know if she got even a little tired.

Once there, Markie checked them all into their rooms with the same speed and efficiency she'd displayed at the airport surprising both Clare and Tina. They had known Markie could manage a household efficiently but never before had they realized she possessed such a multitude of talents!

"I never imagined Markie was so efficient at things like this," marveled Tina. "I'm really glad she came along. Don't think I could have done all this myself."

"Oh, sure we could have handled it. Don't brag too much to her, she'll get the big head and think she's indispensable...of course, she is!"

Once settled in their rooms, Tina and Clare sharing a double and

Markie in an adjoining room, they decided to rest for an hour before heading out for their first taste of Southwestern cuisine. Clare didn't want to admit even to herself how tired she was. She wondered again if she was going to be up to the rigors of this trip but kept her worries to herself.

Tina and Markie had noticed the tired, strained look on Clare's face, but with a knowing look between them, said nothing. They had learned in the past year that Clare was a private person and did not welcome uninvited inquiries or suggestions. If they had ventured to give an opinion on her obvious need to rest, they both knew the suggestion would be met with hostility.

Clare had changed a lot since the incident. Gone was her sweet temper, in its place they often found a shortness that scared them. Preferring to err on the side of caution, they kept suggestions of a nap to themselves even though they were tired after the excitement of the flight and the hassle getting from the airport It was a welcome suggestion from Clare's that they relax in their rooms and freshen up before going out to eat that eliminated the need for them to confess their own exhaustion. Each woman, in their own way, welcomed the comfort of the bed and the comfort of the large well-lit rooms.

It was much cooler outside when the trio got up and met in the hotel lobby almost two hours later and they were glad of the jackets Markie had insisted they pack. The sun was sinking in the west and they saw their first of many desert sunsets, even the city smog couldn't totally destroy the beauty of a colorful display as the western mountains hid the bright sun. It was a magnificent sight, no denying that although marred somewhat by exhaust fumes and dusty air. Smog, though, didn't affect the taste of their first meal in the Arizona capital. Finding a nice restaurant near the Inn, they ordered exotic sounding food, and gorged themselves on spicy Mexican fare.

After dinner, they drove around the city for a short time, allowing Markie to do the chauffeuring. Christmas decorations were still brightly lit and the colorful displays brightened the evening drive. Markie took to her new position as tour guide/chaperone like a duck to water. Even so, she didn't wander too far from the airport and hotel area, stating that she didn't like the traffic and was, after all, a stranger in town. In truth, she didn't drive like a stranger, a point discussed later in the night by Clare and Tina as they prepared for bed. She had pointed places of interest to the girls which made them wonder how she knew so much about the City of Phoenix. Surely she hadn't absorbed all the tourist info from the city guide prominently displayed on the seat next to her?

It was dark when they got back to their hotel but Tina insisted that Clare do stretching exercises for her arms and legs. Clare would have loved to skip the exercises but knew that Tina was right in making the demands that she continue her routine. She unwillingly began the stretching exercises recommended by her therapist, actually cutting the routine short without Tina's knowledge. She was relieved when she finished the modified routine and fell into bed without a shower. In no time, she was asleep.

As soon as Markie got into the room next door, she had picked up her cell phone and furtively punched in the numbers she had grudgingly memorized. When the call was answered, she immediately launched into her report.

"We're in Phoenix now. Everything is OK.…..yes she's OK. Maybe a little tired, but no problems.…No, she hasn't complained about any headache or anything. She did seem a little tired after we ate, but it has been a long day.…yes, I know…I'll keep you posted as promised…We'll be here a couple days at least. She wants to do some tourist things tomorrow.…..yes, I'll call you. *I told you I would*.…yes. Okay, bye."

She stared at the phone held tightly in her hand for a bit after terminating the call. She was too tired and didn't want to continue reporting on Clare's condition. How could she terminate her job as a spy? She wondered what she had gotten herself into with this trip. She hated traveling; hated flying and hated the desert! Turning out the light, she huddled into the sheets and finally fell into a troubled sleep.

★ ★ ★ ★ ★ ★ ★

Clare was in a small room. It was dark and there was a terrible odor of urine and feces. She was in trouble; her head ached and she felt sick to her stomach, when she tried to walk she had piercing pain in her ankle. She hopped over to the door and tried to open it but it was held tightly closed by something on the outside. There was a little light coming through a small metal grate high up on the wall but not enough to allow her to figure out her whereabouts. She could hear faint voices but couldn't understand what was being said, it didn't even sound like English! She was alone and frightened!

★ ★ ★ ★ ★ ★

Clare sat up in the bed, sleep gone. Her body was soaked with sweat. *A hot flash at her age?* She had never been one to have vivid dreams but she couldn't shake the feeling that had overwhelmed her in this dream. Her subconscious told her that maybe this was more than just a dream; perhaps a warning? She tried to remember more clearly what had caused her to wake so suddenly but the dream was almost gone and she was left with a feeling of dread. She walked into the bathroom and washed her sweat-soaked face. The cool water seemed to clear her head as she regained her senses. The feeling of fear subsided as she walked to the small room refrigerator and got a soda. She was grateful for the hotel's courtesy bar of soda and juices because she knew she'd not have been able to leave the room in search of refreshment after what she had just experienced. What had she just experienced? As she sipped the soda, she felt more relaxed and tried to recall the dream and to dwell on the wisp of the terror that had overwhelmed and awakened her.

She remembered a man, two men; one had a hateful threatening voice. Where he fit into the picture she couldn't remember. Only that he was threatening her and someone who was with her. But where were they? She couldn't remember and slowly the dream evaporated from her mind. She gave up trying to remember and finished her soda but continued to sit in the easy chair and stare out the window at the sky. It was dark enough that she could see the plethora of stars in spite of the lights of the city; an umbrella of diamonds set in an inky blackness. She sat there for what seemed hours and finally sleepiness forced her back to bed. She wondered if she'd start dreaming the same troubling dream, but she slept peacefully the remainder of the night.

CHAPTER 4

Clare woke again just before dawn and watched the sun creep over the rugged hills. As the shadows were purged from the desert, a fresh blush painted the land with a rosy glow. She was glad that their room was on the east side of the hotel and that the surrounding area wasn't as built up as much as most of Phoenix. It at least afforded her a view of the sunrise and desert. She'd not given thought to scenery when she made reservations.

She helped herself to some juice from the courtesy bar and enjoyed the quiet for a few minutes longer before she began her morning exercises. This time she planned to do all the exercises that were recommended and then some, making up for her slackness of the night before. She always liked to exercise and then shower. She looked forward to the shower more this morning than usual due to the events of the day and night before; her failure to shower before going to bed coupled with her dream made her feel physically grubby but she knew that the warm shower would really help soothe the stretched muscles and ease some of the tension she felt throughout her body. As she was beginning with the sitting stretch, a repetitive stretch done while sitting on the floor using a bath towel to stretch her leg muscles, Tina sat up in her bed and watched her.

"I bet that exercise would be good for anyone to do to keep their legs in shape."

"Probably."

"How many of them do you do?"

"Usually ten for each leg, I am supposed to do this three or four times a day. Yesterday I slacked off some, so I'm going to do fifteen each leg to start out today."

"Guilt, huh?"

"Not really. I do feel like I can walk a little easier after I do them. Actually, I'm getting better, I think. My therapist isn't happy that I'll be missing some of the ultra sound and heat treatments, but I'll sit in the hot tub tonight and maybe that'll make up for it."

"Is it okay if I go ahead and shower while you exercise? I'll hurry."

"No, you go, I've got several more sets to do, and I'll feel better about working out, if you can call it that, without you in the room. Take your time. I'm in no hurry," Clare lied. She really was anxious to get into the shower and wash away the grime and grit from the day before and the sweat and stink from her restless night but she didn't tell Tina that.

An hour and a half later Clare and Tina met Markie in the hotel coffee shop. Markie was already eating a hearty breakfast burrito and was on her second cup of coffee.

"I was beginning to wonder if you gals were ever going to get up; better order and eat so we can get to those ruins before it gets too crowded. Tourists are heavier this time of year than in the summer when it is so hot not to mention that they take advantage of the holiday season for their vacations. The brochure recommends a full ninety minutes for the tour. When we are finished at the ruins, we can come back here and relax a little before venturing out into the desert gardens again."

"Right," Tina answered for both girls. "We'll just take what she's having," she informed the prompt waitress "but I want ruby-red grape-fruit juice if you have it. Is that okay with you, Clare?"

"Yes, I'll have the same. Except I want just iced water with lemon. That ruby-red stuff just doesn't agree with a burrito, even one made for breakfast!"

Clare looked at Markie. She thought that something wasn't right. "Are you okay with this trip? You just don't seem yourself."

"Oh yes, I'm fine, just had a rough night!" Too hurriedly answered, thought Clare; something just didn't seem right but she couldn't pin down what it was that made her uneasy.

"I'm fine," Markie reiterated without prompting. "Well, maybe a little tired. I don't like flying and I didn't sleep too well last night. I don't know, maybe it's the food or a different bed. People get used to sleeping on one bed and a change is difficult. I probably shouldn't have eaten this burrito this morning either. I'll be okay. Don't you go ruining your trip worrying about me?" She sure wasn't going to tell these girls that she'd entered into a pact with the devil; a pact that required her to make daily reports on Clare's health and well-being to a man who really had no reason to know about Clare's business even if he was a relative. He had told Markie that he wanted to be able to give others in the family encouraging reports on Clare's improving health but for some reason Markie now felt that there was more to his interest than just making reports to family! She'd remembered how Clare had made statements indicating that her long-lost cousin might have been in Portland on the day Tina had been kidnapped. At the time Markie had chalked her statements up to confusion but now she wasn't sure. If she remembered correctly, there had been a couple other times when Clare had made claims of a stranger or a strange vehicle at the scene of an unusual incident. She wondered if maybe Clare's wild accusations weren't more serious than the family and authorities had thought!

The three finished their breakfast in relative silence and paid the bill with Clare's plastic. Clare had made it clear to everyone that she was going to cover all expenses on the trip. Markie and Tina could use their own money for souvenirs but Clare would cover hotel and meals! At first there was disagreement to that part of the plan, but Clare insisted and the other two finally gave in and let her have her way. Leaving the hotel, they headed for Pueblo Grande where they spent the remainder of the morning. After touring the ruins, they scoured the gift shop for souvenirs to take back to their friends in Portland. Clare bought herself a couple CD's featuring Native American flute players; the eerie music seemed to fit her solitary and haunted moods.

After a light lunch, the trio decided to return to the motel for another short rest before their afternoon tour of the Desert Botanical Gardens. The siestas were welcome to them all. It was one of those traditions of the southwest that Clare really enjoyed. She didn't want to admit how tired she was so she was relieved that Markie and Tina didn't balk at the suggestion that they follow the old tradition during their vacation.

Clare hadn't realized how weak she had become during the time she had been a semi-invalid. The time in the hospital and rehab combined with a very lazy lifestyle since returning home had definitely had an effect on her stamina. Most of her activity since leaving rehab had been confined to trips to daily physical therapy and her hated exercise routine which, if the truth be told, she didn't adhere to as strictly as she should have! Although she was free to take breaks whenever she wanted while doing her exercises, she hadn't really pushed herself to stay up and walk after she had left the hospital. Now, things had changed. She had to keep up with others when on a tour as she didn't want to slow anybody down and risk their wondering what was wrong with her. She was more tired than she thought possible and the need for a rest was obvious to her. She just hoped neither Tina nor Markie recognized how fatigued she was. In addition to physical exhaustion, she felt one of the nagging headaches that sometimes turned excruciatingly painful, starting in the back of her head. She was anxious to get out of the sun and lie down before it became a full blown migraine. Once again she wondered how the summer heat would affect her.

When they entered their room, the blinking message light on the phone immediately caught their attention.

"I'll take care of it," Tina offered. "Probably Daddy checking on us, he's so worried." She quickly crossed the room and picked up the phone to check the message as Clare entered the bathroom to rinse off her sweaty face and arms.

"It was Steve calling. I didn't know how long you'd be in the bathroom so I took a number and told him I'd have you call him back. Do you feel like talking to him?"

"Not now," mumbled Clare. "He just can't accept the fact that I need some distance. He just won't give up. Maybe I'll call him tonight before we eat. Right now, I just want to lie down and get rid of this headache before it gets bad."

"Oh, Clare, you should have told us you weren't feeling well. We could have cut our tour short."

"No, I didn't want to do that. I enjoyed the tour. It's just a little thing; I only want to relax before it does get bad."

"You're sure? I was thinking of going down and taking a dip in that beautiful heated pool. Is it okay?"

"Yes, you do that. When you get back, I'll be feeling better and we can go to the Desert Museum. Have fun." With those words, Clare slid under the lightweight spread and closed her eyes against the golden Phoenix sun streaming through the drapes.

Tina, seeing her hide her head under the covers, pulled the curtains, and grabbing her swimwear went to change. She'd give Clare a good hour or so to rest. On her way to the pool, she stopped by Markie's room to tell her that Clare had a headache and ask her to keep an ear open to any unusual sounds from the next room.

CHAPTER 5

It was just after two when Clare woke up from her nap. Her head felt clear and painless. She figured that she'd taken that pill just in time to ward off the agonizing headache that would have incapacitated her for the rest of the day.

Tina was reading a travel brochure and sipping on a soda, her hair still damp from her swim and shower afterwards. "Hi, sleepyhead, how are you feeling," she asked.

"Like I'm ready to take on the world again," Clare answered. She really didn't feel like taking on anything; she really wanted to lay in the bed forever but knew she couldn't do that! She had to put up a front for Tina and Markie. She didn't want anyone to realize how she really felt inside - like a zombie. "What time is it?"

"Almost two thirty. If you want to see those gardens, I guess we'd better get a move on."

"Why did you let me sleep so long? They'll close before we get to see everything!"

"Well, we could stay here another night and go tomorrow if you want."

"No, let me get decent. You check with Markie and see if she wants to go or what….It won't take me long to get ready, how about you?"

"Just run a pick through my hair. It really dries fast in this air. I've not been out of the shower very long at all. I'll give Markie a call. You get dressed."

A knock on the door startled them and they both said "Markie" at the same time. Tina dutifully looked through the peek hole to be sure that they were correct about the identity of their guest as Clare headed to the bath to freshen up.

When Tina opened the door, Markie, her usual energy returned, thrust herself into the center of the room demanding to know if they were "going… or not!" Grabbing their handbags the girls headed towards the door and Markie followed still fussing and fuming about the delay in leaving. After locking the door, the three women left the hotel and headed for the Botanical Gardens in their rented car.

Clare found she could relax as she wandered through the lush garden and studied the unusual plants. She marveled that anything could survive and bloom in the desolate desert terrain. She bought a book on cacti and desert plants before leaving the gardens, the stark simplicity of the cacti intrigued her but it was the beauty of the short-lived blossoms that really entranced her. Seeing the photos of the cacti in bloom made her sorry that they were visiting in near winter rather than the warmer months when the plants were in full bloom.

As they drove through town heading back to the hotel, she leaned back and through the car's sunroof viewed the sky, the setting sun caused vibrant colors within the clouds, on the mountains and even off the buildings. One cloud in particular was filled with iridescent lights making it look like an opal. Clare was amazed at the beautiful colors. Her mother's phrase, "sky-blue pink" popped into her head. She hadn't thought of that term in a good while. It was how her mother had described the clouds and sky when the sun cast the same opalescent light throughout the sky.

"It's like another world. The sun is so bright it almost blinds you. I can see why they recommend polarized glasses. But, I like it. I can't wait to get out of town and really see the country. No noises or fumes, just the desert. Like those pictures in the garden."

They entered the parking garage at the hotel and decided to walk to a small café they had seen nearby. It was just a short distance and once settled at a patio-style table facing the western sunset, they ordered and were treated, once more to spicy Mexican food and music from a mariachi band. They couldn't sit outside due to the coolness of the desert night at this time of year, but afternoon sun made the enclosed patio warm and relaxing. The three women sat and listened to the music while finishing their drinks. The girls had wanted to order margaritas but Markie reminded them that they were both still under 21. She did, however, promise that she'd order them each a drink from room service once they got back to the hotel. She knew Alex wouldn't approve, but what he didn't know wouldn't hurt him. They finished their meal and strolled back to the hotel. True to her word, Markie ordered three margaritas and had them delivered to her room. After the waiter left, she slipped through the adjoining door and once they were closeted in Clare and Tina's room the three women sipped their somewhat illegal treat; pulled out the map and went over the planned road trip for the next day. The intention was to drive to Silver City, New Mexico where they would spend the next night.

"I understand there are some galleries there where you can get nice silver and turquoise jewelry. Of course, you can find nice jewelry everywhere but I'd like to buy from the smaller shops. The local artists appreciate it so much more. You know what I mean? The craftsmen are struggling to make a living from their craft or maybe it is someone who does it as a hobby. It is not easy to get their goods distributed to larger stores so they depend on the people who walk in off the street. It is even more important to buy from the little guys in this strained economy. Anyway, that is how I think," said Clare as she looked through the guidebook.

"There are some Indian ruins too and they say the view around Globe is magnificent. I'm sure there are some mining museums too," added Markie as they sipped their salt-rimmed drinks. Once the glasses were emptied, both Tina and Clare were more than ready to go to bed. Not being used to strong liquor, they were sleepy. Markie told them "good night" and retired to her own room where she once again made her daily telephonic report. When that distasteful task was done; she showered and crawled into bed. She would be glad when the trip was over and she could resume her normal life as a housemother to the small group of college students who rented rooms in Clare's house near the university campus. The care of the household was simple when compared to riding herd on the two girls and making reports to the man she now thought of as a tormentor!

The third day of Clare's trip dawned cloudy. In no hurry to fight the Phoenix morning traffic, they ate a leisurely breakfast and did a little more shopping. The hotel checkout time was 2 p.m. but they were on the road by 11:30 a.m. On their way to Globe, traveling east from Phoenix on Hwy 60, they drove through the area known for the Lost Dutchman Mine. The story tells of German miner who discovered his Eldorado in the rugged Superstition Mountains near Apache Junction but the secret location of the mine died with him and although many had searched for the treasures of the mountains, none had ever found it. There were many variations of the story with many different characters involved.

The travelers were glad the sky was overcast as the clouds helped cut the sun's glare but it also kept the inside temperature of the car at a lower degree during the drive toward New Mexico and once again the girls were glad for the light jackets they'd included in their luggage.

"You should have put a trip to Scottsdale, Flagstaff, Oak Creek and Grand Canyon into your itinerary," said a disgruntled Tina. "This terrain is boring, when you've seen one cactus, you've seen them all. It just looks dead and dry to me."

"Not to me," Clare responded. "I'm sorry you don't like it. I deliberately left out those tourist sites from the trip. I guess that was a mistake. I'm afraid you won't be seeing many of the much talked about desert attractions. I wanted to go to some of the more out of the way places, and that is how my itinerary is set up. We can make changes, I guess if you'd like to be more of a tourist but do keep in mind that we have a very limited amount of time to travel."

"No, you are right, there isn't going to be time. I'm not sure what you're looking for, but I hope you find it. As for me, I'm going to catch a few winks while we drive through this unexciting country."

"How about you, Markie, is it all blah and boring to you too?"

"No, I enjoy the countryside. It's different. I've seen it before, you know, but I don't mind missing the tourist traps. It's nice."

"When were you here?" Clare asked, hoping to learn something about Markie that they had never known.

"Oh, years ago, when I was young and dumb" was her flippant reply.

Clare couldn't help but notice there wasn't much enthusiasm behind her statement. As they drove through the country, she let her imagination run wild. She could visualize Native American's riding their painted ponies through the sagebrush, and cacti; hear the roar of a stagecoach over the dusty roads; and, almost, feel the parched throats of miners as they searched for gold. She allowed her musings to envelope her.

In Globe, they looked at the copper mining operation, an open-pit mine. Old timers told them that, comparatively speaking, the operation in Globe was not nearly as exciting as the old Copper Queen Mine in Bisbee, which was now shut down. Near the mine they found shops selling handmade turquoise and silver jewelry on almost every street corner.

Their goal for the night was Silver City, so they cut their stay short and headed to the junction of Hwy 70 and 90 near Lordsburg. Clare had read about the ghost towns surrounding the area, Stein's and Shakespeare being the nearest but they would have to wait to see them when they came back down and got on Interstate 10 as they returned to Arizona. She was anxious to get to Silver City where she could look forward to a swim and a good meal and a bed.

She couldn't stop looking at the desolate flats along the highway and imaged how difficult it must have been for miners to scratch a living out of the surrounding area. Creosote bushes and yucca covered the level land and signs warning of dust storms that reduced visibility to zero dotted the sides of the highway. Near Lordsburg, they turned onto Hwy 90 and headed toward the Burro Mountains and Silver City. The dramatic change in scenery impressed all three of them. From flat desert, they began to climb and encountered hillsides covered with cedar and pine. Tantalizing names like "Gold Creek Gulch" fueled Clare's already rampant imagination. When she saw the highway marker for the "McComas' Incident" she made Markie pull off the highway and read the story of the Indian massacre and kidnapping of a white boy who was never found! All the history made her want to see and learn more about the early days of the area.

Driving towards Silver City, the Tyrone mining area appeared as a scar on the land. Even though there were reclamation efforts in progress, the high piles of rock and dirt being smoothed and reseeded looked ugly.

"I think a hole in the ground would have look better than this," Tina exclaimed as they drove past the man-made hills.

"There is probably a hole somewhere else. I think the actual mine is off the main road," Markie added. "That road says "Tyrone Mine." This is ugly, though. I'll agree with that. I *know* there is a pit at Santa Rita. That was where the techniques for mining copper were first developed."

"How do you know that?" asked Tina coming out of her boredom.

"Just something I picked up years ago," replied Markie and she clammed up on the subject of her knowledge of the area. The two girls looked at each with puzzlement. It was obvious that Markie was keeping some secret about her past. What, they each wondered, was it?

As they entered Silver City, each occupant of the car seemed deeply engaged in her own private thoughts; Clare fantasized about pioneer life in the old west, Tina wished she were anywhere but where she was, and Markie brooded about those darned telephonic updates she was required to make. The desert was bringing back too many memories for her and she couldn't believe that she'd gotten herself into another mess. They pulled up to The Spa & Salon where Clare had reserved one of the two exclusive guest suites available.

The Spa, in the historic old town section was the picture of an era long gone by with white railed balconies, small-paned windows, and lace curtains. They were taken to the Valley View Suite where they took only minutes to get comfortable. Clare obsessed over the antique claw-foot bathtub in the cozy bathroom room and couldn't wait to get into a good soaking bath.

Tina wanted to find something to eat, and Markie just wanted to work out the kinks in her legs, the result of hours on the road. Each member of the party decided to go their own way agreeing to meet at the downstairs café in about an hour.

Tina decided to take a walk around the old town while waiting for Clare to take her soak. The historic district was picturesque and full of interesting shops. Tina bought a few trinkets and found herself back at their room in the hilltop spa just in time to see Clare emerging from the bathroom looking refreshed and hungry.

Markie was waiting for them in the dining room nursing a cool and refreshing tropical drink. The girls didn't bother to ask what it was because they knew Markie wouldn't allow them to order anything stronger than tea or soda anyway. During the meal, enchiladas with a fried egg on top, they discussed plans for the rest of the time in Silver, as the natives referred to the town, and for the next phase of the trip.

Clare wanted to use her time at the spa for a massage with hot stones and Tina was in for the same treatment. Markie, not into such pampering, settled for a facial and pedicure; the pedicure being a luxury she had never experienced. They scheduled their treatments for the next morning and spent the remainder of the day driving around town, stopping at the Mimbres Museum and other local points of interest.

As evening approached, a light dinner at one of the cozy café's tucked into the historic district concluded the activities. The late lunch had curbed their usually voracious appetites! The girls returned to their suite while Markie, saying she wanted to view the stars, remained on the lovely, if chilly, patio. Tina and Clare were going to make their dutiful calls home to report on their day's activities.

As soon as the girls had left the patio, Markie punched the phone number she had coded into her speed dial and made her mandatory phone call too.

"It's me," she said. "Everything is fine here. No problems.....she seems to be feeling fine. We did some sightseeing today and she seemed to handle the stress well. ……Gee, I'm sorry I can't tell you something that would make you feel better," she spoke sarcastically. "She's doing fine, ok… Yes, I'll let you know if there's any problem. I don't see why I have to call every night. I can let you know if there's something….. okay, okay. Bye." Markie shook her head as she clicked off the phone. *"I don't know how I ever got hooked into this reporting junk,"* she thought as she leaned back in the chair and took a long sip from her Corona! She suddenly wished she'd ordered something stronger than the Mexican beer!

Having reached their room, Tina immediately headed for the bathroom where she changed into her bed clothes anxious to be out of the confining blue jeans she'd worn all day. As she came back into the room, Clare had just hung up the phone after talking to Alex. "He sounds a little better tonight. Not quite so worried," she commented.

"Well, he'll be fine once we get home. I, for one will be too. Clare, what fascinates you about this country? There just isn't anything to turn me on," Tina asked as she pulled the covers back on her bed.

"I don't know. I really can't say. I just like it. In fact, I've got an idea about writing a book and using the desert as the setting or maybe I'll just research local cooking techniques and write a cookbook, I'm falling in love with Mexican food. Have you seen the little ovens behind some of the houses? They are called a *hornos;* I don't know if I said it right but they originally came from the Moors and were used by all the Spanish countries and the Indians, probably by many of the early Americans, for that matter. They are adobe and use wood to cook. It is interesting to read about them."

Ignoring the history lesson on the oven's origin, Tina quizzically asked "Do you know how many cookbooks on Southwestern cuisine there are? You'd be better off writing a fiction story. You could tell the story of someone who was forced to travel the desert and hated it!"

Clare returned the quizzical look. "Are you sorry you came?"

"No, not really; I'm enjoying our time together but I confess I'm perplexed by your reaction to the desert. Anyway, I'm sure you can think of some interesting story about the desert. You've done a lot of reading about it, I can tell; you are overflowing with facts."

"Yes, maybe something actually based on events from history. I found a website that had stories written by people who lived here back when the Apaches were causing trouble. There was one written by an Army lieutenant's wife that was quite interesting. She was the only woman at the site of what became Fort Bayard. Something based on that but totally fiction. I don't know. It's just a thought."

"Do you really think you could write a book? I mean that takes a lot of time and dedication."

"Well, I do have time. I need to do something besides sit around, exercise, and feel sorry for myself. Yes, I think I could do it. I think I just might do it."

"You won't have much time once school starts back up. Have you thought about that?" queried Tina. Clare gave her a strange look in reply; she wasn't ready to go there. Clare wasn't sure she even wanted to go back to school. Tina seemed to read her mind and wisely dropped the subject of school as they got ready for bed. Sleep came easily for Tina but Clare found her mind wandering as she played with ideas for a book.

CHAPTER 6

Once Clare had put her thoughts about writing a book into actual words, she found herself becoming more obsessed with the idea. She bought herself a small notebook and began keeping detailed notes on the things they saw and took numerous pictures with her digital camera. She bought herself a laptop when they arrived at Deming so she could download the pictures and reuse her photo cards. She made notes every day about where they had been, what they had seen, people they'd met, the climate and terrain.

Her impression of the owners of a geode mine near Deming was that they were perfect examples of the grizzled prospectors who once traveled the desert in search of gold, silver and turquoise. She was sure that the present day miners would be perfect characters for her book complete with scraggly beards, crooked teeth, and bent bodies, the result of years spent digging for the nondescript thunder eggs and geodes. She had been surprised to learn that the thunder egg was not synonymous for geode; the thunder egg usually being an agate filled sphere whiles the geode hid glittery crystals of amethyst and quartz within the hollow center.

The day in Luna County was filled with a visit to small local mining museums and a drive to Columbus where they visited the Poncho Villa State Park and museum. It was a good thing they'd brought their passport cards so that they could walk across the border and eat at a local restaurant set apart by its bright pink color, where they also found souvenirs at rock-bottom prices. While Tina complained about the dull, dead desert, Clare soaked in the sights, sounds and smells. The most noticeable odor filling the air was the scent from the creosote bush as a light shower fell on the always thirsty earth during their visit to the Mimbres Museum. Markie dutifully acted as chauffeur and made her nightly report to Clare's unknown snoop. Markie was getting more and more exasperated with each telephone call and frequently in her irritation lashed back at the two girls. In the privacy of their room, Clare and Tina discussed Markie's strange actions. They both realized that when she spoke to them it was sometimes in a voice they didn't recognize as belonging to the Markie they knew and loved! The mercurial changes in Markie's personality became a topic of nightly discussion; sometimes she was still the fun-loving chaperone they knew and loved and sometimes she was more of a gloomy stranger they didn't recognize.

"What on earth is bugging Markie," questioned Tina as they settled in their room after a day of sightseeing around Deming. "She is edgy as can be."

"I don't know and I'm afraid to ask," replied Clare. "I really think it has something to do with some phone calls she gets sometimes. Haven't you noticed how short she answers when she is on the phone"?

"Yes, Now that you mention it, I have heard her speak sharply. Not that she gets many phone calls. I know she talks to Dad sometimes but I'm sure she would never speak to him in that tone of voice. She sounds like she's really being put upon..."

"Maybe we should just ask her about it," suggested Tina.

"Not me," said Clare as she climbed into her bed. "I'm not about to stick my head into that lion's mouth. If she wants us to know, she'll tell us.

"Yeah, I guess you're right. Still, I wish she'd get over it, whatever it is. Did you notice how she acted in Phoenix; like she'd been there before"?

"She did seem familiar with some of the places she took us to, and talked like it was almost a revisit to the area. I don't know what the story is, but if Markie had a secret life that she wants to keep from us, that is her business. She'll spill it if and when she wants us to know about it." With that said Clare switched off the bedside lamps and pulled the covers up to her chin.

Each girl lay in the dark room and allowed her mind to dwell on the questionable actions of their friend, Markie. Soon they dropped off to sleep.

The next morning Markie was her usual chipper self. The doubts of the previous night were quickly forgotten as they left on the first leg of their trip to Tucson. They had two days before they were scheduled to catch their flight back to Portland. Tina and Markie were both counting the hours when Clare suddenly decided to change the planned itinerary. Instead of taking Interstate 10 directly into Tucson, she wanted to take a side road, skirting southward and going deeper into the boot heel of New Mexico.

"It isn't much longer, and it will take us off the beaten track. We won't see the ghost towns I'd planned to visit but there are ruins of an old mining town called Hachita down there and I'd like to see that. I don't imagine there is much left, but it would be better than the interstate."

"I don't see how it could be any different. It's all dead," complained Tina. "I will sure be glad to get back to Portland. It's green and populated. I can't imagine why anybody would live in this country. I'm sure glad they have showers in the motel and indoor swimming pools otherwise, I'd forget what running water looked like - there hasn't been a drop since we left Phoenix except for that sprinkle yesterday. Besides, I have to get back. I need to buy some more clothes before I start classes. Can't go to college dressed in last year's rags!" There was a definite note of sarcasm in Tina's voice. She had never been one to obsess over clothes nor to flaunt her money although all who knew her knew she could afford the finest designer clothes available.

"You'll have time to shop when we get home. I've got to do some things too if I'm to go back to class."

"You mean you are going to go back to college? I thought you'd decided to wait.....I mean that is what you said before."

"Well, I think I've decided now to go back. I want to take some classes to help me develop writing skills. I'm sure I can find some interesting electives that will help in the development of writing skills too. I was taking management and marketing classes and that stuff will be useful no matter what career I eventually decide to pursue!"

"I'm sure glad to hear you feel like going back to class," Markie added. "I thought you were feeling better and that one decision proves it!"

Markie had also noticed how much easier Clare seemed to move and had mentioned it to her father but not to her other regular telephone partner! Clare did her stretching exercises daily and loved the swimming pools and hot baths at the motels when they stopped at night. The limp seemed less exaggerated and her complaints about headaches had stopped after that day in Phoenix. She seemed to have gained stamina as she walked around the old towns, museums, mines, Indian ruins and other attractions. In addition, the sun had given her the hint of a healthy tan. Of course, it didn't take much exposure to the southwestern sun to reap the benefits sunshine even in the cooler months of the year!

"You're right. I am feeling better; seems like I'm not as stiff. Maybe it is the dry climate. I've always heard it was good for arthritis, so maybe it's worked its magic on me. I'm sure I've strengthened my muscles with the walking, and I do feel better about things in general. I just needed a change of atmosphere, I guess."

After they had stopped at Old Hachita which was nothing but a few adobe walls, scrub desert and ant hills, they continued along Highway 9 toward Animas. Clare's new destination was Bisbee and she happily made the change of plans to her co-travelers.

"We'll go to Rodeo, then to Douglas and then to Bisbee. I'm sure we can find a place to stay overnight there. Then we'll stop in Tombstone before we go on to Tucson tomorrow and make our flight the day after so you can say you've been to "The Town Too Tough to Die" and we can see another open-pit mine, Tina!" Clare taunted her sister knowing that she was less than excited about the prospect of seeing another mining town.

"Just what I wanted to see," Tina moaned.

"Oh, now Tina, buck up. You can't come to the Southwest and not visit Tombstone - "The Town Too Tough to Die." Markie giggled as she mimicked Clare's use of the familiar description of the old mining town. Tina moaned again and Clare joined Markie in a good laugh.

In all honesty, Markie was grateful that the end of the trip was in sight. She'd never been impressed by the desert, not even around Vegas, but to baby-sit two almost grown girls on what she considered a cocka-mamie trip was about the least enjoyable thing she had done in years. Of course, she dearly loved both girls and knew that there was a possibility that Clare might have a seizure or some other unforeseen incident related to her head injury and those were the only reasons she'd agreed to make the trip. Knowing that Clare's injury was still too recent for doctors to rule out the unexpected didn't make her enjoy the job any more. Then there were those dammed phone reports. She hated them. They made her feel like some kind of snitch! She would be glad when the trip was over and she was once more comfortably ensconced in her little house in Portland cooking for students! She was going to cut the lines and refuse to make any further "reports" on Clare's progress. Let that nosy spy find some other source of information. It wouldn't be her ever again!

As they covered the seemingly endless miles of desert scrub Clare remarked at how well kept the roads were.

"Why not?" whined Tina, "they don't have anything else to spend their taxes on!"

"I'm sure that isn't true. They have schools, medical services, emer-gency services; things like fire and EMS. They probably have the same expenses as most urban areas - just a lot less people to benefit from them, a lot more area to cover and a lot less tax money to spend."

As they drove into the little community of Animas, Clare was amazed at the peaceful feeling that permeated the community. A new-er-looking school covered a good third of the main street area. The rest of the block was taken up by the post office, a small café and a Baptist Church offering services at 2 p.m. on Sundays. Across the highway from the nearly empty cafe was a telephone office.

"Let's stop at the café and have a burger," Clare suddenly said.

"What?" exclaimed Markie, "I had planned to drive straight through to Bisbee. I got us reservations at the Copper Queen while you kids were looking at dry adobe in that ghost town and I'm sure they have some exotic café there." The last was said with obvious sarcasm.

"Well, I'm hungry now, and I want to know more about this place. Besides, it *is* lunchtime, almost. You could eat something, couldn't you Tina?"

"Sure, I can eat. That's about all there is around here that is fun to do!"

They pulled into the dusty parking lot at the Panther Tracks Café and entered the tin-roofed building. Inside they found themselves in a large dining room with a partition separating the food prep area and kitchen from the tables. To the right were two smaller rooms where they saw items displayed on long tables. There were cosmetics, jewelry, CD's from local artists and a conglomeration of glassware, pottery, blankets, hats, t-shirts and rocks.

Taking a seat at one of the empty tables, and they noted there were several, they each picked up a menu from the table and began to look at its offerings.

"Open Monday through Friday only. Guess you go somewhere else if you want to eat on weekends," said Tina.

"Most people around here do," was the unsolicited reply from a young girl who had stealthily approached their table. "They use the weekend to do shopping and visiting. Not many people stick around here on weekends, hence no business. There is a new place open on Thursday through Saturday evenings. It's called Ghostrider's Grille; it's behind the convenience store. That info is free, just in case you plan to stick around over the weekend." The waitress directed her comment to Tina.

Probably in her mid-twenties, the waitress wore jeans; a t-shirt with "Where the Hell is Animas" emblazoned across the front and long beaded earrings. Her curly blond hair was pulled back into a ponytail. Very little makeup covered her deeply tanned and prematurely lined face.

"What can I get for you today?" she asked.

"What's good?" asked Clare.

"Well, the burgers are specialty of the house. Today we also have homemade enchiladas. Personally, I like the jalapeño burger. You can get the peppers on the side if you're afraid they'll be too hot."

"That's what I want," said Clare, "and iced tea with lemon."

"Peppers on the side" asked the cowboy boot wearing waitress?

"No, I'm brave."

The others ordered and Clare and Tina got up to look closer at the offerings in the "Bargain Barn" attached to the café.

That was Clare's introduction to Animas. After eating their burgers, which Clare thought wonderful, she paid the bill. She pumped the waitress for information about the area as she waited for her change. "Somehow," she thought, "I'm going to be back here. This valley has some secrets and I'm going to uncover them!"

The rest of the trip to Bisbee along Hwy 80 took them past the road leading to Skeleton Canyon, site of Geronimo's final surrender. There at the monument built on the roadside they stopped, read the bronze plaque and took pictures in front of the tall pillar. Continuing toward the Silver Creek area, they edged mountains as they traveled along a twisty, curvy road dotted with scattered houses perched upon the sides of canyons covered in yucca, agave, creosote trees, and desert grasses. Frequent signs warned of deer crossing and curves. The change of scenery seemed to bring new life to Tina.

The quiet was suddenly broken as Tina shouted in an excited voice "Look, there is an illegal"! Sure enough, just to the side of the car was a young man slamming his body to the ground among sharp rocks and dust. He stared at the vehicle as it sped past. It was obvious that he was frightened. His sighting was a surprise and it initiated a thought provoking discussion about the status of immigration reform. As they approached Douglas, Clare was tempted to suggest a side trip to Agua Prieta, Mexico but thought better of it when she recalled Markie's re- action to the stop in Animas and the recent scare they'd had with the sighting of the obviously illegal traveler. "There's plenty of time to go to Mexico later," she thought.

Once they reached Bisbee where extensive reclamation operations were in progress, it was apparent what damage years of mining had done to the natural beauty of the area. There was a long way to go before the area would recover from the ugly scar left by the years of copper extraction. The pit, that had once been a flurry of activity with oversized dump truck hauling copper ore up the terraced roads, was now just a hole in the ground. Markie pulled into the observation area and they all got out to peer into the deep hole from which the copper, that had made the town a bustling metropolis for many years, had been hauled out by the truck loads. The twisting roads were blocked by mud slides that had dried out and precluded any possible usage; desert scrub grew throughout the once pulsating mine. Clare could almost hear the sounds of the machinery as they hauled raw minerals to the surface for transport to the smelter that had once been active in the company town of Playas located near the area they had just left, the Animas Valley in New Mexico.

"That's really ugly, why they don't fill it in is beyond me" was Tina's unsolicited comment.

"Can you imagine how much fill they'd need," responded Markie.

"Not to mention, they'd lose a main tourist attraction," added Clare.

After taking the mandatory photos of the hole, the trio climbed back into the car and headed up the winding road into the town built on the hillsides of Tombstone Canyon. Markie had reserved rooms at the historical Copper Queen Hotel where she was placed in the suite once occupied by movie actor, John Wayne and the girls were assigned to the newly decorated J.A. Jance suite. They decided to freshen up and meet at the Winchester's Restaurant located on site for an early dinner after which they would walk up the canyon and visit some of the artist's shops and galleries.

"I know who John Wayne was," said Tina as they entered the hotel's antique elevator, "but who is this J.A. Jance person?"

"A local girl who has made it big as a mystery writer, she actually lives in Seattle. At least part of the time, the rest of the time, she lives in Tucson. I've read some of her books and enjoyed them."

"Well, I'm not much into mysteries but maybe I'll look her up and try one. Bet there is a store around here where they feature them."

Once settled in their rooms the girls talked with their father and filled him in on the day's activities and the progress of their trip. Markie also called Alexander to give him her insight on the trip and an update on Clare's health.

"She's doing great, really. I don't think there is anything to worry about. She hasn't complained at all about headaches, she seems to have more energy, and she sure loves the desert! Says she's anxious to get home and start back to school."

"You mean she is talking about going back to school?" asked Alex from across the miles.

"Oh, yes. She wants to take some writing classes. Thinks she has an idea for the Great American Novel. You know how that goes. Not that I'd discourage her. If anyone can do it, she can."

As their phone conversation ended Markie recognized a glimmer of the old Alexander Goforth coming through the phone lines. The millionaire entrepreneur she had known once again seemed to come alive. "Maybe this trip will do him good too," she thought as she dialed the second number she needed to call.

All three were up early the next morning. Markie was anxious to get this last full day of traveling finished. She looked forward to spending the night at a motel near the Tucson airport and finally winging their way back to Portland. She would be *so* glad to get the trip behind them and settle back into her safe routine at the sorority house.

Clare hated to leave the quaint canyon town of Bisbee. It, like much of the desert, held an almost mystical attraction for her. The narrow curved Brewery Gulch lined with shops seemed to beckon her. Tombstone Canyon's twisting road made a serpentine path past houses with hundreds of steps leading to small Victorian houses. The houses, clinging to the hillside, called to her. She wanted to take the Queen Mine Tour and see the underground mining operations, but Tina had vetoed the idea. Markie, like Tina, was anxious to get on with the last leg of the trip. There had been some extremely interesting sights, but the desert had quickly bored them both. They declared that they could only look at so much silver and turquoise jewelry and the local pottery all looked alike after a while. They were ready to get back to the excitement of the big city, and the comforts of home. Clare vowed to return someday to see the sights she'd missed.

Subsequent stops at Tombstone and Boot Hill seemed almost anti-climactic. By noon, they were in Benson, a stop on the old Butterfield Stage route and eating in the Horseshoe Café, one of the town's oldest landmarks with its murals depicting cowboys and cattle, providing some of the most unusual décor they'd seen on the trip. . After their quick meal, they headed for Tucson arriving at the Holiday Inn - Palo Verde in about an hour giving them plenty of time for a swim and nap before dinner at a conveniently located restaurant. There was no sight-seeing that night. They repacked their suitcases and prepared for the 10 am flight to Portland. Markie talked the hotel concierge into arranging for the return of their rental car, and returned to her room to make what she prayed would be a final report. She intended to make it clear that she would never again be doing work for *him!*

The anger Markie felt after the phone call didn't dissipate overnight in spite of a good sleep and when Clare knocked on her door the next morning her sharp reply told more than words could say.

"What on earth is wrong with you now," Clare asked. "You've been surly much of this trip, I'd think now that we are going home you'd be happier"!

"Oh I'm happy to be going home alright; happy to have that jerk stop bugging me! Markie, realizing what she'd said, tried to gloss over her words but not fast enough to stop Clare's next words.

"What jerk, who has been bugging you, what is going on"?

"You know what, I'm gonna tell you who, what and everything! I don't like to keep secrets from my family and don't like to spy on them." Before Clare could ask what she was talking about, Markie continued.

"Your cousin from Miami hired me to tell him how you were doing while we were traveling. There, it is out."

"James? You mean James had you *reporting* to him? What on earth for"?

"He said he was concerned about your health and if anything happened he could be wherever we were immediately and offer assistance! Assistance my butt, he just wanted to know if you had any physical problems. He's a worm and I for one wouldn't trust him within ten feet of me! Tears were pouring down the smoke-aged face now as Markie turned towards Clare with hands outstretched, "Clare, please forgive me. I should have never agreed to keep in contact with him but he sounded so concerned at first; said he wanted to keep your aunts posted, that they worried about you all the time. When I tried to stop the calls, he threatened to tell you and to reveal some things in my past that I'd rather not have known."

"I understand, he's worried that I'll live and he'll have to share the inheritance from Aunt Pansy. He's already mad that I turned up to be a valid heir to my mother's portion of the estate and he's hoping I'll kick the bucket so he'll get all of his mother's and all of Aunt Pansy's money too. Your right, he's a worm. But…but what kind of things in your past could make you agree to go along with him"? Clare asked then she added quickly, "don't bother to answer that, it isn't important. Whatever it is, it can't be too bad or Dad would have found out about it long ago. I know he does background checks on all his employees. Let's just forget we ever had this conversation and go on our way home. I'll take care of James' curiosity next time I see him, and I will see him again, I'm sure. There are several things I need to discuss with him." There was a new firmness in Clare's speech, it caused Markie to look at her in a new light and to realize that this girl, her dear friend, was growing up, maturing and she wasn't sure whether she liked the way she was growing or not; only time would tell if the old Clare, kind generous and innocent would reemerge or if it would be a new harder Clare that survived the tragic accident that had changed her life so suddenly.

CHAPTER 7

After arrival back in Portland, the monotony of settling back into a daily routine irritated Clare. Her mind kept returning to the clear blue skies of New Mexico where desert scrub dotted the landscape and foothills stood stark and clear in the distance; it didn't help that the days in Portland were punctuated by cold drizzly rain. Even though her trek through New Mexico had been in the winter, the temperatures were comfortable and as long as she remained inside, the gusty winds had been no problem; in fact, she liked watching the dust devils dance across the semi-barren landscape. She continually found herself searching different web sites for historical information about the Southwest. One day she clicked on a real estate agency that advertised their service area as Grant and Hidalgo Counties "located in the boot heel of New Mexico." As she scrolled through the offerings, one suddenly caught her eye.

The green Palo Verde and ocotillo rock garden in front of a small, neat mobile home seemed to beckon to her. The older single wide was painted to match the desert sand and was trimmed in a sienna red; it looked forlorn yet inviting. Located on 40 acres, Clare at first thought it an intimidating amount of land, but as she scanned photos of the scenery surrounding the living quarters she realized that the vacant land would not require upkeep like the grounds that surrounded her father's mansion. There were no gardens to tend, no trees to trim and no grass to mow. Seeing neighboring houses nearby eased her mind as well. It was obvious that, although the land was unused, it was not totally isolated. As she looked at photos of the surrounding area she saw the distant Pyramid and Animas Mountains which hemmed in the valley. The price, $60,000, was an amount she could easily afford. Without much thought, she called the realtor to talk….just talk. She thought.

Madge Quemado, the realtor answering Clare's phone call, was a pleasant person who, proud of her Mexican and Apache ancestry, was quick to tell the history of the Animas area which included the gruesome details of the attack on Judge McComas, his wife and the subsequent search for his kidnapped son with which Clare was already familiar. Although she had gleaned considerable history from her forays on the Internet, she enjoyed hearing the tales from someone who actually lived in the area. What she heard pleased her.

"Tell me about the property," Clare demanded.

"Well, it is a small trailer, in good condition. It has one and a half baths, two bedrooms, although one is quite small. The woman who owns it lives in Bisbee. She moved there about four years ago to take care of her mother. She only lived in the trailer for about five years. She bought there after her husband had a heart attack so her son could finish high school at Animas. After he graduated, she stayed and kept her grandson until her father got cancer and she moved back to Bisbee to help take care of him. She decided not to move back after her father's death and put the place on the market. It has been empty for about two years."

What about the porches, are they in good repair?"

Yes, they are strong and the roof is good. The trailer is situated so that the front is actually facing northwest. It allows a beautiful view of the sunsets. The water well is about the best in the area. It would make a nice vacation spot, if that is what you want."

"Yes, that is kind of what I want; a quiet place where I can write. But I need to have a place where I can get groceries locally too."

"Well, you said you'd been in the area once. There is the little store; you'd have to get your phone and TV hookup. Most people use satellite TV, either Dish or Direct TV, the phone is a co-op and you have to join but they offer DSL internet, and the electric is actually still turned on, you'd just have to put it in your name. They use propane for heat and cooking and the supplier is local. Oh, and the Schwan's man has a regular route. He comes every two weeks. Why don't I go down, take some video of the place, interior and exterior and send it to you. It will give you a better idea of what it looks like, and then if you are still interested we'll arrange a visit?"

"Hey, that sounds great. I'd really appreciate that."

"I can go down this weekend. I'll overnight the film to you and you should have it by next Tuesday, is that okay? I'm not very proficient on downloading stuff to the Internet but probably can get someone here to help me do that if you want it via Internet."

"No, mail would be great," said Clare. As she hung up her phone, she wondered how she could manage another trip to New Mexico without upsetting her family and missing too much school. She felt a surge of excitement like she'd not known in months. Suddenly she had something to look forward to; something that was safe and secure.

Returning to school for the spring session had been easier than Clare had thought it would be. Her weak leg still ached sometimes, but she was able to get around from class to class easily. Her schedule wasn't heavy and she'd intentionally arranged classes to give her adequate time to rest in between them. She imagined that everyone was staring at first but soon realized that they were far too busy with their own business to waste time watching her and speculating. In fact, she had cut back on her courses, taking only mandatory classes and writing-oriented electives; no extra-curricular activities this year.

Her doctors seemed pleased with her progress at physical therapy; the most recent CT had shown no apparent residual damage to her brain. Her neurologist was considering her his miracle patient of the year. Her headaches had almost completely stopped, for which she was thankful. Her hair, which had been cut short after the surgery, had grown back enough that she could wear it in a more flattering style. She was very glad about that.

Her relationship with Steve was still up-in-the air. He wanted to pick up where they had left off, but Clare wasn't ready yet. They had enjoyed a pleasant dinner only the week before she found the property which was so enticing to her. During the dinner, Steve revealed several things to her.

"My job is okay, but not what I really want to do. I'm thinking of taking a job with IBM. They have been after me for months."

"IBM, does that mean you'd have to move?"

"Yes, they have a position available in LA. It pays a lot more than I make here, I can transfer my credits to UCLA and work on my Master's there. I'd like you to come with me. You can go to school there."

"Steve, I can't. First, I could never live in LA. It is too big and wild. Portland is more than I want. Second, I'm just not sure what I want to do right now. Finally," she said with tears in her eyes, "I just am not ready to pick up our relationship again. I'm not the person I was.....I'm not sure who I am, or what I want. It wouldn't be fair...."

"Damn it, Clare! Let me decide if it would be fair or not! I love you. Isn't that enough?" The unexpected outburst was uncharacteristic of the usually calm, collected man that Clare had to admit she still loved.

"No, Steve, it isn't. I won't tie you down to me when I'm so unsure of what I want to do. I do love you, but I'm still so confused and unsure of myself. I'm not asking you to put your life on hold until I decide. We've been over and over this. There is no future for us.....at least not now. I want to be your friend, but maybe that is impossible considering our feelings. Maybe we need to stop seeing each other....for a while at least."

"Clare, you don't mean that!"

"Yes, I do. If you move to LA, that would make it easier. Just do what you want to do and we'll see what happens. Maybe you'll meet someone there. But I'm not the one for you. Not now. I've changed. I don't know if I can ever trust anyone again. Please understand."

After Steve had left Clare at her apartment, she went inside and cried. She had lost so much, but her trust in people was the loss that was the hardest to accept. She hated hurting Steve, but she just wasn't sure that he wouldn't hurt her too. She had vowed, during those days after coming out of the coma, that she'd never trust anyone again. True, her father, Tina, Markie and even Steve seemed honest and genuine, but then so had Myra; at least most of the time and there was the problem with James. People were too complicated and she didn't want to get involved with them again. That was the thing that fueled her desire to get off alone. To find a place where nobody would bother her, where she wouldn't be vulnerable.

The thought that had at first been just a passing fancy seemed to become an obsession: to get away and start over where nobody knew her or her story. As she surfed the Internet, focusing on the desert southwest, she felt more and more drawn to the area. The receipt of the realtor's video filled her with excitement. As soon as she finished watching the tape, she was on the phone.

"Madge Quemado, please ... Madge, this is Clare Smith. I got your video and I want the place. I am planning a trip to Florida over Easter and could arrange a stop. I'll fly into Phoenix or Tucson, rent a car and drive to Animas. Can we meet somewhere and I'll sign all the paper-work...Oh; it'll be a cash deal. Get the figures all worked up and I'll have a cashier's check for you. Do you want any earnest money, I can send that now?"

They discussed business for a few minutes more and when Clare hung up the phone, she was tingling with excitement. Her own place in the desert! The realtor would be sending her a contract via over-night mail, and she would have to sign and return it with some earnest money. Clare had suggested $5000 and the realtor readily agreed.

It didn't take long to decide which airport to use as her landing point. As soon as classes let out for Easter break, Clare would leave for Tucson, rent a car to drive to New Mexico and meet the realtor at Animas. She was in a quandary as to whom she would ask to accom-pany her. She still felt uncomfortable making such a long trip alone. Her plan was to stay overnight in Tucson, drive to Lordsburg where she'd meet Madge and together they would go Animas for an in person look at the place and if it was acceptable, which she already knew it was, they could complete business then and there. She'd stay overnight at Lordsburg before driving back to Tucson to catch her flight on to

Orlando where she would spend the remainder of her holiday with her aunts, then she would fly back to Portland on Wednesday after Easter and have a few days to relax before classes started up again.

It was a good plan, but whom would she get to travel with her? Markie was tied up with being a housemother for the renters; Tina had been very vocal about her feelings about the desert during their previous trip and wouldn't likely want to go on another quick trip to the Southwest. Besides, Clare really wanted to do this without involving her family. A solution presented itself in a most unexpected way.

Standing in the lobby of the Student Union while waiting for Tina to join her for lunch, Clare studied the ads posted by students. One jumped out at her:

> **Wanted: Someone to travel to Tucson AZ over break.**
> **Share driving and gas expenses. One way only. Call**
> **(718) 397-6363 ask for Mandy.**

Clare couldn't wait to call! The phone rang several times and just as she was just about to disconnect when a sleepy voice answered.

"Hullo."

Clare quickly responded, "Is this Mandy?"

"Yes, who is this?"

"You don't know me, I'm Clare Smith. I'm looking at the card you put up in the Student Union. Are you still looking for someone to go to Tucson with you?"

"Oh, damn. I should have taken that card down. Would you pull it off the board and throw it away for me?"

"You mean you've already got a rider?"

"No, no such luck. I mean my car is kaput and I'm not going. Sorry."

"No, that may be good. Do you still want to go?"

"Yes, sure. Can you drive?"

"No, that wasn't what I was thinking. Can we meet and talk about it. I've a proposition I think you might go for. It would be good for both of us."

"Okay. I have to get going. Have a class at two and I'm gonna be late. How about we meet at Starbuck's across from the Student Union at, say, three-thirty."

"That's fine. How will I know you?"

"I'll be easy to recognize. I have orange hair. I mean ORANGE! Bye, see you later." She was laughing as the phone clicked off.

"Orange hair" thought Clare, *"what have I gotten myself into?"* Removing the card from the board as Mandy had asked her to do, Clare left the building and hurried home where she logged onto her computer and began checking airline ticket prices from Portland to Tucson and return. She knew the costs would have increased since her trip over Christmas but then money didn't pose a problem these days. Clare took a second to dwell once again on the changes in her financial circumstances since her mother's death. She'd completely forgotten her lunch date with Tina until the phone rang and she saw "TINA" emblazed on the screen.

"Oops, I'm sorry," she began before Tina could even speak. "I got caught up in a project and forgot all about our lunch plans. Please forgive me?"

"Clare, I was so worried. You are usually so prompt and when you didn't show up I tried to call but my phone was dead. Had to give it a super charge – in fact I've got it plugged in the lighter in the car now."

"You shouldn't be talking then," chided Clare. "You know that is dangerous! I'll meet you at the Mansion tonight for dinner and we can talk then. See you at six. Bye."

Before Tina could even answer Clare disconnected. She really didn't want to go to the Mansion for dinner or anything else but it was the only way she could think to mollify Tina over the missed lunch. It would also give her a chance to feel out her father's reaction to her plan to move away.

Armed with costs and flight schedules she waited impatiently for the time of her meeting with orange-haired Mandy. While waiting, she silently rehearsed how she would break the news to her father and Tina that she was moving!

Sitting in a booth at Starbucks, Clare watched the front door for the appearance of the solution to her travel problem…she hoped. A few minutes before the three-thirty meeting time, a young girl, dressed in black with bright orange hair entered the establishment. Clare knew it had to be Mandy. She stood up and waved at the girl who nodded in return and proceeded to get a latte before making her way to the booth.

After introductions, which included acknowledgement that Clare was indeed the same person who had been shot during the summer and a member of the Goforth family, Clare set forth her plan. It was straightforward and simple. "I'll pay your plane fare from Portland to Tucson and return if you will drive with me to Lordsburg, stay the night and drive me back Tucson. In fact, I may drive; I just want someone in the car with me. There is the outside possibility that I may have some problem as a result of that injury. I doubt it but want to have someone with me just in case. I'll pay for our motel in Lordsburg and all expenses for the car and meals. I just ask that you don't tell anyone who knows me about our deal. I don't want my family to know about my detour. They think I'm going from Portland to Orlando to visit my aunts."

"You will pay all expenses and the plane fare both ways? I had planned to leave my junker in Tucson and fly back so I have the money for the fare saved up. It would be wrong of me to take advantage of you by letting you pay my fare back."

"No, that's the deal, consider it hush money. You'll travel back alone since I'll be returning direct from Orlando but I'll pick up your fare. I am serious about keeping this side trip secret from my family so I need your promise not to tell anyone and I mean ANYONE!" Thoughts of her Cousin James intruded but she pushed them out of her mind. She'd take care of him while in Orlando"! If you're in, we need to get our reservations made. What do you say?"

"I say you're crazy, but I'm no dummy. I can handle a deal like that. An overnight trip to Lordsburg is no problem. In fact, I have a good friend I could stay overnight with once we get there so you'd be spared the expense of putting me up in the motel. I'd love to see Miranda again; it's been too long since we've visited. I'll call her tonight just to be sure that my dropping in will be ok. You know, if I drove my own car I'd be spending a lot more time on the road than that."

"I guess so, just one question," Clare said. "Why is your hair orange?"

"Oh, that," laughed Mandy. "It was a New Year's costume gone bad. I'm not into drugs or weird things normally, if that is what is worrying you." She proceeded to tell Clare about the party she had gone to and how her hair coloring had backfired.

"I'd never done any hair coloring before. I guess I'll go to a professional and get it fixed before I go home. My Mom would die if she saw it."

Hearing Mandy's tale of the party made Clare recall her experience at the Halloween costume party where she'd met Steve. It had been their first date; a blind date at that. He had dressed as a mummy and her half-brother Aaron had been Count Dracula. Her friend, now sister-in-law, Margaret had agreed to accompany her as Aaron's blind date. Aaron and Margaret had fallen madly in love, as had she and Steve; it all seemed so long ago and unreal.

"Hey, are you okay?" asked Mandy noticing the far-away look in Clare's eyes.

"Huh, oh yes, I'm fine, just remembering my first costume party, the only one I've actually ever been to for that matter. It was a humdinger too, but I didn't have orange hair." Both girls laughed.

At Clare's urging, they made a quick trip to a local travel agency to book their holiday flight. Clare was sorry she'd promised to go to the Mansion for dinner as she wanted to get to know the bubbly Mandy a little better. With that thought in mind, they agreed to meet the following night at one of the local Italian bistros for a meal.

Dinner was a subdued affair at the Mansion and due to the heavy atmosphere Clare didn't broach the subject of her planned trip. She left immediately after eating feigning a slight headache; an excuse that she knew solicited undue sympathy from not only Tina but her father. Mr. Burns, who had uncomplainingly picked her up for dinner, chauffeured her home as he always did. It would have been unthinkable for Clare to have driven herself due to the possibility of "something" unexpected happening. In fact, her father didn't want her to drive at all and would have launched into a lecture had Clare let on that she did drive to classes and short trips around town.

Later that night after relaxing in a dark room to fend off the headache that she had used as an excuse for her early and sudden departure from the Mansion; the headache that had become a reality, Clare pulled out the journal that she had started the year before. She'd not written in it since June. She reread the events from the Halloween party, the holiday with her new family at the Mansion; Christmas with the Steve's family; the Valentine's Dance at the country club where Steve had proposed to her; the excitement of planning her wedding; helping Myra with the Rose Festival and the sudden end to her entries.

Myra! She had ended it all. Clare felt tears swell in her eyes as she relived the scene in the garden on that fateful night. She had tried to put it out of her mind but it was always there gnawing at her. All of it, the accusations, the anger, the hate, the bullet! She knew that she needed to remember it all, to relive the events in order to understand and forgive and admitted to herself that she had put it off long enough. She poured herself a glass of the chardonnay that Steve had left in her refrigerator after their painful dinner a few nights before and returned to her room. Picking up her pen, she began to write…

March 20, 2007

> *It has been so long since I wrote in this journal – I'm not going to recapture all the terrible events that happened since the last entry, nor even the good parts. Suffice it to say, things have changed in my life. I don't know what I want exactly. I am not Mrs. Steven Burch as planned and I doubt I will ever marry Steve. I still care deeply for him, but just don't feel marriage is right for me… Not right now anyway.*
>
> *I am back at school and will finish this semester, at least. I'm planning a trip to New Mexico over the Easter break. I've*

met a girl who will travel with me and I have a feeling that we are going to become great friends; at least I hope so! My original plans to visit Aunt Pansy & Aunt Daisy in Orlando are still on but I'm going to make a side trip too. None of my family (or friends except Mandy, who I have just met) know about it. I am going to look at some property in the little community of Animas. I am going to run away from everyone and everything here and try to regain some sense of what I want out of life. It is a really desolate area but I seem to feel comfortable there. The desert brings peace to me.

CHAPTER 8

Clare was restless. She knew it was the result of thinking about the day of the shooting. After making her short entry in the journal, she sat on the little deck opening off her bedroom with a second glass of wine and went over the events that led up to her injury. The cool night air felt refreshing to her after the stuffiness of the apartment.

Her thoughts drifted back and she remembered that Myra had seemed so friendly and almost loving during the time Clare had helped her work on the Rose Festival.

Both Clare and Tina had been pressed into service to run errands right and left and check mailing lists and orders for the caters and party supplies. It had felt good to be included in the family activities. Clare had missed so much family life in her first eighteen years; no aunts, uncles, cousins or grandparents.

Clare recalled the day following the big event when Tina and she had left the Mansion to return a loaned necklace to a jewelry shop in Portland's Pearl District. Clare had been entrusted with the valuable necklace, but Tina wanted to ride along. *No harm in that!* So she thought, at the time.

It was unusual to meet up with a high school friend on the street but Clare did. As she chatted with Judy beside one of the Benson Bubblers, located throughout the downtown area, Tina volunteered to take the pearl necklace back to the store. It hadn't taken Tina long to complete the chore and Clare had seen her walking among a crowd of tourists clogging the street headed back to where Clare sat with her friend. A commotion in the street had caused her and others, to turn toward the intersection where an accident was narrowly diverted by the quick reactions of one of the drivers. The car, which had almost caused the fender bender, sped swiftly away. Clare recalled that her impression was that none other than her cousin, James Miller, drove the speeding rental car.

It wasn't too unlikely that James could have been in Portland. His mother and aunt, Clare's aunts, were both in town for the festival and her wedding which was scheduled for the first week of July. James was always watching out for his mother and aunt; or *more likely, their money.* That thought had crept insidiously into Clare's mind. She had to admit to herself at least, that she just didn't trust her cousin especially after his sneaky monitoring of her trip to the southwest months before.

Tearing her thoughts from James, she recalled how she had turned to look again for Tina but couldn't find her. Thinking she'd popped into one of the many shops between where Clare sat and where she'd last seen her, she waited and waited. Then she'd gone in search of Tina. When she arrived at the trash can where she'd last seen her half-sister, she spied Tina's pink, bling-covered cell phone in the trash basket. That was when she knew something was terribly wrong!

She called Alex on his private phone, something she seldom did, and told him what had happened. The next few hours were a nightmare. Police and plainclothes detectives had questioned and then questioned her again hoping to unearth something they could grasp that would help them in their search for Tina. An unofficial APB was issued and the family settled in to wait for contact by the abductors - that it was probably a kidnapping was an accepted fact. Alexander Goforth was one of Portland's most influential citizens, owner of a large established shipping company, and worth millions; ransom was the obvious purpose of the assumed snatch.

After hours of questions, Alex and Clare finally left the police station and returned to the Mansion. Everyone was there, Clare remembered; Aaron and his fiancée Margaret, her two aunts, Markie, the Burns', and several of Portland's finest. Unofficially, an FBI agent had been "assigned" to monitor the suspected kidnapping. Monitors were set up on the phones to trace the inevitable ransom call. They waited and waited…

Myra, Tina's mother, was naturally upset. Her history of mental instability worried everyone. What would the kidnapping of her daughter do to her fragile mind?

Clare learned the answer to that question almost immediately upon entering the house. Myra had launched a verbal attack at her, blaming her for the entire incident! She had thrown up events that had happened before Clare was born and reiterated her hatred of Clare's mother. It had terrified Clare and she'd fled to the peace and serenity of the rose garden where she recalled her mother's description of Myra Goforth as a "bitch"!

Alone in the garden, she tried to gather her wits and regain control of her feelings. She loved the rose garden, designed by Myra and enlarged from a small fountain with a few bushes to a gigantic flowering garden covering several acres, sporting statues from all over the world, and earning a place of honor in the Portland Rose Tour.

It was there that Myra had found her at sunset. Clare thought she'd come to apologize, but it only took one look at her ice-blue eyes to know that it wasn't forgiveness she was offering. Clare recalled Myra's revealing words - the kidnappers target was supposed to have been *Clare*, *not Tina*; they had *bumbled* the job and that was unforgivable. Before she'd been able to process the confession, Clare remembered seeing the slow movement of Myra's arm, the gun tightly in her hand, the fear that had overwhelmed her.

Clare remembered vividly her final thought that night, "God, please don't let me die"! Shuttering, she tried to push the memories from her mind. Draining the nearly empty wine glass, she went back inside to her lonely bed and covered up with her old favorite rose comforter.

CHAPTER 9

The next eleven days, although filled with plans and school work, crept past. Finally the day set for the trip to Orlando, via Tucson and points south, arrived. Clare met Mandy at the airport for their early-morning flight having told her family farewell after dinner the night before and assuring Alex that a taxi could do just as good a job at transportation from her apartment to the airport as Mr. Burns and the family limo. It had been a tense evening with Tina and Alex trying once again to understand Clare's insistence that she needed to move "somewhere" to start over. When she told Tina and Alex she didn't want them to accompany her to the airport their confusion and hurt was apparent. It had been with great reluctance that Clare had even agreed to have dinner at the Mansion the night before her departure; the main reason she agreed to the dinner was so she could assure everyone once again that she didn't need them to accompany her to the airport the next day and that she knew exactly what she was doing and why. Her reluctance to include the others, unfortunately, served only to deepen a slowly growing rift between Clare and her family.

Alex and Tina, both realized that Clare had reached a turning point in her life tried to get her to explain why she was thinking of moving, a revelation she'd dropped on them without warning. Her confession that she was unhappy in Portland had put them on notice that things were about to change and they had been trying to adjust to the new ideas Clare had while trying to convince her that it would be the wisest thing if she would reconsider her plans. Neither had been satisfied with the excuses she had feebly offered on earlier occasions and their attempts to sway her from the decision had been the main subject of conversation at dinner the night before. The meal had been strained, to put it mildly, and Clare made her excuses to leave as soon as politely possible. "I have some last minute packing I've got to get done; I have to get up early so I can manage all the security before boarding." Alex and Tina said their goodbyes with heavy hearts. It hurt them both to see Clare so distant and obviously withdrawn but what could they do?

The air trip to Tucson was uneventful and the drive to Lordsburg an easy one, partly due to foresight on Clare's part in arranging for a rental car via the Internet prior to leaving home. Mandy was a good traveling companion; she enjoyed telling Clare about growing up in the desert and Clare with her new enthusiasm for the area was a rapt listener.

"Oh, some years we have locust invasions. They are everywhere. Then some years it is just too dry even for bugs. The rainy season is July and August. That's when we are hit by monsoons. The rains usually don't last very long, but they can be devastating and dangerous if you don't take care. The arroyos can flood and wash a car off the road. It pays to be careful."

After meeting the realtor in Lordsburg Mandy excused herself, and taking the rental car went to visit her old friend who lived nearby. Clare and Madge Quemado drove the 35 miles to Animas where Clare looked over the property she had seen on the Internet and on the video Madge had sent her. There were no surprises in that reality matched the previously viewed scenes exactly.

"I'll need to have some furniture in place before I move in. Can you arrange to have someone to accept delivery if I order it and arrange for it? I'll pay you extra to do that for me."

"Well, I'm sure we can arrange something. Just let me know when and where, I've got a couple of nephews who wouldn't mind a little extra work. They have a truck and I assure you, they are dependable. I've got another set of keys they can use. I'll just hang onto them until you get here then I'll bring them down to you and see how things are going," said Madge. "Do you have any idea when you'll want to move in?" We have a furniture store in Silver where I bought my own furniture. They handle Lazy Boy and you could actually view their offerings via the Internet and order from them or if you have time, you could go to a local store and find pieces you liked and we'll arrange delivery. Just let me know what you want to do and I'll be more than happy to help you."

"I expect I'll be down here the first part of June, right after classes finish up. The sooner the better; I'm going to get some flak from my family, I'm already getting it so I plan to stay in Portland through the school year and leave as soon as I can after then. Your suggestion about furniture sounds good, I'll look into the Internet options. I don't really have time to shop right now. Maybe some of the local stores will have Internet sites and I can order from them. I'd prefer using local businesses."

"The furniture stores in Silver know me so just give them my address for a contact point. I'll help arrange for the boys to pick up and deliver it if you go that route. Also, you can send things by UPS and FedEx but you'd have to be living here to accept delivery. You might just want to use my office address for smaller things you send or order; we'll get them to you once you arrive. I'm sure it is safe to say that the boys will be glad of a little extra cash for playing deliveryman."

"Thank you so much. I trust your judgment. It is so nice of you to help me. I'll have to get some household items too, but I can bring them when I come since I plan to drive. I'll do some in-line searching for furniture and see what I can find and let you know. I wish I had a few more days and could shop while I'm here but I've learned that the Internet is a lot easier on the feet than going from store to store."

The fact that she had developed such trust in Madge on their short acquaintance surprised Clare. Madge was so open and honest though and Clare felt comfortable with her; actually she reminded Clare of her mother in many ways, including the honest smile and sympathetic eyes. That was the only explanation Clare could think of for her easy acceptance of the woman.

After completing business in Animas, Clare returned to Lordsburg and ate at a small café where she had delicious Mexican food and had Madge drop her off back at the Best Western where she and Mandy reunited at the end the weekend and drove back to Tucson. Mandy told Clare about her enjoyable visit with her old friend, Belinda and urged Clare to contact her via the Internet to learn even more about living in the area. She gave Clare the email address for her friend as well as her own before they parted ways at the airport; Mandy with a return ticket to Portland in her pocket and Clare, with a boarding pass for her flight to Orlando.

Landing in Orlando, Clare was greeted by Cousin James. He was still the well-dressed debonair man he'd been several months before when Clare had first met him. He was also as tactless as she remembered but her distrust of him and his motives were at a new height after what she'd learned from Markie concerning his demands for information concerning her summer trip to the southwest.

"What took you so long to get here? Make a stop along the way? I've been on call all week waiting to know when your plane would arrive." The s challenging greeting words reaffirmed Clare's dislike of her cousin. She knew she had a guarded look on her face as he smugly asked the questions. She could feel her suspicions revealed in her face as clearly as if she'd been gazing into a mirror. Evidentially James didn't recognize her strained look for what it was as he continued talking unphased.

"Alex has called twice wondering what was up – you hadn't checked in with him yet!"

"Oh, I'll call him right away." She'd been unable to use the cell while in Animas due to poor reception, and was too excited about her business deal to call when she had gotten back to Tucson. She'd had just enough time to catch her flight to Orlando. She would simply explain that something came up and she made a stop. He knew she was traveling with a friend from Portland to Tucson although he'd never understood the route she'd chosen for her trip. She could tell him the whole story when she got back to Portland. She sure wasn't going to tell James any of her private business this time!

James didn't talk much on the drive to the posh condo owned by his mother and Clare welcomed the quiet. She felt uncomfortable around James and couldn't help but distrust him. She kept seeing him behind the wheel of the car that had caused the diversion when Tina was kidnapped months before. Clare was convinced that the near wreck on the street had been part of the planned kidnapping although the police had brushed off her claim with impatience.

Aunt Pansy was delighted to see her. She didn't even ask why she was almost two days later than her originally planned arrival time. The condo smelled just like Easter with the baked ham, coconut cake and spring flowers; the air was filled with fresh scents and pastel colored vases burst with blooms on every table.

"We've started cooking already but tomorrow morning will be the big day. I've got a traditional meal planned. We always had a big meal when we were home and I'm going to fix one like Mom used to fix! Right now we are decorating Easter Eggs for the egg hunt at the park. We always donate several dozen. They need to have them this evening so the people can hide them early tomorrow. Would you like to help us or are you too tired"?

"No, I'm fine. I would love to help. Let me get my things into the room and I'll be right in. I would like a cold drink though, do have any coke?"

So began the short but relaxing visit with her dear aunts. James had departed as soon as he delivered her but they didn't miss him. While they colored the eggs, the aunts tried, tactfully, to ask about Clare's recovery from her injuries. A .22 shot to the head was no simple injury and they were naturally curious. If it had been a larger caliber shell, Clare wouldn't have been around to tell about recovery!

"I'm doing fine, really I am. The doctors say I'm a miracle and I'm willing to accept their diagnosis. I don't need any special treatment or coddling, the doctors have even released me from physical therapy. I just have exercises I do at home now. Let's just relax and enjoy ourselves. In an effort to divert the conversation from her injuries, Clare casually asked "do you ladies have any plans for a cruise this year?"

* * * * * * *

Easter Sunday was pleasant and the food plentiful. The entire family, James included, attended church at a non-denominational church just a block from their home where Clare was introduced to a plethora of her aunts' friends. If Aunt Pansy and Aunt Daisy seemed to hover over Clare, she tolerated it. She knew how concerned they had been when she'd been injured. They'd cancelled their plans for an Alaska cruise and stayed in Portland until her condition stabilized. She had just come out of her coma when they reluctantly returned to Orlando after securing promises from Alex to keep them posted daily on her condition.

Unlike the trip to Orlando earlier; when Clare had learned of her inheritance from her grandparents, this time she didn't include any visits to the city's crowded nightspots or fancy restaurants, just family and food. It was intentionally a short visit. She wanted to let the aunts see her and know that she was well besides Easter break wasn't long enough for an extended stay. She didn't mention her side trip or her plans to relocate but she did toss out the idea of writing a book, just to get their reactions.

"I originally thought I'd write about the Southwest, some fiction tale about a young bride traveling across the desert but I've decided that I might just compile a cookbook."

"That would be an original offering," Pansy said a little sarcastically. "Have you ever looked at the cookbook department in a bookstore?"

"Yes, I have! This book would focus on the different ways of cooking in the Southwest; the influences of the Spanish, the American Indian, and the Mexican as well as the pioneers."

"Yes, I've seen some older books like that, but I imagine a new one could incorporate the cultures more thoroughly. You could include bits of history to go along with each recipe," added Daisy encouragingly as she threw her sister a questioning look...

They had hashed the pros and cons of the proposed project for the entire evening before Clare was to depart for Portland. Daisy, who liked to consider herself quite a culinary expert, offered to try out any recipes that Clare wanted to send her and give her opinions of the directions and success of the dish, tips and comments.

"Why, that would be wonderful! You know every great chef has a test kitchen and sous chef to help him. Of course, your kitchen would be a little distant, but I'd really love your help. It would be fun." Clare felt more enthusiastic about her plans when the evening was over.

James hadn't shown up for the big family dinner and that, of course, upset his mother. He did call and apologize saying that business had him tied up.

"What kind of business do you suppose that would be?" asked Aunt Daisy. "That man is up to something no good, I just feel it in my bones. He comes up with excuses just like my ex did when he was trafficking drugs."

Clare had felt that there was something James was hiding but not being around him very much, she hadn't comment on it and wasn't about to delve into his nefarious actions regarding her own life! Tactfully she changed the subject.

On that last night Clare would be in Orlando, James showed up just in time to help finish off dessert! They had eaten a light dinner of ham sandwiches and salad. For dessert they were having fresh fruit, a change from the overly sweetened Easter treats left over from Sunday. James peppered his conversation with occasional sarcastic remarks that on the surface were innocent enough, but seemed to mask strong animosity aimed at Clare. She got the distinct impression that he resented her, not only her visit to her aunts, but also for just being alive! There had been no opportunity to take James to task for the previous invasion of her privacy via Markie but she fully intended to bring it up before she departed.

Clare continually tried to tell herself that the bad vibes she got from James were in her imagination. He had no reason to dislike her. The issues they had over her inheritance had been resolved; he had never been blamed by her for any of the problems that delayed her claim to their grandparent's estate, at least not directly. There were unanswered questions about the DNA samples that had gone missing at the lab where his girlfriend had worked but ...

She racked much his negative attitudes up to his own failures at business, love and life. Yet, she couldn't deny that she was uncomfortable around him. Her innocence had been badly destroyed by the summer's incident and she simply didn't trust James!

Other than having to be around her cousin, her visit had been most enjoyable and she thanked God once more for bringing her full circle into a family that loved and accepted her. Clare didn't mind that James managed to miss most of her time with his mother and their aunt but when, due to other commitments, he had been unable to take her to the airport for her return flight she was frustrated that she'd been unable to use that time to confront him about having Markie report to him on her health and activities during their trip to the Southwest. She had to call a cab at the last minute, when she was honest with herself, the less she saw of James Miller, the better she liked it.

On the flight home, she concentrated on how she was going to tell Alex and the other members of her Portland family about her plans to move. She dreaded the confrontation that was ahead. She had to admit that her visit had been a little more stressful than she'd expected. The aunts were so concerned with her health it made her uncomfortable and she knew it was going to be hard confronting the other side of the family about her decision to move to New Mexico. She kept asking herself why she hadn't asked James about his coercing Markie to provide information about her trip. She couldn't come up with a satisfactory answer to that one! As the wheels of the aircraft hit the tarmac, she decided to delay telling her news until school was out, at least!

CHAPTER 10

After landing, Clare took a cab home, unpacked, called Alex to let him know she was safely home and went to bed early. She had one day to relax before classes resumed.

In no time she was deeply asleep and dreaming:

It was a snowy Christmas Eve (how Clare knew it was Christmas Eve was one of those unexplained mysteries of the dream state). The white flakes drifting softly to earth didn't help make the season seem cherry or bright. It just wasn't the same – the same as what?

Clare's dream revealed the answer to that subconscious question as it re-called all the excitement that had proceeded the first holiday with her family; the Christmas before the "accident." Then she had excitedly shopped for gifts, bought new clothes for seasonal events and relished the warmth of belonging to a family full of warmth and love. How things had changed just a few months later!

This year, even in her quiescent state, she recalled, there had been no din-ners, concerts, plays, or romance. There were gifts for Alex, Tina, Aaron and Margaret but her heart hadn't been into shopping. She directed her bookkeeper to add a "little something" extra to Markie's monthly paycheck as a Christmas gift. There had been no lights in the windows of her garage apartment although the front yard of the house had been gaily alight with plastic snowmen, carolers and a nativity scene just as it had been for as far back as she could remember. She knew that if she could have escaped dinner at the Mansion, she would have gladly done so and that knowledge, even in her dream state made her feel depressed.

She recalled how Christmas dinner had been, in spite of the pall that hung over the family, a reasonably gay affair. That was due mainly to the fact that Aaron and Margaret, having flown in from Chicago, had given everyone the best news.

"Let's have a toast," Aaron had proposed as dessert was served, "To a new generation of Goforths!"

"A new generation," Tina questioned, her eyes flashing, "you don't mean…."

"Yes, I do. Margaret and I are going to be parents about July!"

Pandemonium, or the nearest thing to it, broke out. Everyone had been talking at once. It had been the highlight of the evening.

After dinner, gifts were exchanged and opened while carols played over the intercom which piped music throughout every room in the house as well as out into the garden. Nobody walked in the garden this year, though except ghosts of the past.

In her dream, Clare tried to excuse herself early and drive home just as she had in real time. The strain of putting on a happy face had been less than she'd expected, but the discomfort she felt at being in the Mansion again was hard for her to disguise. Alex recognized that she was having difficulty with the festivities. Walking to her, he pulled her into a strong hug.

"Are you okay?" he asked.

"Yes, I'm okay, I guess."

Clare awoke with a sad feeling. The memories stirred up by the dream served to remind her of what all she had lost due to the accident. Lying in her bed, she compared the two Christmas seasons she'd spent with her father; different as night and day. Yes, she was okay or at least she thought she was okay but she dreaded talking to her father about her moving. She'd considered bringing up the subject of relocation at Christmastime but hadn't really decided to move then. Maybe that was why she'd dreamed about that holiday dinner. She didn't know what had triggered the reliving of the past Christmas but it served to remind her that her father did have his other children to help fill the void her leaving would cause. There was nobody to fill the voids in her own life but she was learning to deal with it.

Fortunately, there was one void she'd already dealt with – Steve. Having accepted the job with IBM, he had left town as soon as he was able to terminate his employment with the university. Although he still called her occasionally, he seemed to be accepting the fact that their relationship was over. Sometimes Clare questioned her wisdom in ending their engagement. She had real feelings for Steve but just needed time to reevaluate her life and goals. Steve had been pushing her too fast. She had to admit that she did miss his nerdy laugh and smile. Sometimes when she had trouble navigating the computer, she missed his expertise even more!

After thinking about her dream for a short time, and putting thoughts of Steve out of her mind, Clare easily fell back into a deep sleep that was interrupted by the alarm clock calling her back to the routine of college classes.

It wasn't until the weekend rolled around that she was able to visit her father at the Mansion and that was when she told Alex about her plans to leave Portland. It had actually been easier than she'd expected. He listened quietly as she outlined her search for a new place where she could relax and work on a book. He didn't even interrupt when she confessed the side trip she'd made over the Easter holiday.

She told him that she had been busy on the Internet during the week and had already picked out and arranged for furniture to be delivered and placed in the trailer and that she planned to drive herself to her new home in a newly purchased SUV.

"That way I can take some of my household things and have enough room to haul them. I wouldn't want to ship things I could take myself."

"What about doctors and medical checkups?"

"I've already talked with Dr. Gruyere about that. There is a medical clinic in Animas, and if I need something more than they can provide, he'll refer me to someone in Tucson or I'll fly back here. I'm taking a copy of all my medical records with me so any doctors I see will have my history. I don't think there will be any problem as far as that goes."

"I'm not going to try to talk you out of this; I can tell you've made your mind up already. I only ask that you don't cut us out of your life. We are your family…"

"No, no, that's not my intent. And this isn't a permanent move. I just want a change of scenery. I need to be alone for a bit. 'Till I decide what I want to do with my life. I want to do something worthwhile. I'll be back here once I get my thoughts I order. I'll probably be taking some classes on the internet even while I'm there."

"I don't guess you've told any of the others about this, have you?"

"No, I was hoping maybe you'd handle that for me. I'm afraid they'll all think I'm nuts, especially Tina. She didn't like the country at all when we were down there last year. I just don't feel up to explaining it all to them. I'm not even sure I can explain it to myself. Would you do it?"

"When do you plan to leave?"

"I'm hoping to hit the road as soon as I take my last test, about the twenty-ninth, that will give me plenty of driving time. I'm not going to rush it. I can make it easily in three days. If you can tell the others after I leave, that would be best, I don't want them trying to talk me out of it!"

"Sure, I'll tell them. Sounds like you've got everything arranged. Just remember that I'm here if you need anything. I mean *anything!*"

CHAPTER 11

Several weeks later, Clare watched silver moonlight beam down on the desert outside her window. The scrub trees looked like dark shadows against the white sand. She liked the solitude that the desert gave her. It was quiet and uncomplicated.

In this valley, she wasn't disturbed by the noises of everyday living as she had been in Portland. She had a telephone if she felt the urge to talk to her relatives and friends, Direct TV to keep up with events in the world, watch a romantic movie, challenge herself with a game show and keep up with the culinary competitions that had given her the desire to become a chef. She had once thought she might actually participate in some of the challenges offered by the network. At least that had been one of her dreams before *the accident.*

She made almost daily trips to the post office to check her mail although she received very little mail, or to pick up fresh dairy and produce at the local store. When the need arose, she made the longer trips to Douglas, Silver City, Wilcox, Benson or Deming for major grocery shopping and had even agreed to meet with the neurologist in Tucson for a routine checkup. Alex and his friend, the Doctor, were responsible for that!

The majority of her day was spent surfing the net and working on her first attempt at a cookbook preliminarily entitled, Culinary Diversities in the Southwest. She had hopes that it would be published by the University of New Mexico since it featured recipes spotlighting

New Mexican products and recipes original to the area, if not them; she had no hesitation about going the self-publishing routes.

She remembered the day she'd decided to leave Portland in the hopes of finding her self-confidence once again; she should have been the newly married Mrs. Steven Burch, but was still single Clare Smith. Steve had continued to urge her to marry him as planned but the *accident* had caused her to lose faith in love and the future. His job change and move to Los Angeles had seemed to put an end to his insistence that they pick up their romance where it had been before the accident. However, he did still call and Clare could hear the hope and despair in his voice as they peppered their discussions with mundane things.

Upon arrival in Animas, Clare had set about a quiet life. She needed the time to regroup and reestablish her priorities. She'd promised her father that she would keep in touch with him and more than likely return to Portland in time to begin her junior year at college in the fall. She planned to continue her education via internet courses during her *sabbatical,* as she preferred to think of her move.

It had been quite a surprise to answer a knock on her door one Saturday morning a couple weeks after her arrival to find her cousin James Miller standing on her doorstep. Clare had to shake the chill that crawled up her spine at the sight at her less-than-favorite person on earth!

"James?" she asked incredulously, "what on earth are you doing here? How did you find me? Is everyone alright?"

"Yes, everyone is fine. I had a flight to Cabo San Lucas, and I know this is out of the way, but mother wanted me to stop and find out where you were living and make sure things were all right, fortunately the Lordsburg airport has one runway long enough to handle my plane, and a small car rental facility – not much to choose from as far as rentals go, but I was able to rent a compact and got directions at the grocery to your place. Not much to brag about, is it?" Clare picked up on the sneer in his voice. It angered her. Who was he to judge her living arrangements?

"No, it isn't. But I didn't come here to impress anyone. Come in.

Would you like some coffee or something to drink; I have something I've been wanting to talk to you about."

"Coffee would be great. I won't stay long as I have a long flight ahead back to Orlando. You'd better talk fast." He looked around her little place with an incredulous expression on his face. "You are really out in the boonies. How did you ever find this place?"

"Oh, just driving around during that trip last year, you know the one you followed via secret telephone conversations with Markie!" She continued before he had a chance to reply but saw the surprised look at her mention of his liaison with Markie. "I didn't want much. Just as long as I have a computer so I can work on my classes and write, a phone to keep in touch with family, and a car, I'm happy. It isn't like I plan to live here forever, you know. Just what was the reason for your spying on me during my trip"?

"Spying? I wouldn't exactly call keeping tabs with a sick relative spying," James tried to defend himself as he spoke in a hurt voice. Mother and Aunt Daisy were concerned about your health and still are. I was just doing what they asked me to do by keeping an eye on you. It had nothing to do with me. I hope you don't think I really care what you do or where you go." His voice was testy and short.

"And so you tracked me down here just to keep an eye on my health? Did it ever occur to you people that I just want to be alone and have time to gather my thoughts?"

"I understand that but mother thought you might be planning to become a hermit or something, you know how she worried about things."

Clare couldn't help but resent that her first guest in her new home was her cousin. She had never gotten along well with him and even though he professed concern, she felt uncomfortable having him question her about her life in the quiet desert community.

"Ever see any illegals?" he quickly changed the subject.

"No, I haven't. Sometimes I see things on the highway that I suspect are border patrol related and I see lots of vehicular traffic and helicopters and drones, but I've never been bothered by anything except a couple snakes, spiders, and horny toads and I'm not forgiving you for nosing in where you had no business. Keep out of my private life. I'll stay in touch with your Mother and Aunt Daisy; you don't need to spy on me."

"Okay, don't get your panties in a wad. I'll butt out if that is what you want. Your life doesn't sound very exciting anyway…to put it mildly," James' sarcasm was dripping.

"Not exciting at all but I didn't come here for excitement. I love the peace and quiet. No intrigue, no mysterious phone calls and nobody trying to kill me, and no busy-body relatives, that's all I need"

"Well, I can at least tell mother that you are well and living in a half-way decent place. She had visions of an old adobe shack or something. So, how is the book coming?" The quick change of direction almost caught Clare off guard but she quickly picked up as though there were no hard feelings after their little discussion about his sneaky spy tricks. Did she actually hear a little hint of attitude change in his voice? That was something she'd welcome.

"Pretty good, I think. I've gotten some contributions from the local people with both recipes and history of the area. I'm adding local interest stories to give more depth to the book. There is one tale about a current haunting in the grocery store and grille where you stopped. I'm hoping that by adding the historical and personal interest stories there will be a larger audience for it, don't know yet how it will turn out but it keeps me busy. I have been pleasantly surprised to find several poets in the area and they have been giving me some material to use in my work."

Clare got up and refreshed their coffee. "Would you like a bite to eat before you leave," she asked. "Not that I am trying to run you off, but there just isn't a lot around here and I'm not geared to entertain right now. The grille is only open on Friday and Saturday nights and the other little café down by the post office closes at five."

"No, no, no," James stammered. "I only stopped to satisfy Mom's fears. I didn't intend for you to entertain me. I've seen you and can give a good report to the ladies. They really love you and were concerned,

I'll let them know that I am persona non grata on your premises and that they should contact your directly in the future."

"You are welcome anytime, James. Just don't try to snoop or interfere in my life. I appreciate the concern of my aunts and I'll call them and let them know how things are going; maybe I should call more often. I get so wrapped up in my writing and schoolwork that sometimes I ignore my responsibilities to family. Do tell them I will try to do better. In fact, I'll call them later today and let them know you were here and thank them for their concern."

"That would be good. And I better hit the road. I want to get back to Orlando before dark if I can. I might be cutting it a little close. Clare, let's let bygones be bygones and start over, ok?" Clare nodded her head in a non-committal way as James turned and walked away. She didn't accompany him to his rented car but watched him with a curious expression. Was he sincere?

After he left, Clare sat and thought back over the short visit. James had seemed so different by the time he left; he'd expressed a desire to halt their cold war and that was a surprise in itself, still something about him made her uncomfortable. She knew he resented her because of the money she'd claimed and she had never been able to dismiss the feeling that he had something to do with the kidnapping that had changed her life so tragically.

She put the thoughts from her mind and decided to call her aunts in Orlando. Hearing their cherry voices always gave her a spiritual lift; after talking with James for even that short half-hour visit, she needed lift!

CHAPTER 12

What was it that drew Clare to the window every night? She peered at the silver- shadowed desert, taking in the grey shapes that seemed alive. She knew there was nothing that she could see that was living except the grass, mesquite bushes and tumbleweed that swished with the desert breezes, it was the almost constant winds that made the blowing shrubs look like shadowy figures creeping across the desert. She knew they weren't real people but sometimes the quiet got to her and her imagination took over.

She had studied the history of the area where she lived; from the prehistoric era men had probably wandered the valley, or what part of it wasn't covered by seas long dried up in those millions of years past. Archeologists believed the area near the little community of Animas was the site of prehistoric Indian villages. Shards of pottery and crude implements had been found in caves that dated anywhere from a few years back to centuries old.

More recently, within the last 200 years, Apache tribes had traversed the valley on their migration from the Arizona/New Mexico territories into Mexico. Bandits, like the Ike Clanton gang of Tombstone fame, had used the canyon trails to ambush weary travelers and miners and the area caves as hiding places for their ill-gotten loot. Clare couldn't help but wondered if some of their loot might not still be hidden in the caves around the Wonderland of Rocks in the nearby Chiricahua Mountains. There was a secret history of heartache in the area as evidenced by the ghost towns, lonely graves and tales of death passed down orally from generation to generation. There was even a lonely tombstone on the roadside across from the little grocery not two miles from her home.

As Clare gazed out the window, she saw a blinking strobe light in the distance. It seemed too far away to be on the highway but that was no doubt where it was, probably a state patrol officer giving a speeding ticket to a late night traveler, or maybe a border patrolman stopping a suspicious vehicle looking for "undocumented" aliens or drugs. Being only forty miles from Mexico, there were numerous border patrol vehicles in the area as well as frequent flyover's by drones and National Guard helicopters. She wondered how many illegal aliens were actually apprehended crossing the dry desert. She'd once seen a man flying one of those little gliders over her house. Later she learned that usually drug smugglers used that method to carry contraband over the border to a rendezvous point somewhere in the desert on the American side of the border. The little gliders could fly under radar and meet up with their counterparts, make their delivery and return to Mexico in relative safety. She recalled her conversation with Opal Green, owner of the Panther Track Café, concerning potential immigration problems. She had asked point blank if there were many illegal's in the area.

"No, not really, we sometimes see someone walking along the highway, but we really don't have any problems here. Everyone sort of looks out for everyone else. We're a close-knit community; our main interests are our families and the school. We support the school heavily. Otherwise, there isn't much else we are concerned about."

"But I see so many border patrol vehicles. Do they stop here a lot?"

"There are the regulars. Some of the guys from Douglas, but most of our troops are out of Lordsburg. There has been talk of building a station around here, but nothing has come from it. I imagine if they build anything, it'll be nearer Columbus or Deming. There just doesn't seem to be enough activity in this corner to warrant much investment although a forward operating post would save the Government a lot of wasted money and man hours. It takes the guys an hour and a half each day in driving time just to get from Lordsburg to here and no telling how many gallons of fuel considering how many big SUV's they drive.

I guess Douglas gets more drug traffic than around here, I don't know. They have the San Pedro River to follow in Arizona; here the creeks are dry most of the time, can't get very far without water."

"I guess Phelps Dodge was pretty much responsible for building the school." Clare said. She had read about the environmentalists in Arizona who had won their battle against pollution and made it almost impossible for the mining giant to continue smelting operations in that state. The ore from Bisbee's Copper Queen Mine had to be smelted and in order to avoid a lot trouble; the mining company bought enough land in the boot heel of New Mexico to build a smelter and a town to support it. The birth of Playas, New Mexico brought life to the Animas Valley.

"Yes, they pretty much financed the school when they were open. But when they closed the smelter and moved out, it left us in a pinch. We've been trying to keep the school open ever since. It's a losing battle. Enrollment gets lower every year. They keep trying to pass a tax increase to support the school, but it has failed twice. The state has forgiven bonds a couple times. I don't know how much longer it will stay open."

"Well, maybe something will change. It seems to me that there is a lot of potential around here; seems like something could be done with all this land and space."

"One would hope" was Opal's non-committal reply as she turned to go back to the kitchen. Clare looked around the cozy café. Located next to the high school it naturally displayed a large amount of "Panther" paraphernalia. As the school mascot, the panther was painted on one wall sprinting across the barren desert. Pictures of the school baseball and basketball teams were on display and tee shirts and baseball caps were for sale at the cash register along with the colorful tee shirt like she'd seen worn by the waitress who served them during her first visit to the area. It was obviously not associated with the school; the question emblazoned across the front was simply "Where the Hell is Animas, NM!" Clare had chuckled when she read it and it brought a smile to her face as she gazed at it again.

Thinking back over that conversation, Clare suspected there was more illegal activity in the area than even the locals were aware of or would admit! It seemed to her that this sparsely populated, relatively unpatrolled area in the Chihuahua Desert would appeal to the unscrupulous people who dealt in drug and human trafficking.

As she gazed at the lights in the distance she noted that the strobe was no longer flickering but colored lights continued to glow. As she watched, the lights were suddenly extinguished. It was total darkness, as total as one could get on a moonlit night anyway. It was unnerving. She didn't see taillights indicating vehicles driving off to the east, no headlights showing them heading west. Strange, she thought. Then headlights again lit up the distance and headed into town along the roadway. It seemed funny. Only one set of headlights came toward the junction of Hwy 9 and 338. Shouldn't there have been two sets of lights at least, one going east and one going west? It seemed strange but she didn't dwell on it….then.

CHAPTER 13

Agent Bill Driver entered the already smoke-filled room. He'd known that he'd have to suffer the smoke and smell of cigars when he'd gotten the summons to meet his DEA superiors at a local motel room rather than in an office at DEA Headquarters. The governmental smoking ban for federally owned and operated buildings didn't extend to private rooms in privately owned motels even though the cost of the room, in this case, came out of taxpayer pockets. That was how the cigar-smoking executives managed to get around the no-smoking ban during their planning meetings; they outsourced their meetings to various civilian facilities.

"Well, glad you could make it," Martin Pollen, his direct supervisor said as he blew out a puff of blue smoke and reached for a cup of what was, undoubtedly, not just coffee. "These guys were wondering about you. I told them that you'd be along in time, and here you are, meet Agent Dunbar and sidekick Jim Smart." Pollen gave a nod to the other two men sitting at the small table in front of the window. The natty curtain was pulled tightly closed adding to the darkness of the drab room.

Bill gave Martin a cursory once over; he noted that Martin was still in good physical condition despite his age and the abuse he heaped on himself via tobacco and booze. Bill recalled that Martin was nearing retirement and he, for one, would be glad to see him depart the company. Martin had been Bill's superior for the past three years and it seemed that he did everything possible to make life virtual hell. They had what the psychologist termed a "personality conflict," but Bill just plain didn't like Martin; didn't like his veiled attempts at humor when he criticized Bill, didn't like the way he talked, didn't like his smoking and drinking on the job, and didn't like his extra-curricular activities with high-class call girls.

Pollen was good at hiding his nefarious activities under the guise of undercover work. DEA people were often able to conduct what would have otherwise been considered unacceptable activities using their jobs as a cover up but Bill didn't play games like that, his behavior was always on the up and up, subject to the scrutiny of his friends and superiors alike.

Agent Dunbar moved to the bed and indicated Bill was to take his just vacated seat near the window. He was a heavyset man who was dressed in a black-striped suit and looked sharp as a pin. Bill had heard of him and knew that he was also nearing retirement. He was no longer an active field agent because the agency felt his mental analysis of cases was far more important than fieldwork. He had shrewd sharp eyes hidden by oversized, outdated horn- rimmed glasses, a balding head and stooped shoulders.

Jim Smart, his partner or gopher as he was fondly referred to among the rank and file, was a small, weasel-looking man wearing gold framed glasses and a thin mustache as befitted his disliked moniker. Bill noted how Smart's ears stood out from his head in a comical manner, but he didn't dare laugh, he'd learned years ago that Smart had a tongue as sharp as his pointed ears.

"Enough of the greetings," said Dunbar. "Let's get down to business. We didn't set up a meeting in an out of the way motel just to throw daggers at one another. Bill, we have a job for you; a very important job and very covert."

"Okay, what's up?"

"We believe there is a group of ICE agents involved with a big drug smuggler working in the southwest corner of New Mexico. It isn't a big operation as far as the ICE agents are concerned, but it is big on the Mexican side of the group. You ever hear of Raphael D'Anda."

"Yeah, he's the head honcho in the "Andy" Cartel. They have their fingers in drugs from Columbia, Venezuela and Mexico. He's ruthless and slick. Nobody has ever been able to pin anything on him. It was rumored that he used to be a lieutenant for Noriega but was never taken down."

"Well, he's behind this little Immigration and Customs Enforcement group working in New Mexico. We aren't sure how many of our border patrol officers are involved, but we have a pretty good idea about four. We believe that D'Anda is recruiting a guy from Florida named James Miller to help distribute merchandise smuggled into New Mexico to points in Florida and elsewhere."

"Miller? I don't believe I'm familiar with him."

"He's a small time player from Orlando," contributed Smart as he handed a manila folder to Bill. "Here's what we have on him. So far, he hasn't really done much, just a few drops to get cash when he's been short and could fit it into his existing business activities. He owns a small charter aircraft flying out of Orlando. His mother keeps him pretty well bailed out of his financial difficulties but he gets in too deep sometimes. For whatever reason, he moonlights for D'Anda off and on. Now his cousin has bought some property near Animas, New Mexico. It's a little ranch/farm community in the boot heel, about forty miles north of the border. It's a poor area of New Mexico. Why she chose to buy land there is questionable. There is nothing there anymore. When the copper mines were operational in Bisbee, Phelps Dodge built a smelter and town nearby but the smelter closed when the mines shut down, the town was sold and now serves as a terrorist training center. We think she might be setting up a base for Miller to expand D'Anda's operations in the US."

"What do you have on her?"

"Now that's really the strange part," Dunbar handed a second file folder to Bill. He opened it and looked at the 8" x 10" glossy of the young girl. She was fresh and innocent looking. He'd seen the type before; they usually turned out to be deadly. How looks could deceive! A picture of Melanie flashed across his memory.

"Her name is Clare Smith," Dunbar continued. "She's the daughter of Alexander Goforth, a shipping tycoon from Portland, Oregon area.

She has plenty of money in her own right; inheritance from her grandparents and a trust from her father. She can only access the interest from the trust for the next five years but she has access to the money from her grandparents at will. That inheritance in itself is a story but we don't need to go there. She and Cousin James don't actually appear close on the surface, but that could be a ploy."

"Last June she was shot by her step-mother and pulled off a miraculous recovery. Her stepmother is in a mental hospital and probably won't ever recover enough for trial. Clare, on the other hand, has pretty much cut ties with the Goforth family and become a hermit in Animas. Only recently, she has started seeing James again. That's where you come in."

"Just what is the plan you have for me?"

"Bill, we want to reassign you to the border patrol. You can get to know the troopers there, and get to know Clare Smith. Knowing your history with women, we are sure you can manage to meet and develop a friendship with her, maybe a close friendship. Find out what she's up to, if she and James are involved in this group of patrol officers working with D'Anda. Get as much info as you can as to what D'Anda's scheme is."

"Well, that's a simple enough assignment!" Bill stared at the men in the room and shook his head is dismay, his sarcasm obvious to all. "You think I can just waltz in and cozy into some border patrol conspiracy, hook up with a dame and finagle information to break up one of Mexico's largest drug cartels? Piece of cake!"

"Bill," said Dunbar, "we know you can do this. You've worked with the border patrol; you know their methods and will be able to mesh with the guys in no time. As for the girl, you'll have to work that out your own way. We aren't giving you any deadlines, take your time. We aren't even sure that there is a connection between the ICE agents and Miller or Smith. We do know there has been a connection between D'Anda and Miller in the past, and if he's making appearances so close to the border with Mexico, it's a safe bet they are hooking up again. Exactly what D'Anda's connection with ICE might be is unclear. That is another thing for you to find out. This is going to be a long-term assignment. We figured after that last case, you could use something a little less stressful and figured this would be a change for you... You don't have any family or attachments at the moment, do you?

"No, but that doesn't mean I wouldn't like to have attachments. Sounds like you're putting me in a potential deadly situation. The news is alive with cartel activities in the Las Palomoas area. They don't even have a police force there anymore."

"Don't tell me you're scared," sneered Pollen. "I thought you liked these macho assignments. I always figured you as a double-oh-seven wannabe!"

Bill Driver looked Pollen in the eye and shook his head. How a jerk like him could get to the top of his profession, puzzled him. "Give me what you've got and let me study up on the situation. I assume you have an operation plan prepared?"

"Oh, yes, of course," said Jim Smart as he handed Bill a large accordion file. "Everything is in there. Including some info on disk and we have a laptop computer for your use. You won't get very good cell phone service in some areas down there, but you can get a phone and internet at the local telephone co-op once you find a place to rent. Your contact there will be Marie Sevenstein at the local phone company. She's worked with ICE before. She'll help you find a rental if you need help."

"You mean I have to find a place to stay, phone, TV, everything? What kind of a deal is this?"

"When you see Animas, you'll understand. Most of the border patrol assigned to Lordsburg actually lives in Deming or Silver City, a few in Arizona. There aren't many rental units available, but I imagine you'll find something within a 70-mile radius. We've coordinated with our man in ICE who oversees the area to be sure you are assigned to the proper units. I'll tell you this up front; our contact is one of the top men in the Denver region so your cover should be safe unless there is corruption high up. It is all is up to you." Smart sounded especially smug as he conveyed this information to Bill.

"When do I leave?"

"Look over the info you've got there, and do whatever research you want to this week. We've set your report date as next Monday, said Dunbar, "any problems with that?"

"No, I don't guess so. I'll let you know if there is. I'm sure I have contact numbers in this portfolio; doesn't seem like you are giving me much time to decide, especially if I have to drive myself to New Mexico. It is how many miles; I'm guessing I can file vouchers for expenses like usual?" Not giving anyone time to answer his question, he gathered up the files and gave a curt nod to the three men. Closing the door with a bang, he realized how glad he was to be out of the smoky room and, although he wouldn't have told them so; he was glad to have a new assignment. He was anxious to delve into the files and see what he was getting into this time.

CHAPTER 14

In truth, the inactivity of the last month had weighed heavily on Bill. His mind kept returning to the last night of the last assignment. He found himself continually reliving the nightmare: it had been cold and spitting snow had made driving on the roads around Chicago treacherous. He hated snow and ice.

The plan he was carrying out had been drawn up by a superior officer, one he considered less than competent, and he had only to follow the meticulous laid out instructions. The only problem was that the textbook plans didn't contour to real life! Not to his surprise, things had gone wrong almost from the first.

Of course, weather was against them from the beginning, something he couldn't blame on anyone but the second difficulty was human nature and any person with a background in psychology should have been able to anticipate problems along that line. Bill had surreptitiously funneled all the information he'd gotten from his contact, Melanie, to the men at headquarters just as he'd been directed. But they had failed to realize that even with forehand knowledge; human nature would rule the outcome of events. Melanie…

Just thinking of her name made him get chill bumps all over. She was one of the most open honest people he'd ever met. The story of her involvement in the drug activities of one of Chicago's most notorious gangs was another example of a living nightmare.

Bill recalled the night he had first seen her – the last too. He'd been slowly working his way into the confidences of the gang members for several months. A good undercover operator was vital to breaking the gang and Bill knew how to finagle his way into the most secretive positions. He'd been doing it for a good ten years. To be honest, he was getting tired of the games he had to play to accomplish his goal and was considering making this his last undercover operation. He would gladly accept a desk job when they offered it to him…again. They always offered him a desk job after a big bust. They'd done it in Albany, San Francisco and Miami and he was sure that the Chicago bust would merit another such offer. This time, he vowed to himself, to take it.

As he'd sat in Gill's Grill looking out at the lake on that fateful day, he saw her come in the front door. The room seemed to brighten when the sunlight bounced off her golden blond hair filling the room with momentary brightness and making a halo around her head. Her sky blue eyes gleamed even as the light dimmed with the closing of the heavy door, she wore little makeup but her lips where glossed in a bright pink color that reminded Bill of a peppermint. She seemed to hone onto him like a magnet picking out a piece of metal. Approaching him at the bar, she slid onto the stool next to him and ordered a white wine before she spoke.

"Everything is set for tonight. The package is due to be delivered at 11 p.m."

"Will you be there?"

"Don't plan on it. I'm hoping to be on a flight to Miami by then, I want to get away from this cold place. I hate Chicago in winter."

Only it hadn't worked out that way. Not only was Melanie present at the exchange but she was standing right in the middle of the conflict between DEA and her drug-lord friend. She ended up being his shield as he fought his way through the carefully laid trap intended to put an end to his days of double-dealing. She paid for the one and only infidelity in her life with her life. The scumbag responsible for her death was also killed. The total cost in lives had been great – two DEA agents and a Chicago cop, as well as Melanie and all the drug pushers involved in the night's exchange!

Bill had gone over the plan in his mind repeatedly since that night; it should have worked. Melanie wasn't supposed to have been there. They should have been able to take down the dealers as the exchange was made; it was one of the cleanest deals in which he had ever taken part. The set up was perfect: A meeting in an almost empty underground garage, the dealers and their escorts pulling into an area already staked out by well-hidden undercover DEA and local Chicago cops. When the goods were exchanged, cops would appear and take the bad guys down. But it didn't work out that way. At all!

Law enforcement agents had been stationed at their posts for three hours when the two vehicles arrived. The agents were cold and tired after their wait but the appearance of the black SUVs had caused their blood to start warming as the adrenalin began to pump. They instantly were on alert. One of the vehicles disappeared from sight apparently headed to the next level of the garage, the second parked nearer the central area of the parking level.

The one SUV slowed down and stopped under the lamplight near a previously disabled elevator; of course they wouldn't know the elevator wouldn't work until they got close enough to see the clearly visible "Out of Order" signs taped over the control panel. It wouldn't matter anyway since there was no reason to use the elevator. They were to meet their counterparts at the doors of the elevator. The driver stayed inside the vehicle as four men exited; two took up guard positions, automatic rifles in full view and the other two, each carrying a silver briefcase, walked slowly toward the elevator where two more men stood at attention.

"Snap," "Snap" the sound of clicking locks filled the quiet garage as a briefcase was hastily opened. One man sampled the quality of the product inside the case while another fanned bundles of cash that sounded like the shuffling of a deck of cards. Suddenly, a single voice broke the silence.

"DEA, hands up!"

Then all hell broke loose. The goons at the rear of the parked vehicle began spraying the garage at random; more men, not lawmen, jumped down from an upper level and took up the gunfire that had been cut off when their comrades had fallen to returned gunfire. The dealers and their counterparts ran for the cover of vehicles parked close to their meeting place. Suddenly, there was Melanie being dragged from the back seat of the SUV next to the disabled elevator. She became a shield for the man who now held the case full of drugs. He threw the briefcase down and held a gun to her head!

"Stop firing or she gets it; I know she tipped you guys off. She deserves to die anyway."

Bill could see the fear on her face and could see that she'd already received some mean blows from her paramour – a busted lip and a swollen eye and her blood drenched blouse attested to the fact that he'd beaten information out of her. It all happened too fast. Gunfire was all around him. There was no time to think as he saw Melanie jerk and stiffen as her already saturated blouse turned redder with fresh blood. Then both she and her captor fell into a heap on the concrete floor as he too took somebody's well aimed shot. The gunfire slowed and stopped. A deathly quiet overtook the garage as the remaining DEA agents began to take toll of the night's work. Six dead men plus Melanie on the bad guy's side and two of Chicago's finest and a DEA agent on the good guy's side, plus a couple minor injuries from flying concrete. Bill's last look at Melanie wasn't one of the sunny girl he'd seen earlier that evening, but a pulverized body torn asunder by numerous gunshots intended for her low-life scum-sucking boyfriend; the man who supposedly loved her. It made Bill reevaluate his concept of love as he sipped on a bourbon and coke and turned his thoughts to the new assignment.

CHAPTER 15

Nothing that he'd been told had prepared Bill for the desolation he found in the boot heel of New Mexico. Miles of flat land, desert scrub and alkaline deposits made up the scenery from El Paso on I10 to the Hwy 338 cutoff. Nothing changed after he turned off either. There were a few distant hills, not what he'd call mountains, although far to the west he could see the outline of the Chiricahua Mountains over the New Mexico line in Arizona; few trees or houses broke up the lonely stretch of road. The dusty side roads leading to tree hidden ranches located throughout the area offered grazing for the herds of cattle that dotted the otherwise barren landscape. He wondered how people lived so far from civilization.

When he reached Cotton City, he viewed the closest thing he'd ever seen to a living ghost town. There were several nice homes, a few ramshackle trailers and some empty buildings all surrounded by farm equipment. Tilled but unplanted fields and vacant buildings that once housed the bustling agriculture needs of a cotton-producing community were scattered along the roadside. The only business was called "Santa Fe Ingredients" where he later learned they converted locally grown New Mexico chili peppers into marketable salsa and hot sauce for commercial use but even that enterprise had diminished in recent years as the orders for New Mexico chili peppers had become fewer and fewer. Judging by the number of cars parked in the lot outside the building, he figured the company employed the majority of the valley's residents. What really surprised him were the four churches right on the highway, two Catholic, one non-denominational and one LDS. It shouldn't have been a surprise really. He knew that every city had more churches than they needed. It seemed that every preacher built their own house of worship. It enabled them to preach their version of the Bible!

Just a few miles further, he entered Animas. It was not even as large as Cotton City but with fewer derelict buildings on Main Street, it looked nicer even though it only consisted of a short block.

The red brick post office sported a fresh coat of paint on its sign, the telephone company had several trucks and cars parked in the lot, and the small café next to the post office seemed to be doing a brisk business, if the cars parked in the dusty lot could be considered any sign.

The school appeared to be the newest and largest complex in the whole area. Spread over a large block, it sported a gym and football field as well as what he learned were the elementary, junior and high school buildings; abundant parking areas with mostly empty spots and several modern houses. He learned later that most of the school buildings had been closed off when Phelps-Dodge had closed the nearby smelter. Some of the available space was leased for a local medical clinic and that the homes surrounding the school itself were intended for the school teachers only.

Pulling into the café parking lot between a beat-up pickup and a battered car he inhaled familiar scent of fried foods present near most cafes. He quickly decided that this was as good a place as any to start feeling out the area. Besides the permeating aroma of the area promised something good to eat and he suddenly realized that he was hungry!

Obviously, there had been no interior decorator involved in the design of the café's fifties-style Formica tables with oilcloth coverings. Worn vinyl-covered chairs in a myriad of colors, were scattered around the large dining area. A simple wall separated the kitchen from where the few customers sat. Bill didn't think he'd seen such a varied group of people in any café. There were men who were obviously cowboys; they wore long-sleeved denim shirts, chaps, worn boots and broad-brimmed, sweat stained hats; women who were dressed casually but with taste in slacks and nice blouses; young people who were obviously students wearing levis and t-shirts sporting their favorite ball team or emblazoned with a witty or trite saying made up the lunchtime cliental.

Bill picked out the only empty table set for two and looked around taking in all that was visible. The waitress, who looked like a high school dropout, smiled at him as she handed him the menu.

"What's good," Bill asked.

"It's Wednesday, and our special today is enchiladas. They are good"

"Okay, that's what I'll have."

"With red or green sauce?"

"What do you recommend? I'm not sure what the difference is."

"The color mainly, the green is homemade, the red store bought but its good. They say the red is hotter but I prefer the green myself, both are actually tasty and hot."

"Make it green and a coke to drink."

"You just passing' through? I don't remember seeing you before."

"Not exactly, I'm going to be working with the border patrol out of Lordsburg, just wanted to get an idea of the area before I reported for duty. Don't suppose there are any places for rent around here"?

"Seems like there might be a couple trailers somewhere nearby, I'm not sure if they are for sale, rent or both. Usually they put notices up in the post office; its right next door. You can check there."

Bill watched her sashay towards the kitchen with his order. She was young, but easy on the eyes and Bill was never one to ignore a fertile-looking women.

While he waited for his meal, he took a second look at the rest of the patrons in the café. Two men were obviously real working cowboys and they looked like they'd spent the last week in the scrub on the back of a horse! Both were dressed the same: cowboy hat with a string under the chin, scuffed boots, faded blue jeans, chaps and long-sleeved shirts. It made a lot of sense that they would do everything possible to protect their skin from the sun's dangerous rays and the prickly scrub.

Two women sitting at a corner table appeared almost as shabbily dressed as the men. Long hair tied back at the nape of their necks, no makeup and a tan that a city girl would have to spend weeks in the tanning salon to achieve only added to the effect. The better groomed and dressed women shared a table on the opposite side of the room, as far from the sweaty, grubby workers as they could possibly find, probably to escape the body odors that accompanied the working men. At least that was the impression Bill got as he watched them casually great one another. It was obvious that there were few strangers among the customers of the cafe. Some school kids joked and grabbed at the last fries on one boy's plate. Everyone seemed congenial and relaxed. Well, almost everyone, he noted.

One young girl sitting alone near the door, stood out from all the rest and he recognized her immediately from the photograph he'd seen in Chicago. Her auburn hair was cut short; the light from the front window gave it a copper glow and set off her pale white skin. She gazed out the window and ate her meal slowly, as though her mind was miles from where she was sitting. She was good looking, if young. Too young for him to get involved with, he told himself.

It didn't take long for the enchilada plate to appear, along with a king-sized red plastic glass full of soda. The waitress managed to brush his arm in a friendly manner as she set the plate down.

"Here you are, big guy," she said in a put-on sultry voice. "I think you'll like this. If you need *anything* else, just whistle." Bill watched her again as she seductively walked away. He'd gotten her message.

While he ate, the café slowly emptied out. He watched the patrons and noticed that there was no food left on anyone's plate. The young girl by the door was the last to leave. Without waiting for a check, she took a bill out of her purse, placed it on the table then walked out the door.

There had been a lot of joking and flirting between the waitress and the male customers as they made their exits but nothing too ribald. Again Bill felt that it was obvious that everyone knew everyone else in the small community, there was a warmth and ease among everyone born of time and familiarity. All except the young girl who had been sitting by the door seemed to mesh comfortably. Somehow, he would have to break into her cold shell and get to know her; that would be paramount to getting the answers to the questions he had about his assignment to the area.

Bill watched her get into a newer SUV, the one vehicle in the lot that didn't appear to have dents and scrapes on it but was as covered with dust as every other vehicle. He had just finished the last bite of his enchilada when the waitress appeared at his elbow.

"Did ya' like it?" she asked as she placed his check face down on the table.

"Yes, I did. It was quite good."

"Well, we're open Monday thru Friday, seven to five, closed on the weekends but you can get pizza next door or a steak, burger or something up the road at the Grille, behind the convenience store. They just opened. You can get a beer or a mixed drink with your meal there, if you want, they don't serve beer with the pizza here because it is too close to the school. I'm usually at the Grille in the evenings, doing bartending duty."

"Thanks, I'll remember that once I'm settled. Guess I'll take a gander at what is posted next door and see if I can get a lead on a place. Thanks for your help."

"Sure, my name's Gina. Feel free to call on me anytime." Was it just his imagination or did she draw out "anytime" in a seductive and inviting way?

"Okay, I'll remember that. Good to meet you. I'm sure we will see each other again."

Gina's "I'm sure," was more a promise than a farewell.

CHAPTER 16

After a restless night at the Lordsburg Quality Inn, Bill reported for duty at the border patrol station. He was surprised at the number of Hispanic employees, but rationalized that it was only natural that there would be Hispanics working so near the Mexican border and, of course, knowledge of the language was a prerequisite for working with the agency. He realized his own Spanish was probably rather rusty and he'd have to start working on bringing it up to par if he was going to keep up with the locals! The different dialects made it even more important for him to assimilate speech patterns from his counterparts in the area.

None of the officers at the small office seemed surprised at having a new employee thrust upon them, they had been promised more agents for months; their manpower requirements were far from filled. What really puzzled them was that the man was from Chicago rather than a newly graduated student from the school in Artesia!

"Hey, man, what'd you do to get sent here, step on somebody's toes?" asked the big burley Hispanic on the front desk. He was built like a linebacker and Bill was sure that he was all muscle under the crisp green uniform.

"No, just routine reassignment, I wanted a chance to improve my grasp of a foreign language and this seemed the best way to do it!" The officer at the desk gave him a look that revealed how much he didn't believe that story.

Just then, the door opened and he head officer motioned to him.

"Bill Driver? Glad you are here. Come in and let's get acquainted."

Bill immediately liked Ron Hall, the man who was to be his boss immediately. He was strictly business and that made Bill comfortable.

"I know why you're here," he said, "but nobody else does, or will! For now, I just want you to blend in, get to know the guys. If you are as good a Martin says, you'll pick up a lead and follow it without any help from me. I only ask that you check in with me once a week. You can do that easily enough when you check in or out at shift change. I don't want any written reports or anything, at least not now. You need to keep your own records though because at some time or another there will be an accounting, so, any questions?"

"No, not now, if I think of anything I'll let you know. I'm used to working solo." *Boy, that was short and sweet,* Bill thought to himself as he sat down in the chair facing the man's desk.

"Good. Where are you staying?"

"I'm at the Quality Inn right now, but I think I've found a rental trailer in Animas. I'm supposed to check back with the owner today and finalize the deal."

"That's good. You'll have to drive into work every day for a while at least. I may be able to arrange it for you to have a vehicle assigned for your use in a couple weeks, but that isn't standard operating procedure and I don't want to do anything to draw suspicion to your activities, so you won't be able to keep it at home. You'll have to drive back and forth to work every day just like everyone else. If they ever get that FOP, Forward Operation Post, you won't have so many miles to cover. They've been working on that for a couple years now and it is still all on paper. Your territory will be from Animas to Rodeo, down to the Arizona/New Mexico border then east toward Playas and Hachita. You can touch base with the agents assigned to the Antelope Wells crossing but we don't do much more than run road patrols there as the troops assigned to the Wells usually keep a close watch on their area. They get a lot of activity from the Columbus/Deming region. Smuggling drugs mostly but a few cases of human trafficking. Then there are the individuals who cross the border and head north. You'll get your fill of activity. We usually have a team or two camping in the mountains.

That is where they catch most of the drug smugglers. There is a briefing session in a half hour. Go get some coffee and meet some of the others. I'll formally introduce you to everyone at the briefing. The rest of today you'll need to stay here and familiarize yourself with our local protocol. It's not going to be field work right off the get go."

With that said, Ron Hall, middle-aged and balding rose from his desk in easy dismissal. Bill wondered about the brevity of his orientation; it was almost like there was no reason to acknowledge that there might be a problem within the local unit; maybe there just wasn't anything to say? Somehow he didn't think so. Ron Hall was a respected agent who was ready to retire in a couple years. Bill had that creepy feeling that something just wasn't right with him and his welcome and he didn't like that feeling. It countered his first impression, but he had to admit that their first meeting had been too brief and almost secretive.

Ron turned his attention back to some of the paperwork stacked on his rather cluttered desk; Bill took his leave and found himself at the coffee pot surrounded by other agents waiting for the morning briefing. The men introduced themselves and made small talk as men uncomfortable with someone they don't know will do. Although Bill didn't actually feel tension or dislike, neither did he feel any welcoming vibes from the men he was going to be working with for an unknown period of time – men who would have to back one another up if a life-threatening situation should arise.

"What have I gotten myself into," he wondered? He felt like he'd stepped into a hornet's nest; a feeling that was to increase in intensity over the next several weeks.

CHAPTER 17

James Miller had a head as big as a watermelon. It was honestly earned; he'd spent the night trying to drink Poncho's Bar dry. From the cotton in his mouth and the ache in his head, he was sure he'd succeeded! He justified his binge with feelings of self-pity; he'd been cheated out of a fortune by a wisp of a girl and now he was feeling pressure from Raphael D'Anda, the main Mexican drug lord around Chihuahua, who had it in for him.

Thinking back to the girl caused him to burn. In just a few more weeks, the unclaimed portion of his great-grandparent's estate would have been divided between his mother and aunt. Both ladies were nearing the end of their time on earth and as their only heir; he would have received a substantial inheritance when they died. He wouldn't have had to wait too long … surely! Fortunately, he'd always been able to coax his mother out of money when he wanted or needed it. Now he'd seen the part of his dream where he became independently wealthy float away, he stood to inherit only half as much or less of his anticipated windfall. If only Clare hadn't surfaced! If only Michelle hadn't botched the DNA testing…

He missed Michelle. She was not only beautiful but also exciting. He always had a good time when around the vivacious blond. He missed their sexual experiences – Michelle was accommodating and inventive. He had never had sex as good as when he was with Michelle. Her nymphomania had enabled him to live out all his fantasies. Maybe he should give her a call; she'd always been able to cure his hangovers in the most interesting ways!

Their breakup had been entirely his fault. He had been totally unreasonable about the botched DNA testing issue. Deep down he knew it wasn't Michelle's fault that one of the newly hired assistants had noticed that there was a sample missing from the lab. A person can plan and plan and think they have a foolproof plan, then someone stumbles on the one thing you have no control over. He thought for a moment about calling Michelle and begging her forgiveness but decided he'd better wait to do it when he was in better condition. Feeling like he did now, he'd no doubt mess things up again.

Shaking his head in dismissal, his thoughts returned to the fiasco with his cousin. After the blotched job on the test, he'd had a stroke of good luck when Myra Goforth answered one of his phone calls to Portland. He'd been checking out arrangements for his mother and aunt's arrival and stay during the scheduled wedding. It took just a few words and he realized that Mrs. Goforth was no fonder of Clare Smith than he was! It still amazed how easily he'd coerced Myra that it would be beneficial to both of them to remove Clare from their lives. But that plan, too, backfired thanks to the bumbling idiots hired to handle the simple abduction. James had already lined up a buyer in Saudi Arabia for his cousin. It took some fancy backtracking and extra work to find a substitute body to furnish the perverted middle-eastern potentate before he could get that fiasco resolved!

In the interim, Myra had ended up in a catatonic state in a hospital while Clare, recovering from her injury, ran to New Mexico to heal her wounded pride! At least his involvement in the plot had never been revealed. He had always been lucky.

He sat on the edge of the bed and lit a second cigarette. He knew he needed to stop smoking but he enjoyed the nasty habit. Smoking had first gotten him into trouble in high school and from the sounds he made breathing and his frequent coughing fits, it was going to give him more problems before he left this world. He recalled how he and two other boys had been caught lighting up in the locker room and expelled.

Why that memory entered his head at this time he didn't know. His Dad's solution to that mistake was to send him to a prestigious private military school. He really tried to make good in that school. He had hopes that he'd be able to get into the Air Force Academy if he excelled, but he didn't excel. In fact, he was lucky to graduate.

His grades were good enough, but the letters attesting to his character would have blocked entrance. He coerced his Dad into paying for flying lessons. Just before he got his license, his father died. At least there had been enough insurance money to buy a small plane and partnership in a budding charter service in Orlando. After a few years, he bought out the partner whom he'd never really liked, and was able to run his own business.

That was the one thing he had going for him – his charter business. If only he hadn't started rubbing shoulders with some less than honest men and allowing them to drag him into their nefarious schemes!

James smashed out the butt and lit up again with a smoothness that belied his desire to quit smoking. He knew his apartment, car and clothes smelled of stale nicotine all the time. God knew his mother had harped at him enough to quit. Maybe someday, he thought. The way prices for cigarettes were rising, mostly due to tax increases; he figured he could save a good five hundred dollars a month if he quit. It was something to think about!

Forcing himself up from the bed, he put the barely smoked cigarette in the already overflowing crystal ashtray and made his way to the bathroom. A shower would wash away some of the sins of the night before and then he could think more clearly. He needed to devise a plan to get D'Anda off his case.

One little trip and he was snared in the drug dealers trap. He wished he'd never met the slick little Mexican who swore to every woman he met that he was French! Like women couldn't see through that lie.

He remembered the night of their first meeting like it was yesterday; Michelle had introduced them. The first statement out of D'Anda's mouth was that lie.

"I'm not Mexican," he said. "I'm French"! The man couldn't even be honest about his heritage. Just thinking about it made James sick and gave him another good reason to stay away from Michelle! That first trip was supposed to be a simple charter from Miami to Cabo San Lucas. He didn't know that he was going to deliver D'Anda's cartel members to a rendezvous with death. He wasn't a bodyguard but D'Anda blamed him for letting his passengers fall into the assassins' hands and, more importantly, for the loss of their cargo – an undisclosed amount of cocaine or arms, James never did learn which. So now, as D'Anda said it, he "owed." The only thing James could do was to play along until he could figure out how to break off the association. He prayed that he could just put an end to it after the next trip. He'd hoped that every time D'Anda called him and he honestly had every intention of doing it just as soon as he could finagle it! He already had a plan in mind!

He was late getting to the office and his pert receptionist had a handful of telephone messages and a pot of coffee ready for him. He really appreciated Trina, the efficient tomboyish woman who looked half her age and had a work ethic that could match the most professional secretary he'd ever met, and he'd met plenty of secretaries in their tailor-made suits, carrying their notebooks and wearing fake glasses to enhance their professional appearance. He'd also seen them shuck the same suits to reveal lacy under garments, lusty bodies and insatiable sexual appetites! His relationship with his own secretary remanded strictly business though. Trina was happily *married* to one of the most beautiful women he'd ever seen – what a waste!

"There are three calls from that D'Anda guy and he is getting pushier with every call. How did you ever get tangled up with him? Also, your mom called twice. Said she missed you at breakfast and wondered if you were all right. Are you? You look rough?"

"I'll be fine. Just drank too much; was matching a guy at the bar but I think I had a head start on him; any news on that charter to Atlanta?"

As Trina filled him in on the schedule for taking some local bank exes to a meeting in Atlanta, the phone rang again, "D'Anda" she said.

"I'll take it in my office. Call my mom and tell her I'm here and I'll stop by later. Don't mention my state, she'll harp at me."

With a big sigh, James grabbed the phone receiver as he sank into his leather chair. "Yes, Raphael, sorry I've not called, just got in. A busy morning," he tried to sound glad to hear from the mobster but it was hard.

"Well, I've got another charter for you, this time to Tucson. Next Wednesday. Leave here early and stay over for two days then fly back. You can do whatever you want after you deliver my guys. Go visit that cousin you've got in the area if you want. You can scope that area out. I've got a friend who does some business around there and we might want you to do some *night flying* for us."

James felt an icy chill. What was he saying about his cousin? What did he know about Clare? If it was anything, it was too much. Raphael had been his source for manpower to carry out the failed kidnapping of his cousin, but he'd never filled him in on the details of the failed operation. Suddenly James' need to end his relationship with this man became more urgent. He forced himself to speak as though everything was alright though.

"I can do Wednesday through Friday next week, but I want your assurance that you aren't carrying anything illegal. I can't afford to be mixed up with the law. As for scoping out any place, consider me out. I don't intend to get involved with any illegal activities, understand."

"Ah, James, don't worry, you won't be involved. I wouldn't do that to you. I'm a legit businessman and I only want legit contacts helping me with my dealings. So we are on, right? I'll have my secretary get with your girl concerning flight times, etc. Usual fares, right?"

"Sure, but be advised, I mean what I said about things being on the up and up. I'll take your legit charters, but don't try to slip anything over on me!"

James shook his head as he replaced the phone on the cradle. How could he terminate his dealings with this low-life criminal? He just might do what he'd been considering and turn honest citizen, report what little he knew about D'Anda's activities to the authorities. Maybe he could work with DEA and put D'Anda out of commission for good.

The remainder of the afternoon James spent signing off on vouchers and making flight plans for the Atlanta trip as well as a trip to Tucson. Then he inspected his plane. There was always something to do with the plane. Just as a gardener always found something to do in his garden, a pilot always found something to tweak on his aircraft.

Trina only worked until 4:00 p.m. daily and before she left the office, she walked out to the hanger to let him know she was going. He was glad for the heads up, as he had lost all track of time. Realizing he was hungry, he cleaned up his tools and put them away neatly in their racks. As sloppy as he usually was in his own apartment, he was fastidious in his work area. When he finished cleaning up, he called his mother and offered to bring Chinese if she'd have him for dinner. Of course, she was delighted. She was always delighted.

Pansy Miller was a very attractive senior citizen. She lived with her sister, Daisy, equally attractive but not quite as old. The two women, both single for several years, enjoyed their retirement. Their plans for a summer cruise to Alaska the year before had been interrupted by the tragic shooting of their niece, Clare, just before her wedding. They'd had big plans for that summer and it started with the Portland Rose Festival. As it turned out, it ended with the Portland Rose Festival too! Their niece's wedding had been postponed when the incident occurred and they cancelled their trip to Alaska staying at the ready for a call from the hospital telling them that she'd expired from the gunshot to the head while praying for a miraculous healing.

Fortunately, for them, unfortunately, for James, Clare recovered. James couldn't explain why he still harbored such resentment toward the girl. Her claim to his great-grandparent's money was legitimate and settled; nothing could change that. Maybe it was the way his mother and aunt dotted on her that pissed him off so royally. When she announced that she was leaving Portland for the boot heel of New Mexico, they both got so upset that James had been forced to make a stop to see that she was okay. He had done that on the way back from the ill-fated D'Anda charter to Cabo.

He found her living in a small mobile home in the middle of a desolated desert. Her new home was quite a come down from the elaborate

Mansion she'd had access to in Portland. She seemed content and lacked for nothing...*except maybe brains*! Said she was writing a cookbook and taking on-line classes. His report to his mother and aunt was filled with only positive things. In fact, what he'd told them was true, he had just left out the things he'd heard about the dangers of living so close to the unfenced border, the drug trafficking trails crisscrossing the Chiricahua Mountains, and the arms smuggling from Tucson to points south. No reason to worry the old ladies.

CHAPTER 18

James actually enjoyed the time he spent at his mother's home. He could relax when he was there. It was always clean and the meals were exceptional. The only place where he figured he could get a better dinner was at Kobe's Steakhouse where he ate every Thursday night. He had a standing reservation for a choice table at the steakhouse, lately he'd been taking a different bimbo along to dinner every week. She always paid for her dinner with dessert served in his apartment – the dessert choices had, thus far, been exotic and varied.

Sometimes James felt ashamed at the lustful side of his nature but not ashamed enough to curb his carnal appetite. He figured that as long as he was single and used proper protection, he wasn't hurting anyone with his exploits. At least he hadn't fallen into the drug habit. He'd heard about the dangers of drugs from his Aunt Daisy who had been a player in the game during the heyday of Height-Ashbury and the beginnings of the hallucinogenic drug experience. He knew that it wasn't for him. He might suffer a hangover but addiction and flashbacks were not things he wanted to experience.

Arriving at his mother's apartment, he was revived by luscious smells emanating from the kitchen. "What are you cooking?" he asked as he unloaded the Chinese he'd picked up and headed to the living room to mix a drink. His mother might not drink much, but she did keep a bar stocked with his favorite Jim Beam and coke. "I told you I'd buy tonight."

"Just a simple Korean Fried Rice," said Aunt Daisy. "We only have to fry the eggs. Been waiting for you, so don't get too comfy with that drink. It'll be ready to eat in two minutes and it will go fine with whatever you brought!"

Picking up his already half-empty glass, James followed his aunt to the kitchen where the smells were overpowering. Korean Fried Rice was one of the recipes his father, a career military man, had brought home with him from a tour of duty overseas. It was simple and spicy. James could feel his mouth start to water just at the thought of the fried egg on top of a big plate heaped with the spicy rice, veggie and meat dish.

"So, what are your plans this weekend?" asked his mother.

"Not much. Gonna take it easy. Don't tell me you have something lined up for me."

"No, not really, I have a couple recipes that Clare has sent me to try out. Thought I'd let you be a guinea pig and judge."

"You mean she's still working on that cookbook idea?"

"Yes, and I think it a fine idea. She's sent me some things that sound good. This weekend, I plan to try a tamale recipe. That is something I've never made and I think, after reading her instructions, it won't be too hard."

"Well, I'm sure they will be fine but I don't know how they can compare with this meal! One good thing came out of my dad being in the Army all those years – we learned to eat exotic foods. I love this stuff. Hope you made enough for me to take some home! You can keep the leftover take out stuff and I'll take the fried rice!"

"Of course I did," his mother laughed as she sat down with her own heaping plate.

James studied the two women as he ate. His mother was still slim and spry although her age was really beginning to show. Her eyes were a sparkling blue, reminding him of the sky on a cloudless day, but the lines surrounding them were getting deeper and deeper. She had a smile that reacted to every kind word and was the defining feature of her buoyant character. Sometimes he thought he saw a little hesitancy in her movements but whether this was due to caution or age, he wasn't sure.

On the other hand, his Aunt Daisy still maintained her quick actions. She'd always been the more energetic of the two – a nervous energy. He wondered it her drug use during her youth could explain that. She'd had a much harder life and actually looked the older of the two sisters. There was no denying their relationship though. They had lived in harmony for several years now and they seemed to get along better every year. James was glad that they had each other. It saved him from a lot of worry about his mother.

After the meal was finished, James helped clean the already clean kitchen while his mother fixed him a to-go bag. "That was a really good meal, Mom, as always."

"Well, thank you, son, your contribution made it more of a feast and we really love Chinese too. We missed you this morning at breakfast. You have us spoiled; coming by every morning to cook for us. It worries me if you don't come. Do call if you're not going to be over."

"Sure, I will. I didn't mean to worry you. Just had a late night and overslept. I need to get home early tonight and make up for lost sleep, so I'm leaving as soon as I'm done here. Am I forgiven?" The last was asked as he hugged his mother.

★ ★ ★ ★ ★

James didn't go home when he left his mother's house. He returned to Poncho's Bar, the site of his over indulgence the night before. He liked Ponchos; it was relatively quiet and not a hangout for the prostitutes who frequented other bars on Orlando's strip. There were hookers who came in, that was a surety, but they were high-class hookers more properly referred to as call girls, who usually came in with their customers trying to fool the regulars that they were respectable women, either spouses or a date. James didn't care. He wasn't looking for a woman. He just wanted to think about the dilemma in which he'd found himself. He was tied up with a known drug lord and although he'd told D'Anda that he didn't want to be involved in illegal activities, he knew that he was and he was scared. He might lose everything he had and hoped to have due to his association with the man who was the head of a growing Mexican Cartel.

He had just settled into a small corner booth and was nursing his first JB and coke when he saw the cause of his apprehension approaching. If James had been a woman, or a man of a different persuasion, he might have been attracted to him. D'Anda wasn't tall by any means, at 5'10" he was about the same height as most of the women James dated. His body was slender and rock hard, the result of hours spent in his private gym weight lifting, exercising and swimming. He held many business meetings poolside after his 100 laps in his private Olympic-sized pool. The man had an estate that made the fine homes in the Orlando area look shabby in comparison.

"Slumming?" James asked as the dark eyed, black haired man stopped at his booth.

"Not really, I've been watching for you. We need to talk."

"Okay, talk." James didn't feel like talking to the overly-dressed man but knew he had no choice.

"I seemed to gather that you have a problem working for me. Why?"

"Why? You have to ask why? You are a known drug dealer. Isn't that enough of a reason why?"

"That didn't seem to bother you when I offered you twice what you usually get for a charter to Cabo. Why the change of heart? Have you had any problems with the law since working for me?"

"No, of course not, you'd know if I had, you've got your connections within the police department, DEA, and God knows what else."

"Then what is it?"

"I don't want any trouble, that's all."

D'Anda looked at his gaudy pinkie ring for a moment before speaking. He waved the bar maid off with a flick of his wrist and then he humped over the table and spoke in a low voice.

"I need someone to do a job for me." He looked at James through hooded eyes. "No drugs, I assure you. Just deliver some items to Lordsburg."

"Lordsburg," James exclaimed.

"Shush, not so loud. I don't want everyone to know about our business. It is a simple delivery in New Mexico of items you pick up in Tucson where you are going to take some people next week. When you land in Tucson, there will be some boxes waiting for you. Load them on your plane and fly to Lordsburg. There is a vehicle there belongs to me, you take the vehicle and drive to your cousin's place and visit her. You don't even have to unload, while you are gone, the merchandise will be unloaded by the workers at the airport. They will be servicing your plane and you will give them your keys so there won't be any issue there. It is a small airport and nobody pays any attention to what happens there anyway. When you get back from your cousin's you don't mention the missing cargo, fly back to Tucson for your charter and bring everyone, including your plane and yourself, back to Orlando. It is simple."

"What is the cargo?"

"You don't need to know. It isn't drugs and it isn't bodies. That much I assure you. The only thing you do is fly your plane to Lordsburg and visit your little cousin. You can do that, can't you?"

"If I don't?"

"Your mama might wish you had."

James felt the blood rising. He had never been a physical person but suddenly he wanted to grab the tidy man across the table from him and wipe the smirk off his face. "You are threatening my mother? I wouldn't suggest you do that."

"Not a threat, Mr. Miller. I don't make threats but it seems to me that in the interest of their health, you wouldn't want to cross me. You *owe* me; remember the mess in Cabo? How would you like your mother to learn about your involvement in a massacre that happened in Mexico?"

"I didn't have anything to do with that mess and you know it!"

"So, your mama doesn't. Do this job and we'll be even, I won't ask anything more from you. We'll sever our business dealings. My friends will be at the airport a week from Wednesday at 10:00 a.m. Check your flight plan; remember it is a round trip. You might want to give your cousin a call so she'll be expecting you. You'll need to stay over at her place for the night or somewhere in Lordsburg, whatever you want."

James remained seated as the conniving man retreated from his sight. He hailed the bar maid and she brought him another drink. Could it be that easy? Just one job and he'd be finished with D'Anda. He wanted to believe it but something told him it wasn't that simple.

CHAPTER 19

Eduardo Guerrero stood in the shade of the hanger and looked at the landing strip. Number 12 was the best strip at the Lordsburg airport, the only one long enough to handle any type of small jet. It was paved and maintained regularly, mostly due to the mayor's desire to please the wealthy ranchers in the area. Although the desert might look desolate, several thousand acres of ranchland sustained thousands of cattle on rich grasses and provided more than adequate income allowing the local ranchers to live a luxurious style. They called it Number 12, but there were only three strips total. The other two were suitable for the crop dusters that sprayed the peppers and grains, the main cash crop for farmers.

Eduardo knew that many of the ranchers had lucrative business deals on the side, too. Deals that they would pay a nice price to keep hidden from the public eye, but he'd never been tempted to try the black-market route. He had too much to lose - mainly his life! He remembered the stories he'd heard about bodies being found in the desert; bodies of people who had had noses too big for their faces. He wasn't taking any chances of ending up as coyote and crow food.

The simple truth was that Eduardo liked his life. He had spent four years in the air force, where he learned to be a top-notch mechanic, and could work on everything from the smallest piper cub crop duster to commercial jets. His favorite craft to work on, though, was small charter jets. He was good and he knew it.

The Piss-ant City of Lordsburg had been fortunate that he'd agreed to work for them. The city didn't have any aircraft of their own and no regular service by any airline; but by having him on site, they were able to offer ranchers and professional people maintenance needed to entice them to keep their aircraft at the local airport. He provided a needed service; in return he received a fair wage, was able to be near his family, and could still work jobs on the side to supplement his income. He was content. To keep it operational the airport raked in enough cash from renting hanger space to cover his wage and other maintenance costs.

As a local boy, he knew almost everyone in the county. His father had been a veterinarian and Ed, as everyone called him, had been his assistant until he joined the air force. After spending his time in the Middle East, he was ready to chuck a military career and return to the undemanding life in New Mexico. His G.I. Bill could go unused as far as he was concerned. He had learned enough of a trade while on active duty and further schooling didn't interest him. That line of thinking would have been a disappointment to his father who had always hoped that he would follow his example and become a vet. But when the senior Eduardo became a victim of invasive skin cancer; he gave up that part of his dream knowing he probably wouldn't live long enough to see his son finish school and take up the practice. Ed had made it clear to him that he wasn't interested in following his footsteps. A short time after he was diagnosed with cancer he began looking for a buyer for his practice. Fortunately, he was able to finalize the sale before the cancer finalized him. He was grateful that he had decided to sell. It assured that his wife, Maria, would be able to live the remainder of her life in comfort and, most likely, provide a nice inheritance for Ed when she passed away.

Eduardo knew that his father had made financial arrangements for his mother, yet she continued to live the same frugal lifestyle she had lived while his father was alive. Her modest living assured that he would have a sizeable inheritance upon her death. But he didn't know that. She had given him enough money to buy a nice home, a few miles outside of Lordsburg, when he married Belinda the year before; Ed actually figured there was little or no money left from his father's estate. Ed had been approached a couple of times to help in some illegal operations that seemed to flourish in the quiet valley, but he'd always declined to get involved. There were no financial pressures on him, so no reason to take the risk presented by illegal activities.

It was a cool morning and Eduardo, sitting in the small airport lounge, was just finishing the breakfast burrito and coffee from McDonalds when he saw Alvaro Garcia, the only nighttime guard posted at the airport, approaching. Al was an okay guy but not one of Ed's best buddies. They talked some, were civil to one another' but never shared any social activities.

"Hey, Ed, you wanna make a little extra cash?"

"Maybe, what you got goin'?"

"Just a little job hauling some stuff down to Animas. A guy is flying in this evening with a load, I need somebody to help unload and deliver to a ranch down on 338. Usually I have Jose help me, but he's out of town."

"Sure, I'll help you," Ed replied without thinking. "It's nothing illegal, is it?" he asked after thinking for a second.

"Oh, no, man, I wouldn't be into anything like that!"

Eduardo wasn't too sure about that last statement. He'd heard rumors about Alvaro for a long time. Rumor said that he sold and used dope regularly. Ed wished he hadn't been so quick to accept the job, but it was a little late to back out now! He'd heard that you don't back out on a deal with Alvaro. Some guys had and they'd paid a heavy price. At least, that was rumor. Fact was that Lordsburg thrived on rumors! Ed didn't think that Alvaro was dangerous, not life-threatening dangerous anyway; he'd never seen him violent, but stories abounded that he had made life unpleasant for a couple of Ed's acquaintances. Normally, Ed would have declined the job right off and, thinking back, he couldn't figure out why he'd accepted it this time! It was a decision he would regret…eventually.

Ed was ready to do regular maintenance when the propjet skidded to a standstill later in the afternoon, his tools were handy. The private pilot turned the aircraft and taxied to the small hanger where it would rest until its departure, a common enough action in the small southwestern airport. There was certainly nothing suspicious about a small craft landing, being serviced and parking overnight while the pilot visited friends in the quiet valley. Nothing looked out of the ordinary on the outside of the hanger. Walking the short distance from the hanger door to the aircraft, Ed and Al were ready to unload the unmarked cargo and place it into a pickup truck sporting a windowless shell. The truck was driven by another of Alvaro's buddies who helped arrange long boxes in the back of the truck. It was a simple operation; Eduardo and Alvaro unloaded the cargo and it was hastily stored in the truck shell. The pilot sauntered over to surrender airplane keys, and meet the mechanic responsible for performing routine maintenance and securing the aircraft for the night.

After brief introductions, James Miller handed the aircraft keys to Ed and took another set of keys from Al who pointed to a black SUV near the gate. There were no words exchanged – none were necessary. With an almost loving look at his plane James turned to leave shouting above the wind for Ed to "Lock her up when you finish. I'm going to visit my cousin and I'll be back tomorrow. Leave the keys in the office where I can easily find them." With that, he drove off in the black SUV. The whole exchange had taken less than ten minutes.

Once all the cargo had been unloaded, Al and Pete, the truck driver, grabbed a beer out of the cooler in the back seat of the truck's club cab while Ed locked up the aircraft. He would wait until he got back from the delivery in Animas to perform the maintenance.

He wondered why Pete didn't go with Al to unload and was going to suggest that Al use him for delivery when he heard the sounds of raised voices from inside the metal building. He couldn't tell if the voices were angry or just joking. As he entered the hanger door a few minutes later, he saw Pete leaving in a small dented pickup. Gears grinding, Pete spun his tires, and in a cloud of dust left the area as though the hounds of hell were on his trail! One look at Al's face told Ed that he didn't even want to ask what was going on; it was obvious that the two men had not only had words, but unpleasant words at that. Questions unasked and unanswered, Ed and Al got into the cab of the loaded truck and casually left the airport as they would at the end of any normal workday. Only instead of turning downtown, they headed for the I10 ramp which would take them to the Hwy 338 exit.

The drive to Animas didn't take very long. At 388, they turned south for the last 25 miles of the trip. The speed limit dropped from the 75mph allowed on the interstate to 55 mph on the secondary road, but they still made goodtime.

"It would have been a straight drive to our destination if we'd gone down Hwy 80," Al said shortly after turning south. "In fact, I probably should have taken the back road to Animas, but it would have been a longer drive since that road is so rough." Al was obviously thinking out loud as the men hadn't spoken since leaving the airport. Ed hadn't thought it wise to break into the obviously irritated mood that had come over his companion. "But," continued Al, "there are fewer border patrol vehicles and seldom a check point on 338. Hwy 80, you get hassled all the time, not just border patrol either, state police, county sheriff, too." They buzzed through Cotton City and straight past the Animas post office and Telephone Company, taking a right at the First Baptist Church onto Hwy 9 going west. Ed had figured they'd continue on 338 South to one of the bigger ranches in the area but by turning on 9, they were going toward Rodeo and Arizona. Border patrol vehicles regularly patrolled the area but since it was late afternoon, the shift change was in progress so most of the agents were reroute either to Lordsburg to end their shift or hadn't yet made it to their assigned areas to start a new one. They'd passed several vehicles headed to Lordsburg as they traversed 388 going south; those they had just seen gave Al a high-five but didn't stop him as he headed toward the secret rendezvous.

Upon reaching the Hwy 80 intersection, Al turned towards Rodeo, another spot in the road that would be missed in a blink, but before entering the community, he headed towards the Cave Creek area. Ed was familiar with the area. He'd often camped at Cave Creek and was still in awe of the magnificent scenery. It was a good distance to the mountain park in Arizona, but Ed enjoyed it. Shortly after passing through Portal, they entered Federal land, and left pavement behind. Signs warned of illegal activity in the area, but neither man commented on them.

Ed had decided there was more to the delivery than Al had told him, simply, because the privately owned property around the park area couldn't exactly be considered ranches! Yes, there were vacation homes, but they weren't headed in that direction. Instead they drove into a dead-end canyon.

Al pulled onto the dirt track that thinned out to nothing at the base of a small mound, surrounded by monstrous boulders and rock walls that reached hundreds of feet into the darkening sky. Exiting the vehicle, Al began to scale a small rocky hill. When he was about ten feet up, he pulled back huge tumbleweeds revealing the mouth of a small cave. There were many caves in the hills in the area, but Ed had not been in many of them. In fact, most of them were openings in the rocks visible from the ground but inaccessible to humans! He'd heard some more adventurous hikers had found arrowheads, pottery chards, miner's tools and even unexploded dynamite in them. But that was before they were designated off-limits by the park service. The dynamite found was usually old and unstable as it had been in the deserted caves for many years. The other finds bragged about over beer were rattlesnake nests!! Fortunately, nobody had ever suffered injuries resulting from the more dangerous of the finds.

"Okay, let's start packin'," shouted Al. "This is where we are to leave the stuff. Someone will be along later to pick it up. Our job is done when we store it here."

"I thought you told me you weren't doing anything illegal? This seems like some kind of smuggling to me. What's the truth?"

"I tol you the truth, I'm just delivering cargo to a pickup point. Man, I don't know what it is and don't want to know." I get my money tomorrow and you'll get yours. No questions, ok, man."

"OK, this time. Since I'm here and already involved, but don't expect me to do it again," Ed responded as he carted the first of the four heavy crates up the hillside to his accomplice.

The entire cargo was unloaded and secured inside the little cave within minutes. Ed was relieved as he watched Al replace the large tumbleweed over the cave opening. He pulled off his heavy work gloves and threw them into the back of the truck.

"Man, I mean it. Don't ask me to help you again!"

"Ah, don't be such a chicken. Nobody is gonna bother us. Everyone is taken care of already, if you know what I mean."

"No, I don't know what you mean. The border patrol is hot and heavy around here. I hear about busts every week. What makes you think you can get away with this shit?"

"I think I can get away with it because the border patrol won't bother me. You saw how they waved when we passed them. You think they are gonna wave one minute and stop me the next? I tell you, the people who make these deals have the border patrol in their pockets. The busts you hear about are people who aren't smart enough to grease the palms of the right people. Man, where you been burying your head?"

It was another quiet ride back to Lordsburg. When Al stopped at the airport to let Ed out at his truck, tension was still thick enough to slice with a knife.

"Just don't ask me again, understand?" said Ed.

"Yeah, I understand. You just don't blab anything or you'll be sorry, *you* understand?"

Ed slammed the door and turned to get in his own truck ignoring the mental nudge to check out maintenance on the locked plane that was nagging at him. He told himself everything would be okay till morning and he'd get up early and do his job.

"Man, I mean it. You know too much now. My people will be keeping an eye on you, so don't do anything stupid?"

CHAPTER 20

James drove away from Lordsburg and stared in wonderment at the desolate countryside south to Animas. Why anyone would want to live in a place like this was beyond his comprehension! At least the roads were good and the SUV was a top-of-the line model that glided smoothly over the miles. In no time, he found himself at his cousin's back door.

"I use the back door as most people would a front door," she had told him on his first visit. "The front door opens onto the big porch and I use it more like a backdoor. The trailer is situated funny and it works better this way." She was waiting for him on the small back porch having heard his car and seen his dust trail long before he turned off the motor. The porch belied the desert environment surrounding the trailer with hanging plants, potted palms, and flowering pots almost hiding the view outside the small room. A huge Devil's Ivy was centered on the glass-topped table set in one corner, with two plastic chairs cozily placed on each side. The chairs had colorful cushions that matched the one on the simple wooden bench scooted against a wall. Clare was drinking a glass of iced tea as he approached the porch and didn't bother to get up. She had a pitcher of the iced beverage ready to pour into an ice-filled glass for him.

"I see you didn't have any trouble finding me again," she greeted him.

"No, but I don't know what you see in this place."

"That's its charm; there is nothing here. No traffic, no noise, no nothing. I am not required to do anything I don't want to do, go anywhere I don't want to go, or see anyone I don't want to see."

"Except me," James said with a little unveiled sarcasm, he wasn't sure if she had intended her reply as sarcasm or not. "Here I am, the unwanted visitor, right?"

"Wrong….you are always welcome," Clare spoke sincerely, more sincerely than she really felt. She'd resolved to put the past behind her and try to embrace a warmer relationship with her cousin. "In fact, I'm really glad to see you. I'm a little worried about Aunt Pansy. She seemed a little off last time I talked to her. Is she okay?"

"Just the same old Pansy as far as I know; she gets a little goofy sometimes, usually after a couple glasses of wine. Was it late when you talked to her?"

"Yes, I guess it was, at least by Florida time. I forget the time difference sometimes. I've got some dinner cooked, hope you like it. It's a new recipe I'm trying out for my cookbook. I'm really glad to have a guinea pig."

James was surprised at Clare's almost warm reception and even more at the pleasant smell that greeted him as he entered the kitchen. He was directed to the cozy living room and in short order offered him a Jim Beam and coke. He wondered where Clare had gotten the alcohol but didn't ask; he knew she had friends and money enough to get anything she wanted to get. He had to admit he was impressed by the neat clean rooms and the tantalizing aromas that wafted through the air.

"I remembered you drink Jim Beam so had one of the people from the grille buy me a small bottle. Usually I don't keep liquor in the house. Well, maybe some wine sometimes if I can coerce someone old enough to buy it for me. I usually have them buy two of whatever I want and give them one. I know that isn't exactly legal, but one has to do what one has to do!" It was as if she'd read his mind.

"This is great. If you want some beer or wine, I can run up to the store and get you something while I'm here."

"No, that's okay. I don't drink much anyway. But I am thinking about trying to make some wine one of these days!"

"Oh, yeah, homemade wines, now that would be a real treat!

"Really, it wouldn't be that hard. I found a recipe for wine using frozen grape juice or, I can order kits on the Internet. I may have to lie about my age if I go the Internet route; I don't know. I'm thinking about it, that's as far as I've gotten. You relax and I'll get dinner on the table. It won't take long." While Clare finished up the meal, the two shared chit-chat.

"The ladies were glad to learn that you live in a decent place. They had visions of a crumbling adobe filled with snakes and spiders. I had to describe it in detail to them after my last visit."

"You did? Clare laughed. "Well, there are a few spiders, but I've found some super spray that takes care of them. As for snakes, I've seen a couple on the road but so far none here. Actually, I don't wander too far from the trailer and I've got a clear view to the car. I don't go out at night. I understand that is when the snakes move around. You know, I'm surprised they worry about me."

"You shouldn't be. They think a lot of you. They found a missing link and don't want to lose you again. You have heard how their sister's disappearance affected them and when you were shot, they were devastated! I'm glad you recovered, for their sakes."

Did Clare catch some sincerity in his voice? James had never particularly liked Clare and the truth was that the feeling was mutual, but something had changed, there almost seemed to be friendliness in his manner. Maybe he'd made the same vow that Clare had made?

It was easy enough for James to visit with Clare while she worked due to the openness of the mobile home. After a pleasant meal, he settled down to watch back-to-back episodes of NCIS, one of his favorite TV shows while Clare cleaned up the kitchen.

"I do wish I could get a dishwasher installed," she lamented. "I'd have to surrender an under-the-counter cabinet to do that and I can't give up that storage space though, so guess I'll have to learn to live with dishpan hands and rewash sometimes. I'm not the best dishwasher in the world; that's for sure."

"Maybe you could get one of those little countertop things. I've seen them in books?" suggested James.

"Oh, no, that would be as bad as losing the under-the-counter space! I'll just rough it."

It was almost dark when James retrieved his bag from the SUV. He kept his eyes to the ground as much as possible remembering Clare's words about snakes being more active at night; he wasn't any more anxious to meet up with a creepy crawly than she was! When he was finally in his room he realized, that he was more tired than he thought and decided to go to bed early. The large bedroom had an entrance from the front porch of the mobile home and was cooled by a portable water cooler; the steady hum of which lulled him to sleep in no time. Clare, on the other hand, sat in the dark living room wondering what had really brought James to the boot hill of New Mexico and marveled at the change in his attitude towards her.

CHAPTER 21

About the same time James retired, Ed got home from his excursion to Animas after stopping for a couple beers at the local tavern. He found Belinda sitting up in their small kitchen nursing a glass of iced tea.

"Where were you," asked his wife.

"Just ran an errand. I should have called you, sorry."

"Your dinner is in the microwave. I'll warm it up and then we need to talk." As Belinda moved towards the microwave, Ed grabbed her in a bear hug.

"No! Let me be!" she cried out. Her voice sounded angry, something Ed had never heard from her before. He looked at her in shock.

"Hey, I was just a little late. I was trying to earn some extra cash. It isn't like I was out drinking or something like that."

"Oh, I know. I believe you even though I do smell beer! I'm sorry I'm so bitchy. It's just that I'm really not feeling too well. I've been sick all day."

"Hey, Baby, take it easy," Ed was immediately concerned. He and Belinda had been trying to make a baby for several months; could it be time? "You don't have to wait on me. I can fix my own food. Sit down if you don't feel good."

Belinda gave him a quizzical stare as she placed the plate of quickly reheated roast beef, potatoes, gravy and green beans on the counter.

"It's okay, it only takes a second and I can manage. What you want to drink?" Even as she asked the question, she was pouring iced tea into a beer glass filled with crystal-clear ice. Setting it in front of him, she took a seat across from where he sat at the kitchen bar.

"Sorry, it's a little dry. If I'd known you were going to be late, I would have kept it warm. I just didn't know when to expect you." She was contrite as she spoke and near tears.

"What is wrong with you, you said you didn't feel well? Don't tell me you are finally pregnant." The hope in Ed's voice was obvious but disappeared when he looked up from the meat he was cutting. She had a stony look on her face and tears rolling down her cheeks.

"Baby, what is it? What's the matter"?

"I…I was pregnant. I thought I was, but wasn't sure. I'd even gotten one of those over-the-counter tests and it was positive, but I wanted to see the doctor before I told you. Today was my appointment, but when I got up this morning, I was spotting … just a little. I've heard that sometimes that happens early on and that it probably wasn't anything to worry about, I went ahead to work and then to the doctor's at two. He was about to examine me when I began having really bad cramps – it didn't take long for everything to gush out. It was horrible."

"Honey, you didn't call me? Why didn't you call me? I should have been there?"

"I *did* try to call you. They told me you'd left already, with Alvaro. I called your cell and it went to voice mail. I left you a message, *why didn't you call back?* I didn't know what to think. I didn't think you even liked Alvaro."

"I don't. I was down Animas way and the phone coverage is spotty there. I probably have a message on the phone; I didn't even check it when I got back in an area with service. Oh, God, I'm so sorry I was down." Ed wrapped his arms around his wife and held her close. He stroked her long black hair and wiped the tears from her face. "Shouldn't you be in bed?"

"Yes, I guess I should, but I wanted to be up to tell you. The doctor said for me to take a couple days off work and then to check back with him next week to be sure everything was ok. He wants me to go see a

GYN doc in Silver too. They are supposed to call me with an appointment tomorrow."

Ed took his wife in his arms and walked her into their bedroom where he helped her undress for bed. Belinda was such a tiny thing. Only five foot two and trim as a model. Her body was the first thing he'd noticed about her – typical male reaction to the sight of a sexy woman. Her mild, quiet manner and sweet personality had captured his heart on their second date. It hurt him to know she was in pain, not just physical but emotional too.

"Hey, you just rest. I'll call in tomorrow and stay here with you. You gotta get well and then we can work on more babies. This kind of thing happens all the time from what I hear. I'm sure there was a good reason for you to lose the baby; maybe something wasn't growing right. God knows what he is doing."

With those comforting words, he snuggled up beside his wife on the bed and hugged her to him until her soft breathing told him she was asleep, and then he slipped out of the bed and quietly cleaned up the kitchen. He poured him a shot of tequila and gulped it down, then went to the bathroom where he took a quick shower and crawled naked into bed beside his beloved wife.

CHAPTER 22

Life for Belinda Salinas had been not been exactly easy but neither had it been hard. Her parents had entered the United States in the dark of night by swimming across the Rio Grande just north of Ciudad Acuna, after a long and arduous trip from El Salvador. They were fleeing poverty, persecution, and the civil war that was tearing their homeland asunder. They had not been members of the elite class in their native country nor had they been compesinos (peasants surviving below the poverty level without benefit of electric or water). They were almost middle-class citizens, at least as middle class as possible in Ecuador at the time. They were well-educated teachers who saw what was happening in their country and didn't like it. They didn't side with the military-led Government of El Salvador under President General Carlos Humberto Romero nor could they, in good conscience, side with the Farabundo Marti National Liberation Front (FMLN).

They made their decision to flee the country only after members of the dreaded ORDEN, a private military death squad, made a nocturnal visit to the small town where they taught children of the poor to read and write. They were not the targets of the squad that night but they saw all civil authority in the village massacred as well as the old priest who had fathered his flock for over 40 years.

Miguel Salinas later said that night had been "es la gotaquequebro el vaso" (the straw that broke the camel's back). He finalized plans to flee to the United States. Two weeks later he and his wife of two years left El Salvador in the dark of night and traversed the Central American jungles and deserts of Mexico for the next six months, used whatever transportation they were able to obtain, begged for food and shelter, and bartered their way north with the few personal items they were able to carry in three suitcases. The trip was about 1500 miles and cost them all their meager savings as well as jewelry that had been family heirlooms that were irreplaceable.

By the time they arrived at Ciudad Acuna, Chahuila State, Mexico, they were exhausted, but buoyed by the thought their journey was so nearly finished. The wading of the Rio Grande with their few remaining personal items was "un sopado" (a piece of cake), according to Miguel.

Once in the United States both Miguel and Marta, his wife, fell to their knees and gave a prayer of Thanksgiving. For the first time in months they felt safe. It was that night, on the sandy banks of the Rio Grande that Belinda was conceived.

Task number one was to apply for political asylum; they would never be safe returning to their native country. The U.S. had already granted Temporary Protected Status (TPS) to citizens of war-torn El Salvador, a policy which continued in effect through 1992. Miguel and Marta made their trip north during the hot, humid summer of 1980 and were among the earliest refugees to take advantage of TPS. Once they were no longer classified as unauthorized migrants and given proper documents for work, the couple began to rebuild their lives. Fortunately, they were able to find work in short order through a program sponsored by the Catholic Church.

Although Miguel and Marta were happy that their daughter, Belinda was born a U.S. citizen, they were not immediately able to give her the security they wished for her. Not being fluent in English was a big drawback to success in America so both parents enrolled in English as a Second Language (ESL) classes. Neither Miguel nor Marta ever considered raising Belinda in a Spanish only speaking household. They took all the steps required to become citizens of the United States, but they both relived the nightmare trip from Ecuador and their dark-of-the-night river crossing even while sleeping soundly in their new

Texas home. They were proud as they took the oath of allegiance to the United States as required for citizenship.

Miguel had foresight enough to forward his teaching credentials to friends in the United States long before the actual time for fleeing his native country arrived and he was able to obtain teaching certification after presenting them to the appropriate sources and taking additional classes at the University of Texas to meet the teaching qualifications required in the U.S. After teaching in Texas for several years, Miguel and Marta accepted positions in the Animas School District located in New Mexico's boot heel. It was here that Ed had met Belinda. Her parents were taking care of the small Catholic Church in Cotton City, New Mexico in addition to their teaching duties. By doing the menial janitorial chores required to maintain the building and grounds of the small facility, they felt some satisfaction towards repayment of the debt they felt owed to the church for the help they'd received upon their arrival in the United States years before.

Ed and Belinda were both students at the Animas High School. Ed went to Animas by choice. The school, with an excellent athletic department, held championships status in most sports. Under the financial sponsorship of the Phelps Dodge Corporation, the student athletes were well outfitted and respected throughout the state.

Ed had already decided on his Air Force career by his senior year, and he asked Belinda to marry him before they graduated. She accepted with no reservations and they began dreaming of their life together. It was understood that Ed would go into the air force for four years and learn a trade (he'd already decided he wanted to be a mechanic) and when he came back to Lordsburg they would be married. Belinda accepted a receptionist position at the small clinic in Lordsburg and waited for him to come home. There was never any question in either of their minds that their life together would be perfect.

Except for the death of Ed's father, their plans went just as they expected. It was a long wait for the wedding, but their big day finally arrived and Miguel Salinas proudly walked his daughter down the aisle of the small chapel he cared for in Cotton City.

Never for a moment had Ed considered taking part in any of the illegal activities that flourished in the boot heel area. Never, at least until after Belinda had a miscarriage, and he learned of her more serious health problems.

CHAPTER 23

Belinda hadn't wanted Ed to accompany her to the Women's Clinic in Silver City, but she could think of no good reason to keep him from driving her. She hated the fifty-mile drive into the Gila and normally would have been happy to have him drive. This time, though, she had a very uneasy feeling about the outcome of the trip. She had considered asking her mother to go with her, but she didn't want to worry her parents with her health problems so she reluctantly relented and let Ed be her chauffer. She vowed to keep her recent miscarriage from her parents until she knew that she had a clean bill of health and could assure them that they would have grandchildren eventually.

Belinda was carrying a heavy burden of guilt in that she hadn't been completely honest with her husband about the urgent need for the appointment with a specialist. It wasn't as simple as a little checkup by a gynecologist to be sure she had recovered from her spontaneous abortion. The doctor in Lordsburg had taken a good look at her medical history and had some concerns. He wanted the GYN doctor to rule out female problems as the source of her frequent headaches and irregular menstrual cycles, and to confirm what he actually suspected was Belinda's problem. The doctor's tone of voice wasn't reassuring to Belinda, she'd been living with dread ever since the visit. She felt sure there was something the doctor hadn't told her. She hadn't told Ed about all of her pains and discomfort for the past few months; there was no sense in worrying him unnecessarily; she could worry enough for both of them!

The drive through the mountains was normally quiet and relaxing. Belinda found herself thinking about the history of the area. As they following Hwy 90 through the scrub pines and into the hill country, Belinda began to mentally review her studies of history and culture of native Apache Indians who had roamed the Southwest for centuries. The Indians had seen their culture destroyed by white men and were reduced from a proud People living off the land, to thieves and murderers as they struggled to maintain their freedom. During their last one-hundred years of independence, they had been forced by the white man to live like hunted animals while prospectors robbed the mineral wealth of the countryside.

The Apache, like all of the Southwest Natives, had known how to live peacefully with nature but thought the white man only knew how to pillage and plunder the countryside; digging holes in search of the silver and gold hidden in the rocks, streams and hills; polluting the water, and destroying the symmetry of the pristine hills and mountains. Belinda shared the feelings of loss the Indians felt as they were driven off their homelands onto reservations in areas that proved inhospitable to them. After Geronimo's band of outlaws was subdued, most of the natives were removed to Florida where they couldn't survive in the humid swampy atmosphere. Those that were fortunate to live through the relocation procedures were eventually moved again to Oklahoma where most of them died. To this day, there is a legal battle over the Apache desire to remove the remains of Geronimo from Fort Sill in Oklahoma to his homeland in New Mexico. Belinda was angry over what the white men had done to those people but she lived with that anger, just as black people lived with their anger over the legacy of slavery. When she actually thought of how hard life was in the desert southwest, she had to admit that she would have hated to live in the inhospitable land as it existed a hundred years ago. The Indian walked up to 50 miles a day through the scrub and heat to escape the soldiers and farmers who wanted to exterminate them; lived on cacti, nuts and berries, and slept in the open subjected to Nature's whims. No, she preferred her comfortable life in the twenty-first century.

Many times Belinda had begged her parents to tell her what life had been like in their native El Salvador, but her father shared only good memories. It was up to Belinda to learn the bad things through her own research; what she read about the poverty of that small South American nation made her want to cry. She understood why her parents, like many, had fled and started a new life in the United States.

"Wonder if they will ever reopen the mine?" Ed's words broke into her thoughts of the past and she realized that they were passing the Tyrone Mine cutoff. "It's sure a shame all those people lost their jobs. I don't know what this world is coming to; then closing all those car dealerships! Can't believe they closed the one in Silver too. Closing the one in Lordsburg has almost broken the city. There aren't hardly any businesses there now. If we didn't have the border patrol headquarters, it would probably become a ghost town! Yeah, then we could make it into a tourist attraction – I can see it now: "Modern Ghost Town on Interstate 10," Ed spoke the latter in a sarcastic voice.

Belinda looked at him with questioning eyes, why on earth did he dwell on the negative? He always brought up the bad things. That was another reason she didn't want him to come into the doctor's office with her. He didn't need to hear anything more negative!

Digging in her purse, she pulled a sheet of folded paper. "You can go down to Wal-Mart while I'm in the clinic. That will save us time. The cooler is plugged in so be sure you put the cold things in it. Oh, and get you some new boots. If you're going to be traipsing around the desert with Alvaro, you'll need better boots. Your old ones are losing their soles."

"I hope you aren't getting too much. That cooler keeps it okay but it isn't very big." Ed was referring to the handy hot/cold chest they'd gotten for a Christmas gift from Belinda's parents. It ran on AC/DC current and was perfect for shopping when they made trips to Silver City or Deming. With only one grocery in Lordsburg, the variety was limited and the prices high! "What makes you think I'm going 'traipsing around the desert' with Al anyway?"

"Just a thought, after the other night, I got to thinking about it. He always seems to have plenty of money and I've never heard of him having a steady job, so he must have something going for him. It wouldn't hurt if we could save a few dollars by your doing odd jobs for him."

"And what if it isn't legal? Asked Ed, as he pulled into a parking space on the hilltop overlooking Silver City. "You still want me to do it"?

Belinda didn't bother to answer but gave her Mexican husband a cold stare, and opened the door quietly getting out of the car. "I'll be sitting on that bench if I get done before you get back; if you get here first, park where I can see you."

Ed watched his wife as she walked up the hill to the clinic entrance. "Wow," he thought. She was a fierce woman when riled. "It must be something in her blood," he thought. He laughed to himself, fierce and feisty, that described them to a T. *Fiersty* was what they should name their baby; a combination of the fierce South American blood from her and the feisty Mexican blood that flowed through his veins.

CHAPTER 24

Bill Driver was getting nowhere in his quest to find irregularities in the operations of the Lordsburg Border Patrol office. He had been paired up with several different officers for a day or two at a time; had gotten subtle hints of irregularities among some of the team, but never enough information to lead him to any one person who might be covering up illegal activities. His covert reports to Martin Pollen had been non-informational in their content. Martin, who had not expected immediate results, simply told him to "Hang in there. Someone will let something slip."

Settled into the small mobile home near the school in Animas, Bill spent most of his evenings reading or watching TV. His weekly excursions to the local Ghost rider's Grille for dinner and a couple drinks were the only break in the boring week.

Sitting at the bar on Friday, the same week Clare entertained her cousin; Bill tried to strike up a conversation with Gina, who, true to her word, was tending bar. She wore a green tank top this night; an extremely low cut neckline that showed off her full bust to good advantage. The bar was busy, jokes filled the air, and the clash of balls rang throughout the building as pool players at the end of the room yelled for refills for their beer mugs.

Bill had ordered a plate of appetizers and was patiently waiting for his Mexican dinner, the weekly special. Placing another Corona before him, Gina smiled her come-hither smile.

"Have you gotten settled now?" she asked.

"Yes, as settled as I expect to get. I don't think I'm gonna stay here too long; just not much action."

"I can show you some action, if that is what you are looking for." Her offer was clear. Bill was tempted to take her up on it. Then he saw the reflection of Clare Smith in the mirror that covered the length of the bar. She was peering into the bar area from the dining room. Picking up his glass, Bill turned and faced her. She looked lonely and confused. Sliding off his stool in two quick strides he was at the bottom of the three steps that connected the two rooms.

"Hi, I'm your neighbor. Live in the mobile home across the road from your place, Bill Driver," he said extending his hand. "Are you here for dinner?"

"Yes, that's the idea," Clare spoke softly as she returned his handshake. She'd seen this man when she was sitting on her porch. He seemed quiet enough but Clare wasn't sure she wanted to have dinner with him, if that was his intention.

Bill marveled at the warmth and softness of the porcelain white hand she offered him. It was a short handshake; merely a touch, but enough to cause his heartbeat to increase quickly.

The redheaded waitress appeared behind Clare carrying Bill's dinner, "Up here or at the bar?"

"At a table up there, if Miss Smith will join me, I hate to eat alone." He looked questioningly at Clare who quickly decided he was right; eating alone was no fun.

"Yes, it is lonely eating alone. I'll join you Mr. Driver." She turned with the grace of a ballerina; no hint of the imbalance in her stiff leg, and followed the waitress carrying Bill's dinner to the only two-person dining table in the area. "I see you are having the special, it looks good. That is what I'll have, and a coke." Her soft voice fell smoothly on Bill's ear. He took in her youthful appearance; short auburn hair, simply done, smooth face with only a hint of lipstick, and simple yet stylish clothes. What would he find to talk to her about?

Gina appeared at his side with the remainder of his appetizer and the coke ordered by Clare. She glared at him as she set down the plate.

Surely, she wasn't angry that he had decided to eat with Clare, he thought. Oh well, if she was…she was. Somehow, he didn't care. Her type would get over her anger very fast. He'd been around too many like her; a one-night stand, hoping it would turn into something more permanent. Bill Driver wasn't looking for anything permanent and a sit-down dinner with this lovely girl would satisfy his needs more than a fling with the waitress!

Talking with Clare was the hardest thing he'd tried to do in a long time. They really didn't have anything in common, other than the fact that they were both new arrivals to the area. Bill couldn't let her know the extent of his knowledge about her; her past life in Portland, or even that he was aware that she'd just moved to Animas. He was grateful when Clare picked up the conversation.

"I see you drive a border patrol truck sometimes, so I guess you work for the patrol, anything exciting going on around here?"

"Just the routine stuff since I've been here. I know you hear about lots of smuggling, drugs and stuff on TV but there isn't much activity here. At least not on my watch, guess I've just been lucky so far." He couldn't tell her about the real reason he'd been sent to this hell-hole, as he thought of the valley. "They did stop a character with about 5 k's of coke last week over on 80 near Rodeo. That's about the most excitement I've seen. Tell me about yourself, lived here long?"

"Oh no, I just came here to regroup. I had some bad experiences last year and needed time to think and sort things out. I'm working on a book and taking some on-line classes. I don't know how much longer I'll even stay in this area. Sometimes I wonder what I'm doing here."

"Sounds lonely, is that what you wanted?"

"At the time I first came here, yes. Now, I'm not sure, but I'm going to stay here through the summer at least. Maybe by the time school start again next fall, I'll be ready to go back to the university."

"The university here in New Mexico?"

"Oregon. I'll be a junior next year. I came here from Portland."

At least that was a breakthrough. Bill could now ask questions about her family, and he did. Surprisingly enough, Clare was very forthcoming about most of her life in Oregon. She didn't mention the kidnapping of her half-sister or the subsequent shooting, but she didn't need to. Bill just had to be sure that he didn't spill the beans and tell her something that would let on how much he really knew about her.

When Clare's meal arrived, Bill ordered his third Corona and they quietly ate. The Ghost Rider Special was a little different from other Mexican combination plates he'd eaten. This large platter consisted of a burrito, taco, chili relleno, tamale and the usual beans and rice; the homemade salsa was hot and spicy and the tortilla chips thin and crisp. It was a good meal.

There was a moment of awkward silence when Clare finished her dinner. They sat and looked at each other out of words. Fortunately, the waitress approached the table and tried to entice them to some homemade chocolate pie with whipped cream. Bill declined using the beer as an excuse and Clare declared she was stuffed.

"Just give me my bill and I'll be on my way," was her way to put an end to the evening.

"Let me get it."

"No, I don't think so. This is a Dutch treat."

With that, she reached for her handbag and rummaged through her wallet extracting a twenty and placing it under her plate. "Thanks for the company, it has been pleasant. Maybe we'll get together again soon."

Bill emptied his Corona as he watched her leave the dining room. He looked toward Gina at the bar. She was turning her charm onto a cowboy drinking tequila shots and beer. Bill knew he'd lost his chance for a nightcap with her. He didn't really feel much loss though, as he placed a more than adequate amount to cover the bill under his plate and headed for the door. His big night on the town was finished. Maybe if he hurried he could catch a nine o'clock movie on HBO. He was grateful that they had satellite TV in the valley or he'd go nuts!

CHAPTER 25

Several weeks later, James Miller was relaxing at Poncho's bar, as had become a habit. His easy mood came to an abrupt end when Raphael D'Anda approached his table and without invitation, took a seat. James wasn't happy when D'Anda told him that he had another job for him. "I thought we were through," he chided.

"Ha, you'll never be through! What you think this is a game or something? I have enough on you to keep you working for me until one of us dies and then some."

"Look, I don't want to be involved in your *business,* get someone else."

"Ah, but there is no one else who can do it like you, you know the routine and have a perfect reason for being in the Lordsburg area and you owe me. It is simple. The trip will be a week from today."

"What do you mean, 'I owe you'. I don't owe you one damn thing and you know it!"

Ignoring the outburst, D'Anda continued, "this time, you fly to Dallas, pick up my man, then to Lordsburg, unload the man and cargo and go your way. There won't be a return passenger. I don't care if you visit your cousin or not, but the car is there if you want to use it." That said D'Anda slipped an envelope across the table towards James that he knew held his pay and more precise instructions. As D'Anda stood up from the table, he looked at James with those piercing eyes, "Don't be stupid. Remember, I know where your cousin lives too!"

"Don't make threats against my cousin, or any of my family," James said barely able to control his temper. "I can cause trouble for you too and if anything happens to any one of them, I will. To hell with whatever you might do to me, I'll be sure you get yours first. D'Anda, this is the last job I will do for you, I mean it. Don't come to me again or you'll wish you'd never started with me! I don't know what you think you have on me but I assure you it won't stop me from getting you if you hurt any of my family or friends!"

D'Anda gave James a stare that, coupled with a snide grin, said he didn't believe a word of what he'd just heard and stalked out of the quiet, neon-lit bar.

James sat back down and finished his drink. His hands were shaking and his stomach tied up in knots! He was sick and tired of D'Anda and his demands. How dare he threaten his family! James decided he was going to take D'Anda's operation down. He pulled his wallet out and searched for a business card he'd carried in his wallet for a long time. He'd never thought he'd use it, but in light of recent events he knew now was the time if ever there was one!

CHAPTER 26

Clare woke to the ringing of the phone. It was early for her. She usually stayed up late working on her cookbook or playing Scrabble on the Internet. There was no reason for her to get up early.

"Hello," she answered groggily.

"Clare, its James, did I wake you up?"

"Yes, you did," she mumbled her reply.

"Say, I'm sorry, I forget about the time difference. I'm going to be in your area tomorrow, is it all right if I come down? I won't stay long, no overnight this time. I just want to visit a bit so I can tell Mom and Aunt Pansy that I saw you. They are always asking how you are doing. I think they worry about you out there by yourself so close to the border. They hear all the stories of drugs and there was that shooting nearby that made headlines."

"Sure, come on out." *Why was he being so concerned*, Clare wondered? "What time. I'll have us something cooked. It is the least I can do."

"Probably mid-afternoon, but don't go to any trouble. I'd be happy with sandwiches. I just want to clear my head some. That country does have a soothing effect."

"Okay, I'll make it light. See you tomorrow."

James hung up on his end thinking that Clare had been short with him but then he had woken her!

Clare hung up her phone and asked herself if maybe she hadn't been a little short. But, he had intruded on her dream! She stretched and took a deep breath remembering the warmth she'd felt in someone's arms.

She wasn't sure who her mysterious comforter was but she could still smell his cologne in her imagination. Slowly the memory faded away. I may as well get up now, she thought. I've lost the train of thought. *Funny, but James almost sounded concerned!*

Just as she got her toothbrush in her mouth, the phone rang again. She let it go to the answering machine.

"Clare, its Steve, give me a call. I just want to talk with you. Let you know how my new job is going…hear your voice. I love you."

Steve was the one person she couldn't convince of her happiness with her new lifestyle in New Mexico. He should have been settled himself in a new life in California, working for IBM, meeting young women and living high; but he continued to call her and profess his love. Clare had to admit, she sometimes felt the old desire for Steve but she just wasn't ready to rekindle their relationship. She didn't think she would ever be able to go back to things as they had been before the *accident*, as she still referred to her injury.

* * * * * *

Steve replaced the receiver and shook his head. He didn't know if Clare would call him back or not. He could never tell what she'd do. Gone was the old Clare, dependable and thoughtful; she'd been replaced by someone he couldn't understand, someone he couldn't seem to get through to. He missed her so much. He'd tried to get her out of his mind since he'd moved to L.A., but that was easier said than done. Just as he thought he was going to enjoy an evening with his newfound friends, he'd catch a word, a laugh, or see auburn tresses across the room and his heart would flip-flop. It wasn't getting any easier with time. He'd always heard that time healed all wounds, but he begged to differ. Never would he get over Clare. He could only pray that he could win her back somehow…sometime.

Shrugging into his jacket, he gave the quiet phone one last long look and headed to his new job, in his new office, with his new secretary who had made it clear that she was available for him anytime for anything. The only problem was that Steve wasn't available for her!

CHAPTER 27

Clare looked at her long neglected journal. She had barely written in it since she'd left Portland early in the year. She had made mundane entries as she settled in her new home, introduced the people she'd met in her narrative and described the changing landscape as she'd seen the effects of wind, rain, and sun on the desert and mountains. There were descriptions of some of her failed attempts to make some of the more complicated recipes she'd experimented with prior to inclusion in the book but overall, she'd neglected her journal.

Glancing over the pages she'd written previously, she was inspired to write about her feelings:

July 1, 2007

I've been living in Animas for almost four months now and I enjoy the peace and quiet so much. Sometimes I just sit on the porch, wrapped in a blanket – the nights in the desert get decidedly cool – and gaze at the stars. There is very little traffic on Hwy 9 late at night except for the border patrol passing or large semi-trucks taking a detour around the weight stations on the interstate.

Sometimes the patrol cars park just out of my sight but I can follow the lights shining into the desert as they search for interlopers from the south. I don't think they ever arrest any.

It is so quiet and I can think… I try not to dwell on the events of last June but it is hard not to. I feel like I was betrayed by life. I thought I had everything I'd ever want -family, money, security and Steve. Then it was all destroyed by jealousy. I can't understand how everything went wrong so suddenly!

I miss Tina and Alex most and, of course, Markie, Aaron and Margaret too and Steve! How could I not miss Steve? We had such fine plans. He calls me every week and always asks me to join him in L.A. He really likes his job there but says he feels "incomplete," I guess I do too if I would be honest with myself!

Steve can't imagine how hard it is for me not to just run to him and pick up where we left off! It would be so easy to drop all my concerns on him but I can't do that. I have to find myself before I move forward and involve anyone else in my life.

I've met a really nice man here in Animas, Bill Driver. He is older than I am, but not too much older. I don't know how I really feel about him. He makes me feel special again. I like being with him but I know that I'm not ready for the kind of relationship he wants. He's much more experienced than I am and I'm sure a good night kiss would not satisfy his needs.

I feel that he has experienced the same kind of hurt that I have experienced. It scares me but we are comfortable together. We have a quiet, undemanding relationship but I don't think it will ever progress further than that. I don't plan to allow it to progress!!

CHAPTER 28

Telephone tag was not a game James liked to play, especially with a Federal agent. He wasn't exactly sure how to go about what he was doing and would have rather talked to anyone but Martin Pollen but he didn't know anyone else involved in undercover drug operations. He'd met Pollen during a raid on a party where he'd been an unwitting guest. Pollen had helped him handle the legal tangle and James had escaped with only a few lost hours to questions and answers and a promise to give Pollen a "heads up" if he ever stumbled upon anything that seemed it might be interesting to the DEA. James respected the man's integrity even though he didn't personally like him and had vowed he'd never be calling him. Times had changed since that night and James found that the thought of helping the DEA wasn't as repulsive to him now as it once was.

He'd been trying to contact Pollen for two days and was really getting pissed by the run around given him by clerks and secretaries, maybe it was a sign that he shouldn't try to trip up D'Anda in his plans? Hell, James didn't really know what D'Anda's game was but he had figured out enough that he felt confident he could give info to the Feds that would close him down. Of course, he would insist on immunity for his help.

When he *finally* conferred with the agent, he was referred to a local yokel, Ben Taylor. Ben, so Pollen told him, had a thick dossier on D'Anda and would be more than happy to be the recipient of any and all info James could give him. If it was something the higher ups needed to know, Ben would fill them in and he'd hear back if they wanted more....

After James 'talk with Pollen and the brush off, as he considered the referral, he almost backed out of the idea of going to DEA, but then he recalled the sound of D'Anda voice during their latest conversation and his not-so-idle words: *"Ha, you'll never be through! What you think this is a game or something? I have enough on you to keep you working for me until one of us dies and then some."* His tone made it clear that his words weren't hollow and that what he said was as an unmistakable threat.

The telephone call to Ben, unlike his attempts to contact Pollen, was readily accepted and as he talked to Ben Taylor, who was all business, he realized that turning informant wasn't going to be as easy as he'd thought. He would have to play along with D'Anda for a while longer while the DEA checked out his story and made plans for a hit; he'd have to keep Ben informed of all his activities until the sting could be arranged. The logistics of planning a bust over several states would involve more men and time than James had anticipated. By the time he had heard all that was involved, he regretted making contact in the first place! He had wanted out of D'Anda's mess and here he was being sucked in deeper and deeper. It was enough to drive a man to drink. But, for once, he didn't want to drink.

★ ★ ★ ★ ★ ★

James handled two more shipments for D'Anda before he heard again from Taylor. During the interim, he wasn't sure if he felt relief at not hearing from the agent or aggravation at the delay by the Feds in taking action on his offer of help. Taylor's call instructed James to meet him at their pre-designated meeting place, a small café about a block south of Poncho's. The cryptic text message told James to meet Ben at the cafe at 6:30 P.M. on a Tuesday night. He was on time; Ben wasn't.

"Sorry I'm late, got caught up in some last minute stuff," was the only explanation offered as Taylor scooted into the booth. Ordering a coffee and apple pie, the small balding man, ice blue eyes hidden behind thick glasses, wasted no time getting to his purpose.

"There is a man in Lordsburg named Bill Driver. He's working

with the local border patrol office and he is your contact in Animas."
With those words, he pushed a folded slip of paper across the Formica
table to James with one hand while he shoved a huge bite of pie into his
mouth with the other. "He actually lives very near your cousin down
there…." He said as he followed his pie with a gulp of hot black coffee.

"Hey," cut in James, "I don't want Clare caught up in this mess! She's
got nothing to do with it. I don't know what you guys are thinking…"

"She's not involved I assure you," Taylor said in a calming voice. "I
was just using her location as a point of reference."

"Just so you understand." James' mind was spinning. He didn't
want to involve Clare in any of this. It was bad enough that D'Anda
had already threatened Clare as well as his mother and aunt without
the Feds hinting at some involvement. He wondered how everybody
seemed to know about his relationship to Clare anyway. James had
finally acknowledged his guilt at the part he'd played in the botched
abduction plot the year before and was trying to earn Clare's trust; he
didn't want any more guilt as far as Clare was concerned!

"Now," continued Taylor speaking in a rather exasperated voice,
"you need to arrange a meeting with Driver. You and he will coordi-
nate the time of the next delivery. You give Driver the info and he will
arrange the bust. You won't be involved in the actual action except for
the involvement you have now in the pickups and deliveries, he'll decide on which end of the operation he wants to act. After we get what
we need, you'll be notified and we'll arrange any protection you might
need. I doubt you'll need any. We don't plan to involve you unless we
have to. It's possible we will have to pull a fake arrest just to make the
bust look legit, if we do, we will get you out quickly. We've got your
statement all typed up for you to read and sign, and it will be delivered
to your office tomorrow. You will have time to read it, sign it and return
it. It gives all the particulars of our agreement with you. Nothing will
be done to protect you until we have it in writing, understand?" James
listened to the little man with open mouth. He rattled off the info like
it was prerecorded!

"Yes, I do. What if I don't agree with the statement"?

"You will. We have made all very clear. Your words were transcribed exactly as you told us. We made sure of that. We still have your taped info if you want to make a comparison. If there is any question, call me. Listen, we want to put this scum-bum out of business as much as you do, maybe more. We aren't going to screw you. You're the first person with enough guts to come forward, just hang in there."

James looked at his own unfinished pie. His stomach was churning. Was this was really the end? "Okay, just don't screw me up."

"No prob, man. You aren't the only one risking everything. This may be our only chance to get him. We don't want to screw up anyone or anything." Folding his napkin next to empty plate, Ben stood up, "thanks for the pie and coffee. Watch for our deliveryman."

When he was gone, James continued sitting in the booth for a few minutes trying to collect his thoughts. He was up to his neck now and he would come out of the deal as either a free man or a dead one! Those were the only options.

CHAPTER 29

Bill Driver drove the green and white Border Patrol vehicle down the deserted Hwy 9 toward Hachita. In the passenger seat sat Jamie Wells, his partner for the week. Along this portion of the curvy highway they were surrounded by rocky hills and desert scrub; a few cattle grazed or lazed near rusty water storage tanks scattered along the abandoned railroad bed. The small groups of cattle ignored vehicles barreling along the roadway. Occasionally a snake slithered across the road or the remains of a jackrabbit that had failed to hop out of a vehicle's way provided a tasty meal for errant crows or buzzards. Railroad ties were piled up at irregular intervals having been pulled up and stacked when the copper smelter at Playas had been closed; but the winding trail where the railroad bed had been still crawled across the landscape all the way to Douglas and Bisbee. The anti-terrorist training site, now located at the abandoned smelter town, had no needs of railroad ties.

Bill watched the countryside hoping that he might see some movement amid the creosote bushes, gullies and washes that peppered the landscape. He was always anxious to see signs of illegal activity during routine patrols but usually had his hopes dashed as the desert scrub hid activity too thoroughly. They did get to see action but it was when they got a radio message telling them of a tripped monitor located in the outback or a call for help from members of patrols mounted on horses or four-wheelers. Many times those alerts ended up being a herd of deer or javelina rather than the illegals the patrol watched and waited to capture.

Jaime Wells, was one of the older and more experienced agents assigned to the Lordsburg area and Bill enjoyed working with him more than with any of the other agents he'd been partnered with in the weeks since he'd come to the border patrol.

Not a big man by any means; when the two of them walked together, it was a Mutt and Jeff cartoon come to life! Jaime was short, squat and walked with a swagger born from years of trying to keep up with his longer-legged counterparts and riding the horses he favored for desert patrols. Although his legs were short, he was able to move with lightning speed; Bill had learned that on their first day together when the rattle of a Diamondback interrupted their trail discussion. Before Bill knew what had happened, Jaime had picked up a large rock and chunked the venomous reptile. They cut off six rattles and a button to add to Jaime's collection. Bill had never even seen the danger!

Even more important to Bill was the almost encyclopedic amount of information Jaime had about survival in the desert. He could identify all the native plants, provide histories of specific areas and give tips about where to look for illegal's coming and going. He knew of hidey-holes that most people would never notice and had the proverbial eagle eyes. Bill decided early on that Jaime was the one man he wanted to back him up in any operation. Jaime had nearly 20 years with the agency and it had given him more field experience than all the agents in the Lordsburg office.

It would seem that Jaime should have risen to a much higher position than he held, but he explained his lack of progression by saying, "I don't want the headaches of management. I joined the patrol to do just that, patrol. I'm happy with what I do. I am pretty much my own boss; I have my assignments and work them as I want. Nobody bothers me anymore. I'm not a smart-assed kid trying to make a name for myself. I just want to finish up my time and retire."

Besides being informative, Bill found that Jaime was entertaining! He had a repertoire of jokes and tales that would keep one on the edge of his seat laughing and wiping tears from his eyes for hours. His practical jokes were the source of entertaining conversation and bantering in the stationhouse. The other agents had already warned Bill about the poker games in which the men sometimes indulged. A particularly memorable one involved flatulence and peanut butter! Bill intended to ask that Jaime be permanently assigned as his partner. After he managed that monumental task, monumental because Ron Hall was famous for his determination to keeps his teams rotating, Bill planned to let Jaime in on the real purpose of his assignment and seek his help in finding the renegade agent or group of agents who were working both sides of the border. Bill was confident that Jaime was as honest as the day was long and knew deep in his gut that he could count on him to help and to do it without spilling the beans about Bill's actual assignment.

"I'm having a cookout at my house on Sunday," Jaime said interrupting Bill's thoughts. "Why don't you come? It will give you an opportunity to meet some of the guys in a more relaxed atmosphere. You can bring your girl too, if you have one."

"That sounds nice. What can I bring besides *my girl* since I don't have one?"

"No girl? Surely you've met someone since you've been here!"

"I really don't have one but there is someone I might bring if I can tear her away from her writing project."

"Oh, a writer."

"More like a wannabe writer. She's really too young for me but she's been through a lot and I think it might do her good to get out and socialize a bit. If I can talk her into coming, I'll bring her."

"I'll give you a map to my place; it isn't hard to find but like most of the places around here, you drive and drive. I live pretty far north of Lordsburg, near Silver, little place called Cliff. Makes it a slight drive to work, but it's a little cooler there than here and we get more rain. The wife likes it. We've got about ten acres and a couple horses for the kids. They like the school and that means a lot."

"Must be nice to have a family," Bill said a little sadly.

"You don't have anyone, do you? I mean, you never talk about a family. Everyone speculates…."

"No, my folks are dead. I tried marriage once but it didn't work out. Guess I'm too involved with the job – doesn't mix well with family. Maybe someday I'll find someone." Bill found himself picturing Clare Smith in his mind even as he spoke. He chuckled to himself. Like *that* would ever happen! He was way too old for her.

"Something funny?"

"Not really, just dreaming."

The conversation was interrupted by the crackle of the radio. A National Guard helicopter patrolling the area had seen some suspicious activity just south of their location. Jaime acknowledged the info and headed toward a roadside parking spot where the patrol often caught illegal's crossing into the U.S. It was the end of conversation and back to work for the two men.

Sitting in the hot vehicle was the really bad part of this job. Bill had already swilled two bottles of ice-cold water when Jaime grunted and held out the high-powered binoculars to him.

"There they are, ready?"

Bill peered into the desert scrub and finally made out two figures cautiously darting from creosote bush to creosote bush. It was hard to see them due to the height of the grasses, chamisa and creosote bushes but by watching the movements of the desert scrub, he could follow their progress towards Hwy 9. Jaime got on the radio to request more backup and the two men quietly exited the vehicle. They would wait until the travelers were nearer the road before interrupting their flight. The two officers checked their firearms and crawled under the barbed-wire fence. There would probably be no need for the weapons. Usually the interlopers were just poor Mexican peasants and were seldom armed with anything more dangerous than a pocket knife. Only when actual smugglers or coyotes were involved in a crossing were weapons warranted.

Slowly and quietly, the two agents made their way about fifty yards into the desert where they waited for the illegal crossers. The capture was easy.

The two Hispanic men, tired and sweaty, put up no resistance when confronted by the two officers. They simply hung their heads and asked for "aqua, por favor," as they dutifully held out their hands for cuffing while eying the bottled water in the agent's backpacks.

"Señores, han estado antes ustedes aquí," questioned Jaime. He needed to know if the men had been in the country before. If they had, they would know the routine and they wouldn't have any fear of what might be ahead. If they were first timers, the border patrol would easily have the upper hand and it would make the procedures for processing the aliens and returning them to their homes much easier.

"No Señor, jamás hemos estado aquí."

"Ha, they say they have never been here before. Liars."

As Jamie prepared to load the men into the back of the truck, he informed them, in their own language, that they would have their journey finished by the United States government. .Inside the small cell that made up the bed of the truck there were hard metal benches where the interlopers would sit during their ride to the processing center. The only comfort was the minimal air conditioning, the shade and the cold water bottles that each man gulped down quickly.

Just as they were closing the doors, their counterparts drove up and Bill's cell phone rang. He missed the greeting given to the new arrivals by Jaime but picked up on the frustration in his voice. It had taken them longer to arrive than was desirable; Bill figured that Jaime was telling them about that in no uncertain terms! Fortunately, there had been no problems on this pickup.

Answering his private cell, Bill had to admit that he was glad that the Agency had finally decided to supply him with a satellite phone for his use in this desolate desert area. With a locally purchased one, he constantly dropped calls and in many places had no service. The satellite phone was always able to hone in on some signal so missed and dropped calls were things of the past.

One of the things the local citizenry was crying for was better cell phone coverage. Additional towers in the hilly regions would enable residents to get help when they spotted intruders at their stock tanks or cutting their fences. It was not unusual for ranchers to come across a group of people in an arroyo while checking their livestock. One rancher had run into some drug smugglers and paid for his find with his life! That had caused an uproar that continued to grow! Another still had a case in the courts resulting from actions when he held a group of immigrants at bay until the border patrol arrived to take them off his hands. His evident mistake was holding them at gun point even though they were trespassing on private land.

Looking at the phone, Bill didn't recognize the number shown on caller ID but expecting a call from a new contact, he promptly punched the "talk" button.

"Hello."

"Is this Bill Driver"? asked the voice on the other end of the line.

"The one and only."

"James here."

"Okay, I'm ready. We can meet wherever you want, whenever you want."

"I'm going to be in Lordsburg on Friday. How about we catch lunch at KFC, I should be there about one o'clock."

"Sounds good to me, I'm looking forward to meeting you. I'd like a break in this job. It has been monotonous so far."

CHAPTER 30

Eduardo and Belinda, had fallen into an uncomfortable routine relationship with one another since Ed had been taking on extra work with Alvaro. Belinda still didn't feel like her old self, since the miscarriage she had been irritable and distant. Matters weren't helped any by the inconclusive results from the myriad of tests that the doctors had been performing. Ed had been pre-occupied trying to decide if he should continue to work with Al and wasn't available to discuss Belinda's fears. Ed knew that Al was involved in something shady and that what they were doing wasn't legal, but he didn't know what they were delivering to out of the way sites throughout the boot hill, and interrogations of Al brought no answers to his questions.

One afternoon several weeks after her miscarriage, Belinda left work early and was trying to relax. As she drank a cool glass of tea and thinking about what she could fix for dinner that was easy and quick, the ring of the telephone interrupted her thoughts. Inexplicably, she felt the cold hand of dread clutch her heart and with a shaking hand reached for the phone.

"Belinda Guerrero?" asked the very business-like voice.

"Yes, this is she," she answered, her intuition telling her who it was even before the caller identified herself.

"This is Marie at Gila Regional. Doctor Davis would like you and your husband to come in to discuss the final results of the tests you had last week. Can you be here at two tomorrow?"

"Tomorrow?" asked Belinda with a sinking feeling. She knew it was bad news. She'd been steeling herself for it since she'd lost the baby and had a variety of tests done at the community hospital. It seemed that the results of one test had immediately required another test to confirm or rule out one or another finding.

"Yes, he can work you in then. He wants you to come as soon as possible."

"I'll be there. I don't know about my husband. Does he have to come?"

"The doctor wants to talk to both of you but if he can't make it, you do need to have someone else along. The doctor may want to do some more tests and if he does, there is a possibility you'd need a driver," said Marie. She hated this part of her job, trying to get a patient into the office so that they could receive life-changing bad news. The latest test results had finally confirmed cancer cells in Belinda's cervix. It was Stage II or III and surgery was called for immediately, then probably chemo and maybe radiation. Her odds for beating the disease were not as good as they would have been six months ago, but Dr. Davis would do everything in his power to save her. He put his whole heart and soul into saving his patients. That was why Marie loved him.

"Just tell me when and I'll be there," Belinda said. "I don't know if Ed can get away or not, but I'll bring someone. It isn't good is it"?

"I can't speculate on the results; the Doctor is the only one who can tell you that. I'm sorry, I just make the appointments, and we'll see you at two tomorrow then..."

"Sure, I understand, I'll Be there," Belinda said as she replaced the phone with a sinking feeling.

The next day Belinda and her mother headed to the clinic for her meeting with Dr. Davis. Her mother had been confused and hurt when Belinda had called her and told her about all the problems she'd been having but was a rock for Belinda to lean on. When they went in to see the doctor, their worst fears were realized. The doctor took his time and explained in detail the disease that was ravaging Belinda's body, the treatments available and her prognosis for survival both with and without the prolonged, expensive treatments. They left the doctor's office with what seemed reams of literature and a decision to make. The drive back to Lordsburg was spent in rehashing all the things each one could remember from the visit and speculation as to what Belinda should do. Both knew further treatment was required, delay wasn't an option and money was something they'd manage.

"I'll help you pay for treatments if it is necessary," her mother assured Belinda. "You just need to get well. That is what we want," was her parting statement as she dropped her daughter off at the cozy house that had once held such hope for the family.

Belinda didn't know how she was going to tell her husband of the death sentence the doctor had handed her and needed time to think of a good way to tell him of their dilemma. Ed had been so distracted lately...

She hadn't really accepted the news herself, how did she think she would be able to tell anyone that she had vaginal cancer, Stage III. Surgery was tentively scheduled for early Monday, just four days away; the one decision she and her mother had been capable of making on the basis of the day's visit. She fondled the prayer beads of her rosary, held tightly in her hands, and prayed. It was all she could think to do. So absorbed in her prayers she didn't even hear Eduardo when he came into the house or into their bedroom.

It only took one look at Belinda for Ed to know that something was terribly wrong! Her usual calm face was drawn and pale. He'd know her for too many years not to realize that whatever was bothering her was very serious. He dropped his baseball cap to the floor and quickly sat down next to her on their queen-sized bed. There was no sign of distraction in his voice as he spoke to her.

"Honey, what is wrong?"

"I...I don't know what to say," Belinda stammered. Tears were rolling down her face unchecked now. Ed felt a shiver.

"Tell me, whatever it is; it can't be so bad that we can't handle it together."

Belinda stared deeply into Ed's dark eyes. She saw genuine concern and love there. She fell across his lap and broke into gasping sobs. Eduardo allowed her to cry herself out before pressing her to tell him what was wrong. He had enough patience and wisdom to know that he would never get the full story until Belinda had cried herself out.

CHAPTER 31

The same afternoon, Ron Hall picked up the red line in his office; a secure telephone used only for special calls. It was connected directly to his bosses in El Paso, Albuquerque and Denver but they seldom called him and he never called them. His call was to another agent this time, his Miami connection, Ben Taylor.

Ben had been with DEA for almost 20 years and was ready to retire. He needed only one last big bust and the accompanying bonus to make it a very comfortable retirement. He had been looking for something that would pay him well, endanger him not at all, either physically or financially and take little effort. He was lazy on top of being crooked.

The perfect deal had just magically materialized out of thin air. He still couldn't believe he had been presented with a statement signed by one James Miller, a statement that implicated Raphael D'Anda, the head of a cartel dealing in arms, ammunition and drug smuggling. He only had to decide who would be best to alert to the proposed DEA bust; someone that would be willing to line his pocket in exchange for the information! He didn't want to go directly to D'Anda who was the target because it might implicate him in a way that would prove dangerous. No, he wanted to keep his involvement out of the deal and work through a third person. No sense in taking unwarranted chances at this point in the game. The most logical person was Ron Hall; another 20-year agent who had found himself assigned to the hellhole known as Lordsburg after a bust had gone bad in Miami's Little Havana area. Ben and Ron went way back, having worked several cases together. It was pure luck that Ben hadn't been reassigned after the fiasco in Little Miami. He owed Ron for not telling his superiors about his involvement in the bust gone wrong. Ron had taken all the heat. Now maybe Ben could make it up to his friend.

Ron had accepted the Lordsburg assignment gladly, knowing that he'd actually been lucky to get any assignment instead of being removed from the Agency, but he harbored a deep resentment that others involved in the failed bust hadn't been similarly reassigned. True, he hadn't ratted out any of his cohorts, but he did hope that one day the circle would come full swing and he'd be repaid for his silence. At the time of the failed incident, Ben wondered if Ron would have been better off leaving the agency instead of going to the Desert No-where, but now he was grateful to have someone he knew in the Lordsburg area. After cursory greetings, Ben filled Ron in on the basics of the Miller statement and the tentative plans to bring down another drug ring. Ron agreed with Ben's conclusion that this could be the deal that they had been waiting for to make their retirement dreams reality.

What he didn't tell Ben was that he was already aware of D'Anda's activities in the Lordsburg area – had been aware of them for quite some time, in fact. D'Anda's payoffs had made life easier for Ron, and in return the local border patrol. Following instructions, officers didn't interfere with D'Anda's activities. It was already a cozy deal but if the plan to curtail D'Anda's activities succeeded, it would mean the end to the lucrative arrangement. Because of this, Ron downplayed the fact that he expected he could make more out of this information than Ben could imagine. Raphael D'Anda didn't like snitches and would pay well for information exposing informants or would-be informants. Ron ended the call with a Cheshire-cat grin on his usually glum face. Things were looking up…

Ron had realized that there was more to the assignment of Bill Driver to his sector than just the routine transfer of a tired border patrol agent and with this new information, he had his number. It was unthinkable that he had a DEA agent planted in his organization! That angered Ron, and he felt grim satisfaction knowing that he could bring the smug S.O.B. down. He'd play Driver's little game a little longer and see what more he could ascertain of the plans DEA was making to bring D'Anda down, and then he'd help lower the boom! Things wouldn't go as the Feds hoped, but they would sure go in Ron Hall's favor!

CHAPTER 32

Ed left for work early the next morning. He knew he would have to talk with his bosses to get time off so he could be with Belinda during her surgery and subsequent treatments. His heart was heavy as he knocked on the metal door to the airport manager's office. His boss would work with him to give the time needed so he could be with Belinda when she came home from surgery, care for her through the chemo, and whatever other things were required, he had no doubt of that. The only thing that really bothered him was how they would get the money to cover their co-payments from the surgery and treatments. Al had to admit that he'd not been a very good saver. His insurance was adequate for routine needs but a catastrophic illness would cause even the most thrifty person difficulties.

Of course, there was his mother. Ed knew she still had some money from his father's insurance that she was keeping for an emergency. This was an emergency but he didn't want to take his mother's meager savings. There was always the chance that she would need it for herself sometime in the not too distant future.

Belinda's parents had managed to save a little money too but he'd never ask them for help; Miguel and Marta had worked too hard and had too little to expect them to pay for their daughters illness, even though Marta had made it clear that they were more than willing to help financially.

Without meaning to, he thought of Alvaro Garcia. Maybe he could get some more work helping him. Al had paid him well the times he'd worked with him. Far more money than the meager work he'd done had warranted. He dismissed the idea as quickly as it entered his mind. He didn't need that kind of trouble. Al was into something illegal and it wouldn't do Ed any good to end up in prison or dead! He sure wouldn't be there for Belinda either way. No, he decided, he would work something out. They would get through this together.

CHAPTER 33

The desert can be merciless at times. The white-hot sun beats down on the parched earth baking the ground into one big brick! It was the early Mexican explorers who taught the indigenous Indians of South America how to make the bricks, which became the traditional adobe structures that dotted the deserts of what we know as the southwestern United States. These structures, many of them with only partial walls remaining today, were ideal for capturing the heat of the sun, storing it and releasing the thermal energy to keep occupants warm during cool desert nights. Early Indians had already been using adobe; sand, clay and water made into a mortar and strengthened with sticks, straw or dung mixed together in baskets to make their structures. When they learned how to mold bricks, the building became easier. The desert climate seasoned the bricks quickly and the aridness allowed them to develop into a strong building material that could withstand the ferocious winds and blowing sands that plagued desert dwellers. Only torrential monsoon rains could destroy the adobe buildings that dotted the countryside.

Bill Driver had rented a mobile home that was attached to one of the oldest adobe structures in the Animas area. The double-room building was huge! There was no way Bill was going to buy adequate furniture to turn the comfortable front room into the room it could have been. The 12-inch thick walls kept the room cool through the hottest days and radiated the stored up heat to keep it warm in the chilly nights. If he was unfortunate enough to be in the area in winter, he could always use the huge fireplace, which dominated one wide wall. There were still gas light fixtures on the walls, but Bill was satisfied with lamps situated on the two end tables next to the old sofa that was dwarfed by the length of the room.

With no intention of making the rental a permanent home, he didn't bother putting a rug over the old black and red checkerboard pattern asbestos tile covering the floor. He could sit comfortably on the sofa and use his laptop and that was all he needed. A previous resident had supplied a 20-foot telephone line that was perfect for his computer connection. He used his satellite phone for most of his calls leaving the landline phone for incoming messages, routed through the answering machine, from his boss in Lordsburg. The system worked perfectly for him. In fact, the Internet service in the Animas area was far better than he'd had at his old place of residence! He vowed to never again use dial up Internet!

There was only one other piece of furniture in the room, if you could call a 19-inch Sony flat screen setting on an old sewing machine cabinet furniture. While he had invested in a Direct TV package, he seldom watched the tube except to catch local and national news and the weather. The weather coverage, he learned quickly enough, was not what he was used to having. His choice was either Tucson or Albuquerque as his main news/weather source and the Tucson stations stopped weather coverage at the New Mexico/Arizona line and the Albuquerque stations didn't mentioned much about weather for the boot heel area and touched on the Silver City and Deming area only barely. He turned it on more for noise than to watch the poor selection of what was called "entertainment."

Local news had turned out to be another joke as the only news he actually received was of the happenings in Albuquerque and the northern part of New Mexico. The boot heel area just didn't warrant any attention. Once in a great while he'd get a blurb of info about some happening in Silver City, Deming, Columbus or even Las Cruces. He could have opted for Tucson as his main source of service but that would have given him less news of southwest New Mexico than the Albuquerque stations did. The TV stations in both states seemed to stop their news coverage at the state lines. It was discouraging but he had gotten used to it. For National news, he preferred CNN and Fox anyway.

Bill had been contemplating his existence in the forlorn area and nodded off on the lumpy sofa. He had been on patrol with Jaime all day and they had picked up two more undocumented people near Rodeo. The men, both under 21, were tired, dirty and hungry. When they saw the border patrol vehicle cruising south along Hwy 80, they quickly hit the dust but not before eagle-eyed Jaime saw them. Looking into the panic-stricken eyes of the two young men, Bill found a strange sense of sympathy come over him. He couldn't blame these men for seeking a better life north of the border. He wished again that the immigration process could be streamlined so that the necessity for people to sneak into the United States could be eliminated. It really angered him when he heard the stories of how smugglers were charging thousands of dollars to transport individuals across the border. Many of the poor people were left in the desert both dead and alive!

Most of the undocumented visitors who made it safely into the States were happy with jobs that the average American didn't want anyway. Being agreeable to lower pay, as offered in chicken plants and on farms, employment provided them with money to send home to their families in Mexico and other South American countries where the living expenses were considerably less than in the U.S. and salary followed suit. It also filled a labor need for businesses who found it difficult to maintain a workforce. Unfortunately, the two young men they had apprehended, who knew no English, would be shipped back across the border at the expense of the taxpayers and return via another crossing within a matter of time. It was a no-win situation no matter how you looked at it.

Of course, the drug smugglers were another matter and their presence at the border was not only illegal, to say the least, but dangerous. Farmers and ranchers in the area were constant in their reports of damage and theft. Then there were the robberies. It was another situation completely and one that Bill hoped he could help resolve.

It seemed he had just dozed off when the ringing of the landline caused him to jerk awake. It took a second for him to get his bearings in the dimly lit room and then he reached for the phone.

"Hello" was his first groggy word.

"Bill, this is the Big Man from Denver, how goes it?" Bill recognized his DEA bosses voice immediately.

"Mark, hi. I'm fine, you?

"Let's cut the crap. I'm not fine and neither are you. Things are just as screwed up around here as before you left! I'm just calling to give you a head's up. You hear from your stoolie down there yet"?

"If you mean that Miller guy, yes. He's not the most informative *stoolie* I've ever known, but I guess we can work with what little he gives us. I'm still looking for some leak here though." Mark's choice of words to describe James Miller was irritating to Bill but he didn't comment.

"Okay, we've gotten some more info on D'Anda. Seems someone in DEA has ties to the D'Anda Cartel and have ratted out our informant. The word on the street is that D'Anda plans to make an example of Miller on the next run. See if you can ferret out something more and stay on your toes, this could be the big break we need. There should be some reaction among the patrol informant there in Lordsburg and if we are really diligent we may be able to close this gap in security."

"Sounds good," commented a more awake Driver. "It just hit me, why did you call on this phone? I thought we were going to use the satellite phone to communicate, you know taps and so on…"

"Actually, we think the cartels have developed some high tech tap techniques themselves. They seem able to listen in on satellite connections. Hence, we are going to change our methods. We have a few tricks up our sleeves too, and one is a device that allows us to determine if a phone is tapped when we call. Your land line is secure."

"Damn, you're feeding me a line of BS!" Bill was astounded. "Tell me it isn't so."

"It's so." Modern technology and all that. Just be careful. I'll be in contact soon. Oh, by the way, we suspect that the mole in the patrol is someone pretty high up. That's another reason we are going to eliminate contact through the office. From now on, any really important stuff we will relate to you directly. Bye."

Bill gave an absent-minded farewell greeting and sat on the sofa in a still groggy stupor. What had he just heard? The bad men in the world were getting too high tech for him. If the DEA suspected a higher up in the Lordsburg office of being involved in the smuggling operation, it could only be Ron Hall. He was the only person with the connections to get info that could be compromised! Bill didn't like what he was hearing. He'd developed a liking for Hall. Suddenly his mind wandered in another direction. He had the thought that the world was moving too fast for him and maybe it was time for him to make a career change?

CHAPTER 34

Clare celebrated the six-month anniversary in New Mexico by having dinner at the Grille. She enjoyed the solitude of the desert and loved the weather, except when the winds stirred up the dust that choked and covered everything with a grainy residue. She had almost finished collecting the recipes she wanted for her cookbook. She had baked, fried and grilled all of them and was happy with her efforts. She had even taken digital snapshots of the finished products and was busy arranging the offerings in order for presentation to a publisher. That was the problem now…finding a publisher.

Knowing that she always had the option of self-publication made things easier for her but she really wanted to go with a traditional publisher. That was the only way she could see to get the distribution and publicity needed to turn her work into a successful book with reasonable sales.

She had just ordered the Grill's specialty when Bill walked in and approached her table. She was once again overwhelmed at his good looks. Suddenly she felt light headed and her stomach was trembling. She hadn't had such feelings since she'd met Steve and she wasn't sure how to react to them. Maybe it was a sign that it was time to rejoin the world?

"Mind if I join you"? He asked her, his smooth voice almost a caress.

Clare took a quick look around the almost empty dining room and then gave him a look that said there are plenty of other empty places, but she found herself inviting him to sit down.

What was the attraction to this man? He was definitely out of her league. Not only was he older than she was but he was also so much more experienced! Clare felt that he was dangerous, yet in a typical female fashion, she embraced the danger.

Never having been promiscuous, Clare sure wasn't about to change her style now. She knew that if she allowed a relationship to develop between Bill Driver and herself that the day would come when she would have to tell him that she'd never had sex and didn't plan to engage in such behavior until she had a wedding ring on her finger! She remembered the pledge made with Steve just a year ago. Somehow, she thought, Bill Driver just wasn't the marrying kind!

Bill caught the glimpse of sorrow that flashed through Clare's eyes as she remembered happier times. "A penny for your thoughts," he said.

"You wouldn't get much for your money. I was just remembering an old boyfriend."

"Ah, a rival for your affections! What can I do to make you forget him?"

"Nothing, I don't want to forget him. My memories bring me comfort. I'm not even sure I'm not going to go to him and beg him to take me back," she quipped, knowing that she'd never have to beg Steve. He was the one doing the begging!

"Well, maybe I can at least give you something else to think about. How about going to a bar-b-que with me tomorrow? One of the patrol agents is having a get-together at his house north of Lordsburg. I'd like to take you along. I think you'd like it."

"Oh, I don't know. I wouldn't know anybody…."

"No, but you could meet them. It would do you good to get out among people and have some fun."

"Have you been talking to my Dad? You sound just like him."

"Sorry, no, I don't know your Dad. In fact, I don't know much about you at all." Bill flushed as he told the lie. He knew all about Clare Smith, her family and history. She probably knew things even she didn't know!

"Well, if I went to a party like that and it's a big IF, I'd have to take something. I've been working on a chili relleno casserole that I think is pretty good; wouldn't mind getting some feedback on it. What time would we leave?"

"How about noon?" Bill asked as Tina, the waitress, brought Clare's Ghostrider's Burger. Tina brushed Bill's sleeve unnecessarily as she handed him a menu and gave him one of her already well-known "come hither" smiles.

"Thanks," Bill said acknowledging her service and touch. "Could I have beer?"

"Sure, you can have whatever you want," Tina said suggestively.

"Just beer now and one of those sandwiches like you just brought her."

Bill watched her as she seductively waltzed away from the table. He shook his head. "Boy, she sure tries hard to get me into the sack," he said without thinking.

Clare gave him a hard stare and he immediately apologized.

"She has been after me since I hit town. I'm sorry if I embarrassed you."

"That's okay, I guess some people have a much more active life than I, but this life is my choice. I needed peace and solitude and sure found it here."

Conversation ceased and Bill watched as Clare devoted her attention to the juicy burger smothered in mushrooms and tangy sauce.

"I warn you, this isn't the easiest burger I've ever eaten, Clare said, but it is undoubtedly one of the best, might be easier with a knife and fork."

Bill learned firsthand just what Clare meant when he began eating his own sandwich a few minutes later. Clare was nearly finished with her sandwich when Bill's was delivered, but the tasty meal disappeared swiftly from his plate. It was obvious that he hadn't had much to eat during the day.

"I see what you mean about the knife and fork," Bill smiled as he cut up the burger. "This is really good though, must be the booze in the sauce!" They finished their meal in silence punctuated by the sound of knives on china. With perfect timing, Tina approached just as they were finished with their entrée.

"No dessert," declared Clare before she even asked. "I'm stuffed. Don't think I've ever had a better gourmet burger. That could hold its own against any burger anywhere I've ever been!" Bill waved Tina away and smiled at Clare as he reached across the table to wipe a drop of sauce from her chin. "Yeah, it is good." So we are on for tomorrow, right."

"Sure, I'll get up and make a couple casseroles in the morning. They should go well with whatever is on the menu. I'll be ready when you show up."

Picking up both checks, Bill placed his hand over Clare's as he shook his head, "My treat this time. I'll see you about noon." With those words he went to the bar to pay the tab; when he turned back around, Clare was nowhere in sight. Her car was turning onto the highway as he walked out the door. He was surprised at how let down he felt that their evening had ended so suddenly. He wanted more from his relationship with Clare. Maybe tomorrow would bring about some positive changes!

CHAPTER 35

It had proven to be a very interesting day. Clare's chili relleno casseroles had been a hit at the bar-b-que. Jaime's ribs and burgers were fantastic and his wife, Lana, had prepared old-fashioned American potato salad with a twist that interested Clare's culinary side. The unique dressing was made with cream cheese rather than the usual mayonnaise! Jaime's baked beans had just a hint of smoke and were made with a spicy root beer based BBQ sauce that had been developed by a friend of his. Its spicy flavor topped off a meal that was a hit with everyone.

In addition to Clare and Bill and Jaime and his lovely wife, there were at least six other couples enjoying a cool afternoon on the patio. The party seemed a real success but there existed an undercurrent that caused discomfort for Clare. She couldn't pinpoint exactly what was out of kilter, but something was! She was experiencing the same feelings she'd had in Portland when she had been around Myra – an undercurrent of distrust and anger. She sensed that Bill picked up on it too and resolved to talk to him about it on the way home.

By the time they started the drive back to Animas; Clare was exhausted and actually fell asleep before they reached Lordsburg and Interstate 10.

Bill watched her as she slept. He was entranced by her and feelings were being stirred that he hadn't experienced for a long time but maybe that was just because he hadn't been around a desirable woman in a long time! He knew she was much younger than he was but that didn't seem important any longer. Many women preferred older men and he had realized that Clare was more mature than other women were at her age. At least he thought she was! Heck, after what she'd been through anyone would have grown up fast!

When they took the sharp turn off I10 onto 338 South, Clare woke up. "I'm so sorry I fell asleep. I don't usually do that. Guess all the fresh air…"

"Don't worry about it. I enjoyed watching you so relaxed. You usually have a wall around you, tense; it was good to see you at rest."

"Really, you think I've got something to hide, or what?"

"No, no, I didn't mean that. It's just that you don't let anyone get close to you. You seem almost scared to allow anybody to get to know you. I think you relaxed with Lana today though. You liked her didn't you?"

"Yes, I did. She's a very smart woman, friendly and not nosy. I enjoyed meeting her and Jaime."

"That is very important to you, isn't it?"

"What?"

"The not being nosy part."

"Yes, it is. Not that I have any big secret to hide but I just prefer not to have anyone digging into my life. The other couples were a little more clannish. They didn't make me feel welcome. For that matter, I didn't see the guys falling all over you either." Clare had managed to give a glimpse into her thoughts and turn the conversation away from anything personal in one sentence. Bill had to admire her talent for steering the conversation away from her life.

"You're right. They're tight group." Bill followed her lead and picked up the conversation about the party as though her private life had never been mentioned. "Jaime had hoped the party might break the ice some but it didn't work. I really think those guys have something going together. Don't ask me what, but I plan to find out."

"That sounds dangerous. Maybe they are involved in some underhanded operation…you know, using their positions in the patrol to cover for something."

"What makes you say that?" Bill had the same thoughts but he hadn't put them into words. "What gives you such an idea?" Had he spoken too sharply?

"Oh, just a thought, I see some strange things out my window sometimes, lights, cars. It makes me wonder if there isn't some hanky-panky going on. We are only fifty miles from the border, after all."

"Clare, do me a favor, don't *ever* say those things to anyone else. You could say something that might put you in danger."

"What? Are you saying that there *are* things going on right here in Animas?"

"Like you said, we are only fifty miles from the border. We pick up drug smugglers frequently and illegals too. Yes, there probably is a lot more going on than we know about and even more than you can imagine. Just don't say things like that too loud, promise."

"Sure, but don't scare me. I'm enjoying living here. I tell myself it is peaceful, quiet and safe. Don't destroy my image."

"I don't mean to do that. I just want you to be cautious. You do lock your doors at night, don't you?"

"Of course," Clare laughed and the tension was broken. The remainder of the ride passed quietly. When they arrived at Clare's house, Bill walked her to the door; they stood in the dim light of the yellow glow from the light and for a moment Clare thought he was going to kiss her but with a quick peck on the cheek, he excused himself. Clare stood and stared after him wondering why he hadn't pressed her to let him come inside? Maybe he wasn't as interested in her as she'd thought. Maybe she'd read his intentions all wrong!

Sitting in the dark living room after Bill drove away, Clare gave a few minutes to quiet contemplation of the day's events. It was a day to remember. She turned on the lamp and reached for her often-neglected diary...

June 2, 2007

Had a wonderful time at a small BBQ with Bill Driver today. It was actually fun to be around people again! Of course, the party wasn't large – nothing to compare with the big shindigs that I used to go to in Portland (after I became a member of the Goforth family anyway). Bill is really a nice guy but I think he is hiding something; not a bad side but something more serious. Maybe he's a secret agent? A 007 wannabe! That would be a corker. He is suave and debonair and yet simple and down-to-earth. I'm sure he has had some experiences that would make my hair stand on end! I was surprised he didn't try to turn the day into more – like a night! But he was quite the gentleman depositing me on the back porch (which I use as a front door) with just a slight peck on the cheek and a "goodbye"! I came inside feeling cheated! It is the first time in a long time that I wanted to be near someone. I came inside and tried to call Steve but he didn't answer. I didn't leave a message. He'll see the number; I'm sure and call me before the weekend is out!

NEDRA J. BURCH

CHAPTER 36

Even as Bill and Clare were driving through the desert toward Animas, admiring the red blaze of a desert sunset, Alexander Goforth sat at his antique mahogany desk in his paneled library, not looking at the collections of leather-bound, first edition classics but staring at the smooth, rich mahogany top of the desk with a frown on his handsome face.

He had aged in the past year. Always younger appearing than his true years, he now showed every one of the near fifty he'd spent on the earth. His eyes no longer glowed with the lively fire that had entranced many a woman; his chestnut hair was liberally sprinkled with gray where it had once only been only a feathering over his temples; and his once enticing smile had turned into a perpetual frown, worry lines were permanently etched into his forehead.

The events of the previous June would have caused anyone to change and although Alexander Goforth was a giant in the shipping world, a leader among the philanthropic, and a highly respected member of the "movers and shakers" of society, he had not escaped the ravages heartbreak and sorrow could wreck upon the human body. People remembered how he *used* to be and shook their heads in dismay at the man he now was.

Alexander didn't pay attention to those who queried him about how things were going; he just gave them civil answers that said, "Leave me alone" without hurting their feelings or exposing himself to their sympathy. He didn't need sympathy. He needed Clare!

There had been so many changes since the accident that sometimes he thought he must have been dreaming it all. Having Myra institution-alized was not new but the circumstances that precipitated this, her current situation, were so terrible that he often thought he imagined them. Only he knew he hadn't. Myra drew nearer death every day. He couldn't see how she could last much longer in her present condition.

Once she had been a beautiful woman, a vision to behold as she graced the dance floor in form-fitting gowns wearing diamonds, ru-bies or emeralds bright as her eyes, laughter tinkling like crystals on a windblown chandler, smiling a warm and sensuous invitation seconded by her soft voice filled with desire and mystery. Now she was a fragile shell threatening to shatter with the slightest breeze. She spent her days gazing out the window with lifeless eyes, lost in her own torment, and her nights in a dreamless darkness that nothing could penetrate. She was a frozen image of a woman, possessing no warmth, no feeling, and no desire. If not for the high-dollar medical team watching carefully over her, feeding her through plastic tubes and providing necessary services for basic cleanliness and sanitation, she would have expired long ago. Even with the level of expert care and treatment given her by the finest team of providers, her time was slowly ending. Alexander had acknowledged this fact but didn't want to see the end in spite of the need to know that Myra had been released from her self-made hell.

His son, Aaron, had managed to escape Portland and the fiasco that had changed the Goforth family so suddenly and irrevocably. He and his new wife had fled the city and started over in Chicago, where he was chiseling out a successful career and starting his new family. Alexander was grateful for that glimmer of light. He looked forward to visiting with Aaron and Margaret in the near future.

Bettina, his daughter, had seemingly recovered fully from her or-deal at the hands of kidnappers. Counseling had helped but Alexander felt that it was her possession of the Goforth stamina that made her ancestors successful traders and dynasty founders, that was the source of her recovery. She was a comfort to him, no doubt, but he couldn't refuse to let her have the freedom to live her own life. As a college freshman, her days were filled with new friends, activities, studies and even a love interest. Bettina had never had a serious boyfriend before so although he was afraid that she'd end up heartbroken when she saw the shallowness of her new friend, he was glad that she was able to form a relationship at all! When he considered all she'd been through in the hours before Myra and Clare's *accident,* he could only marvel that she appeared so normal.

Clare, his love child, was another matter altogether. No denying that she'd suffered the most physically and possibly the most mentally as a result of the incident of the previous summer, but Alexander still had trouble accepting the manner in which she'd decided to cope with the tragedy. It was unthinkable to him that she could recover by hiding from life in barren land miles from civilization, friends and family. He felt that she would heal more quickly and completely submerged in a warm loving environment. But Clare had other ideas.

When she had first told him about her decision to move to the boot heel of New Mexico, he had thought it was just a fancy and would pass. He hadn't realized how much thought she had given the idea or how determined she was to escape Portland and all the memories that lingered there. Her new hermit-style life in the desert allowed her to continue her education, pursue her newly found dreams for a career as an author and ignore the pressures that society demanded of a Goforth active in Portland society. When he was honest, he fancied such an escape for himself!

Alexander failed to recognize his own dropout attitude toward his social obligations; obligations that he had once relished, were anything other than normal. In his own way, he was escaping into another realm just as Clare had. He'd heard people suggest that very thing to him but he quickly steered the conversations in other directions so that he didn't have to deal with his own inadequate response to the tragedies that had invaded his once vibrant life.

He couldn't evade this latest threat though. Word from his friends in the boot heel was that there were things going on in the area that could pose a danger to his Clare. It terrified him every time he heard news of more cartel violence in Arizona and Mexico. The fact that

Juarez was fast becoming the murder capital of the world didn't help him ignore the unease he felt at having Clare so close to the border.

He shook his head. His listless brown hair, a tangled web, belied his once immaculate grooming as it fell into his eyes. He stared at the telephone, the instrument of the disturbing news that, without his knowledge, was about to shake his world up again!

CHAPTER 37

After Clare had dropped the bombshell that she planned to move to the little-known community of Animas, New Mexico the prior December, Alexander had utilized his net of informants to ferret out all he could about the area. He let it be known among his acquaintances that he had a personal interest in activities in the area. He didn't have to have any other reason. His long-time friends were more than happy to supply him with information and to provide on-going updates. Up to now, the information had been mundane to say the least.

A small community where once Phelps-Dodge had been King now held on to its survival by the grace of some cattle ranches, old-family spreads; and struggling farmers who raised paltry crops of grain, alfalfa, and New Mexico peppers. Every year someone else left the valley and sought a new, more prosperous life elsewhere. Rumors of an agricultural resurgence by a large California-based conglomerate kept others hanging on to their dreams of a more profitable life.

It appeared that it was truly a sleepy little community until Alex received a phone call from Jay Davis. An old business acquaintance, Jay had once represented his families shipping interests with Alexander's company. His family owned large potato farms in Idaho and at one time had operated a conglomerate of cotton farmers in Cotton City, New Mexico; an area located about thirteen miles north of Animas. Jay still had family living in the area, older folks who couldn't see relocating even though their farming days were long over. They lived in the quiet valley, allowing the once productive acres they owned lie fallow.

Cotton had ceased to be a crop some thirty or more years ago and they were too old to plant the chili peppers that kept the area in the green. They did allow some alfalfa fields to be planted and cut each year and the income from that high-dollar crop along with dwindling savings allowed them to live comfortably.

Jay knew, however, that Alexander Goforth wasn't interested in his family history. The information he had for him had come from other sources. His great-nephew and namesake worked for the border patrol. Stationed in Lordsburg, he'd passed along some of the more trustworthy gossip he'd overheard in the office. Information he thought his great uncle's old friend might be interested in.

Everyone knew there was business in illegal activities along the entire U.S./Mexico border so it had been no surprise to the border patrol agents working in the Animas area when activity picked up along their segment. The cartel activity in the Columbus and El Paso crossings had naturally driven coyotes to find less patrolled routes. Antelope Wells was one site that was a natural recipient for some of the business, another site was less well known. South of Animas the cartel had managed to find another crossing area that was actually safer than the Antelope Wells site. This was not a recognized crossing; it was much more easily hidden from the drones and helicopters patrols by the small hills and scrubby desert plants.

Smuggling routes across the Animas valley were old and well used, having been trails traversed by Geronimo's wild band on their forays into the United States from Mexico and back; also the Clanton Gang, well known around Tombstone, Arizona as ranchers, smuggled contraband to Mexico through the valley. If the rocks along the path could talk, there would probably be many hair-raising tales told!

Small groups of men on horseback could easily traverse arroyos and enter the U.S. without detection. Once in the mountains they could off load their cargo and hide it in the numerous small caves that peppered the area. For the same reason, they could locate already hidden contraband, usually weapons and munitions, and cart it back to Mexico where such items were not easy to buy, at least legally! By using different trails, they were able to minimize the telltale tracks that were often identified by agents patrolling by land and air and keep their operations secret and secure! Their evasion tactics were continually changing and the border patrol couldn't keep up with them.

The patrol wasn't ignorant of these new operations in the Lordsburg area. They were slowly building their personnel resources to deal with the larger threats. Jay had heard that was why Bill Driver had been assigned to the unit. On his heels, three other agents had recently reported to the area, and the Lordsburg station inventory of weapons and vehicles had received a hefty augmentation. Jay had passed this information to his great uncle knowing that he would forward it to his friend, Alexander Goforth who had a personal interest in the area. The latest chatter indicated that there was well organized smuggling traffic starting at the Lordsburg airport and heading south. A big sting operation was being planned with the help of the pilot bringing the contraband into the area; a pilot named James Miller.

Alexander had perked up as soon as he heard the tale of the smuggling operations. He was already wary about the situation around the area where Clare lived and didn't want her in an area where there might be danger from angry drug cartel members, but when he heard the name *James Miller,* his blood began to rush through his veins! It could only be Clare's cousin piloting the plane. Clare had told him about James' frequent visits to her in Animas. She had wondered why he had suddenly developed such an interest in her life. James had told her that her aunts, his mother and aunt, were concerned about her well-being and he stopped so he could give them honest reports on her situation but Alexander now knew the real reason for his visits and it filled him with fear.

Every time the phone rang, he hesitated to answer it expecting to hear that Clare had been the victim of some vandalism, massacre or kidnap plot perpetrated by a Mexican drug lord. Activities along the southwestern New Mexico border had been headlined in papers and on news stories on every TV channel. He continually begged Clare to return to Portland but she insisted that everything in the Animas area was "quiet and peaceful." Alex knew that it wasn't…

He always looked at the caller-ID screen before picking up the receiver and this time he relaxed as he saw it wasn't from New Mexico. It was, however, the hospital. He recognized the name, Mary's Wood, and knew that they would only call if it concerned Myra. He steeled himself for the worst.

CHAPTER 38

Myra had been on a steady downhill trend since her admission those many months ago. Alex couldn't understand what kept her going. She was fed by tube, sat all day in a wheelchair and stared at the lake. She didn't talk, didn't move. She appeared to be a vegetable, but there was still a lot of brain wave activity. The doctors didn't know what was going on inside her head but the amount of activity belied her apparent dispassionate face, her lifeless eyes and listless body. Just to look at her one would never know she wasn't a life-sized porcelain doll placed in the chair. Even her breathing was barely perceptible!

Fully expecting to hear the news that she had expired, Alex was prepared for the worst. However, the administrator gave him the opposite news. Myra had snapped out of her self-induced catatonic state! She was asking for Alex!

The drive to Mary's Woods seemed to take twice as long as usual. Alex mused over the events of the past months as he drove. The doctors had never been able to give him a suitable explanation for Myra's condition. That she didn't want to face reality was an easy out but it didn't explain anything. There had been many times when Alex wished he could have hidden from the realities of life as easily as Myra had but that thought was unrealistic. He had responsibilities, Tina needed him and so did Clare even though she didn't realize it.

The nurse opened the door to Myra's suite. Her rooms were as far removed from institution-looking rooms as could be imagined. The wheel chair in the corner, the institutional tiled floors and the IV tree holding bagged liquids snaking down the tube attached to Myra's body were the only indications that the occupant of the cozy room wasn't living in an upscale home. Discretely hidden were the cameras that maintained 24-hour surveillance and the bank of monitors that normally recorded bodily functions. Myra was lying in her bed and appeared asleep. As Alex entered, she turned her head in his direction and gave him a weak smile.

The smile didn't do much to mask her weakened state. She looked like the slightest movement would cause her thin, white skin to crack. Blue veins showed on her face and in her hands. Her fingers looked like the bones of a skeleton held together by flimsy rubber gloves; he took her hand in his, it was icy!

"Alex," she croaked. Her voice was dry, raspy, and weak. "I'm so glad you made it. I don't have long and I've got to explain it to you."

"There is nothing to explain. Not now, you need to rest and get strong. We can talk later…"

"No! I have to tell you the truth. I don't have long…don't want long. I've cheated you, cheated us. I'm so sorry. Listen to me, please."

I'm so sorry for all the pain I've caused you. The loss of Tina…"

"Tina is fine," Alex told her.

Myra's eyes overflowed with tears at these words. "Fine? Tina's fine?" she questioned.

"Yes. She is in school and doing okay. She'll be glad to know you asked about her."

"They didn't do anything to her? Those men…?"

"Nothing serious, the kidnappers kept her hidden for a couple days and then let her go. The police found her and after an overnight stay in the hospital, she came home. She's doing fine now." There was no reason to mention that the kidnappers had given her several injections of a knock-out drug and Alex still worried that there might be some delayed after effect from the drug!

"Oh, thank God. I was so afraid I'd killed her. That's why I killed Clare. Oh, Alex, can you ever forgive me, I've been so selfish?"

"Clare is okay too. She isn't dead…"

"You mean I missed? I remember the gun, pulling the trigger and her falling. Blood spattering. She's alive?"

"Yes. She was wounded and took a while to recover but she is living in New Mexico and is doing fine. Sometimes she has headaches but she is doing well."

"I've been thinking about it all, for so long. I was wrong. Wrong about it all. If I had stepped aside when you first asked me for a divorce, back when you and Rose first started seeing each other, none of this would have ever happened. I should have done it but I wanted you. I didn't want to share you with anyone else."

I didn't want to see Aaron and Tina lose part of their inheritance to Clare just as I didn't want to share you. I told myself I was going to have to get rid of her to protect them, but that was a lie. I just wanted to…."

"It's alright now, Myra. You just rest. Everyone is alive and well. In a few weeks, you'll have a grandchild. You need to get strong so you can hold him."

"A grandchild?"

"Yes, Aaron and his wife, Margaret. Do you remember Clare's friend Margaret? Aaron and she married and they are in Chicago now. Aaron is working for a large landscape design firm. You need to rest now; you need to get strong so that we can go visit them after the baby is born."

"No, that won't happen. What I need to do is tell you the truth, the rest of the story."

"No, you just need to rest." Alex looked at the woman he had once loved and felt his heart twist. There had been a time when Myra had been the light of his life but now he could only feel sympathy for the emaciated shell of a woman lying on the bed.

"James, did they get James," she whispered.

"James? What about James," asked Alex, suddenly interested?

"It was all his idea. He wanted to get rid of Clare too. He didn't want her to inherit his mother and aunt's estates. He arranged for the kidnappers. I just had to be sure Clare was where he needed her to be when he needed her to be there."

"Myra, I hear what you're saying and I don't like it. James has taken a real interest in Clare's life recently. Do you think she's in danger from him?"

"Yes. He wants her dead. I wouldn't go along with murder so he said he'd just have her kidnapped and shipped out of the country. They were supposed to take her to the Middle East or somewhere and keep her there."

"They? Who?"

"I don't know. Some people he'd worked with in Florida. Drug smugglers, I guess. I don't know. He hired them. I don't really know what they were going to do. Yes, I do. No matter what I tried to tell myself, I knew that Clare would end up dead at the end of the road or wishing she were dead. He couldn't take a chance of her coming back. But you said she was fine…"

"Yes, she is fine. You don't worry about her. Just rest and get strong. I have to go now, but I'll be back later. Thanks, Myra. Thanks for telling me…"

"Forgive me, please. Tell me you forgive me."

"Yes, Myra, I forgive you. I understand your fears and I forgive you. Now you rest."

"I will Alex. I can rest now. I love you." Almost before the words had left her lips, Myra closed her eyes. Alex looked at her face. It seemed peaceful at last. They say 'confession is good for the soul' and it looked like it had worked for Myra. Little did he know that she would never again open those once-beautiful eyes. Myra died peacefully in her sleep within minutes after Alex left the room.

He got the phone call on his cell just as he was pulling onto the highway and turned back to Mary's Wood immediately. There were things that required his immediate attention. He signed papers and gave instructions to the staff for the removal of the body to the mortuary without showing the inner turmoil he was suffering; however, he lost all composure when he realized that Myra had died on the exact same date that Rose Simpson had died!

"Mr. Goforth, are you alright?" asked the charge nurse as she waited for him to sign the final release form.

Alex pulled himself from back from the thoughts that had suddenly engulfed him. "Yes, I'm fine. It's just that it is so ironic that Myra died today."

"Ironic, I guess you could say that. We have expected it for a while but actually she seemed to be rallying."

"You don't understand. It's just that I lost someone else on this date; someone who also played a very important role in my life. It was two years ago but…" his voice drifted off and was replaced by the scratching sound of his signature on the form. As soon as he finished signing, he stood up and excused himself. He had to call Aaron and Tina and… Clare.

★ ★ ★ ★

The telephone call telling about Myra's death was not a surprise to Aaron. That she had hung onto life for so long was more of a surprise to him. He told Alex he would be on the next flight to Portland. He wasn't sure if Margaret would accompany him but they would check with the doctor and if he felt the trip would pose no problem for her pregnancy, she would make the trip.

Alex had just finished the phone call with his son when he saw Tina in the doorway. Her eyes were full of tears. How much of the conversation she'd heard he didn't know but from her tears he knew that she'd heard enough to know of her mother's death. He held out his arms and his daughter fell into them, sobbing her heart out. They sat in the dimly lit library for a while and then Alex half carried Tina to her room and tucked her into bed. They would visit the funeral home once Aaron arrived as a family and finalize the arrangements for the burial service. Alex still had one person to call though, and he wasn't sure how to approach his daughter, Clare.

As he dialed the phone there was heaviness in his heart unlike any he had ever known. He broke to news to her knowing that it would take more than Myra's death to bring Clare home.

There had never been a close relationship between the two and after the *incident* whatever had existed was destroyed. It also bothered Alex that he knew Clare would be thinking of her own mother on this date and missing her. How could he expect her to come to Portland for his wife's burial when his wife was responsible for all the hurt and pain Clare had experienced throughout her life and especially the injury of the past year? He wasn't surprised at her words after he told her of the recent demise of his wife.

"I'm sorry Alex, really sorry. I know it hurts you, and Aaron and Tina and I'd like to be there for all of you, but I can't see myself crying over the woman who tried to kill me. Please understand…"

"Of course, I understand." Alex felt his heart breaking again as he heard Clare's refusal. He had hoped his fears were unfounded and she would agree to attend Myra's funeral. Surely it was not unusual for a victim not to want to pay their respects to their attacker! Alex had just hoped that maybe Clare would come home for Aaron and Tina, for him, not actually for Myra.

"There is more that I need to tell you." Alex continued. Clare noticed the exhaustion in Alex's voice and felt guilty at her refusal to return to Portland just to offer her support but she couldn't see making the trip. Not now at least.

"Myra woke up before she died. I talked to her. She begged forgiveness for what happened. She thought both you and Tina were dead and she begged me to forgive her. I told her that you were both all right and that eased her mind somewhat. I forgave her, of course. Then she told me about the plot…"

"No, please, I don't want to hear about it"

"But, you need to know…"

"No! I'm trying to put it behind me. I don't want to talk about that night, or anything leading up to it; maybe someday, but not now. There is nothing you can tell me that will change the past. Just save it for some other time when I can deal with it."

"But Clare, you don't understand, there is something you need to know. It does affect you now, your life …"

"NO! I won't listen. I'll call Tina and Aaron, talk to them and give them my condolences just as I give them to you, but I don't want to hear anything about the shooting! I'm just not ready!"

Alex jumped at the sound of the phone being slammed down. He felt that it was so important Clare know about James' involvement in the plot to kidnap her. He had already told the Portland police, they were reopening the case, and looking into the allegation of James' involvement but Alex knew that James was making inroads into Clare's new life and it scared him. What if James still wanted Clare out of the way? He had been able to plan a kidnapping once. How much easier would it be to affect a sinister plot now? Alex was going to have to call in some favors to assure protection for his daughter!

Clare had slammed down the phone receiver without really thinking. She was surprised by her own vehement response to Alex trying to talk about the year-old incident. She poured a glass of wine and sat in the quiet dark room until her internal shaking subsided then made the obligatory phone calls to her siblings. It was the only thing she felt she could do.

CHAPTER 39

Clare could feel no genuine sorrow at the news of Myra's death but she did have genuine empathy for Aaron and Tina's loss. She remembered how heartsick she'd felt after her own mother had died just two years before. It was shocking that Myra had died on the anniversary of her own mother's death. Life was strange, to be sure. After a restless night, she spent the entire day thinking back over her life since her tragic and sudden mother's demise. Things had looked so gloomy for her and then a ray of light filled her life with unexpected surprises. She suddenly had a family, money, more family, a lover and then disaster!

Clare had been emotionally drained after talking to her relatives. She couldn't understand why she had gotten so upset with Alex and the memory of her explosion on the phone ate at her. Even if what he had to tell her was just fabrication from his own imagination, she owed it to him to at least listen to his concerns. Alex had always had Clare's best interest at the forefront of his actions. She felt a nagging fear that she should have listened to him. That he had something that was important for her to hear. She almost picked up the phone to call him and apologize but her fierce independence wouldn't allow her to do it.

It had been a week since the bar-b-que at Jaime Well's place and suddenly she felt alone and lost, a feeling that had been coming over her more and more often. Clare usually ate at Ghostrider's Grille on Saturday but she didn't feel like running into Bill so decided to go to the Grille on Friday instead. The memory of the previous weekend was still vivid in her mind and contributed to a new restlessness at night. She had to deal with emotions that she didn't want to acknowledge; was she developing feelings for Bill or was it simple loneliness? Although she really didn't know Bill that well, she knew he'd be able to see that she was distracted and that would require explanations that she didn't feel up to making so she made up her mind to leave for dinner early. She arrived just after the Grille's opening time, 5 p.m. and sat at her usual two-person table hoping that Bill wouldn't decide to come in for a drink and stop and sit with her.

In the kitchen, located just out of sight of the dining room, loud voices rose in anger. "I can't do it all by myself, I need some help. If you don't hire someone that I can depend on to help with preparation, someone who can do the job decently, you can look for another cook!"

"I can't afford to hire someone else." Clare recognized the voice of Tom, the owner of the café. "I've got my own son doing dishes, bussing tables and other odd jobs. He works for peanuts and he tries to help you whenever he can, doing whatever he can but what do you expect from a twelve-year old? If you quit, I'll have to find someone else and I hate to do that. You are good, the best cook I've …"

"I'm more than a cook – I'm a chef! I spent two years going to culinary school to learn the ins and outs of the business. I've worked in some of Albuquerque's top restaurants, and in Phoenix and Tucson too."

"I know, I know. I'm lucky to have you but the truth is that there isn't another decent café for a hundred miles. It isn't as if you could leave here and get another job. Just be patient, I'll see what I can do. If nothing else, I'll get my Mom to come in and help you. Is that okay?"

"I'll give you two weeks. If I don't have someone by then, I'm history."

It might have been an exaggeration to say that there wasn't another decent café within a hundred miles, but Tom was desperate. If he lost Chef James, he didn't know who he'd get to fill the loss. Decent cooks were hard to find in the sparsely populated valley!

As things quieted down, Clare had a thought. Why don't I volunteer to help? I can use the experience, I can learn some of the tricks of the trade from a trained chef and I don't need the money. As Tom walked past her table on his way to the bar, she held out a tentative hand to stop him.

"I overheard you talking to your chef in the kitchen and I'd like to volunteer to work with him."

"Do you have experience," he asked tentatively.

"Well, not exactly. I'm planning to go to culinary school myself (*where did that idea come from, she wondered*). I'm a quick learner and I have studied a lot about cooking. In fact, I'm in the process of compiling a cookbook that I hope to have published soon."

"I don't know. He wants somebody with experience besides I can't really afford to hire anyone right now."

"Oh, I'd work for free! The experience would be invaluable to me and to be honest I really don't need the money."

Tom looked at her quizzically. "Don't need the money, must be nice."

"Don't get the wrong idea, I can use the income just like anyone, but right now, I'm, shall we say, 'secure'. That could change but I don't see it happening right away. Why don't you see if he'll talk to me about it at least?"

Clare realized that she had given a peak into her private business and wanted to end the talk about money quickly. It would be best if people didn't know about her finances, she was sure.

"Okay, I'll have him talk to you. It might be a little while as he is busy preparing some takeout orders right now and, of course, your dinner."

"That's fine. I'll wait. And, can we keep the salary thing just between you and me. I'd rather it not get out that I'm working for nothing."

"Sure, if that's the way you want it. We'll work that out later too. I don't like the idea of someone in my kitchen who isn't a paid employee. You know there could be ramifications, insurance, health department certs, stuff like that."

After Tom walked on, Clare thought some more about what she had just done. Taking on a job had never even entered her mind before but she could see how it would benefit her greatly. The experience of working in a real kitchen was something she had planned to do once before, when she was in Portland. She already had some insight into the operations of the business through the classes she'd taken in hotel and restaurant management the prior year. She was an avid watcher of all the cooking shows that flooded the TV channels, and had read many books on food preparation. Her work on her own cookbook had given her insight into cooking for a few or a crowd. If the chef agreed, she'd pick his brain and learn everything she could about working in a commercial kitchen. It could only be a plus for her.

She was relieved when the chef himself served her dinner. "Understand you want to talk," he said as he placed her plate before her.

Clare looked up at the tall, skinny man who ruled the kitchen. He couldn't have been much older than she was! Milky blue eyes were set in a face that was long, lean and thin lipped. He had close-cropped blond hair, wore a chef's coat and pleated cap that proclaimed his position.

"Yes, if you have time. I overheard you saying you needed someone to help in the kitchen."

"And you have experience?" he asked. Clare noted that he was talking down to her as a teacher might talk to an untried student but resolved not to let that turn her from her goal.

"I'll be honest, I've never worked in a commercial kitchen but I've studied a lot of books, watched a lot of shows and taken some classes in restaurant and hotel management. I'm a fast learner and not afraid of work. I love to cook and would appreciate the opportunity to learn the basics from a professional, like you." She'd added the last just to flatter him. It seemed to her that he needed some flattering. She'd already realized that this man had an over-inflated ego and needed someone to fuss over his accomplishments. He reminded her of some of the kids she'd known at college – timid and insecure.

"I'm a chef and I don't have time to teach an amateur," was his sharp reply.

"Just give me a chance, that's all I ask. Tom can keep looking for someone to help and when he finds them, I'll leave. I don't think you'll be sorry. I handle a mean knife." Clare tried to cajole the chef.

Looking at this fresh-faced girl, Chef James, actually liked what he saw. Just a few years younger than he, she displayed the same intensity he'd once felt for cooking. An intensity that had burned out after in a being passed over for the third time in as many years for the job of head chef. Even though she didn't have experience, James felt an urge to give her a chance. What the heck, what could he lose, if she could dice veggies, she'd be more help than he had now.

"Okay, I'll give you a chance. Be here at three o'clock tomorrow and you can start. I won't have much time for training but I'll show you once what I need done, then it'll be up to you."

Before Clare could utter a simple "thanks," he was striding back to the kitchen where a couple orders had piled up. Clare sat back and looked at the attractive plate he had so recently plopped before her. If she could learn anything from him, she'd be better off than she was now. She cut into her perfectly cooked steak and thought about the new turn her life was taking.

CHAPTER 40

Ed was very sure that what he was about to do was a not a good thing. His gut told him to walk away and forget the venture with Al. Still…

Belinda had done well with the surgery but now, faced with weeks of chemotherapy, he could see her falling deeper and deeper into the unfathomable realm of depression. It tore him apart. She not only had the treatments to fear but also continued to worry about the financial drain her medical condition was putting on them. He had talked to the oncologist and it had been decided to give her some anti-depressant medication in the hopes that she would be able to deal with the stresses that her condition was instigating.

Alvaro Garcia drove into the parking spot outside the front window of KFC just as Ed had convinced himself that he needed to leave. Al was late as usual and as Ed saw him jump lightly from his customized pickup, he felt his adrenalin rush. It was easy to see that Al had a lucrative income from some source; always well dressed, cash at hand, driving a fancy vehicle and talk about free time. He never seemed to be in a hurry or concerned about getting to work. Ed shook his head as Al stopped by the booth.

"Hey man, sorry I'm late. Just give me a minute to grab a bite then we can talk business," not waiting for an answer, Al sauntered to the counter as though he owned the place! Ed shook his head again and felt heaviness come over him. Did he really need to do this?

They talked in low tones. That alone made people curious to hear the conversation but with Alvaro Garcia as one of the participants in the conversation, people nearby were straining to hear any stray word. Everyone in Lordsburg knew, or at least thought they knew, that Al was the man to go to for anything illegal to be found in the area. He wasn't exactly respected among the citizenry but it was common knowledge that you didn't give him any reason to single you out and, more importantly, you didn't cross him. Ed had heard stories but he didn't really know if any of the rumors that surrounded Al were true. He had no reason to believe them. On the other hand, he had no reason NOT to believe them.

Alvaro Garcia hadn't grown up in the boot heel area. He had just materialized one night at The Silver Spur, a local bar. Strutting to the bar, he attracted the eyes of every woman in the bar just as a magnet attracts metal shavings. Dressed to the nines, his wardrobe was a sharp contrast to the dust-covered jeans and faded denim shirts favored by the locals. No scuffed boots for him but lizard skin shined to a tee! What he lacked in stature, he made up for in style.

"So man, you wanna work for me now? I can get you in on a good job that is coming up shortly."

"I'm considering…"

"You are either in or you are not. It is that simple. I need someone to help me with a delivery on Saturday – you in?"

Ed couldn't help but hesitate. He was fighting an internal battle and knew he was losing. "Yeah, I'm in. Where and when do you want me to meet you?"

Details of the pickup were sketchy as Ed expected. Al didn't stay safe in his profession by revealing any more than absolutely necessary about his activities. The men finished their meals and parted ways with a date for Saturday night. They would meet at the airport; that was all Ed knew as he left to go home. He carried a 3-piece dinner for Belinda and he hoped she'd enjoy it. She was barely eating and had already lost more weight than her lithe body could spare!

Alvaro watched Ed leave with the dinner for his wife. He envied Ed but would never let it show. Sure, he wore nice clothes, drove a top-of-the line vehicle but if the truth were known, he didn't have a pot to piss in!

Alvaro Garcia was just biding his time; hoping that he could get out of the business he'd become embroiled in and start a new life somewhere. He wanted a wife and family. He'd give up the fancy clothes and flashy vehicle for a peaceful life in a New York minute! He was beginning to feel stressed but it wasn't from the job he did, it was from the physical need he had for the drugs that had enslaved him. He hated it and vowed to himself to check into rehab as soon as this job was finished. He had to turn his life around!

★ ★ ★ ★ ★ ★

How does one deal with the fear of death. The diagnosis of cancer earlier in the spring had been a shock to Belinda. At first, she couldn't believe it. She was too young. There had never been any female cancer in her family as far as she knew. Of course, there wasn't much knowledge available about her relatives left behind by her parents when they fled El Salvador those many years ago. She knew there had been aunts and grandmothers but after arriving in the states, her parents had lost contact with everyone still in El Salvador. One of the prices paid for freedom and safety.

Belinda had thought a lot about her diagnosis and its implications. But the doctor's tests had been thorough and there was no question that she had stage 3A uterine cancer. Surgery was only the first step in the treatment plan.

Dr. Davis had performed a diagnostic hysteroscopy in his office and carefully removed suspicious tissue for analysis. The treatment he laid out was detailed and aggressive: first surgery, a radical hysterectomy; radiation, brachytherapy, the insertion of radioactive implants through the vagina in the cervix and uterus; external radiation, at the Silver City cancer center five days a week for seven weeks; and chemotherapy, an intravenous drip also administered at the cancer center twice a week for three months.

When Dr. Davis and his counterpart, Dr. Krantz had first outlined the plan of treatment, Belinda's denial changed to anger. She didn't understand why she had to have such aggressive treatment. Wouldn't the surgery take care of everything? She knew there would never be any children for her and Ed. Wasn't that enough punishment for getting this dumb disease? Why did she have to go through all the other stuff?

Quickly she tried to bargain with the doctor but he patiently explained why he wanted to take such an aggressive approach.

Belinda's cancer had spread too far for them to be sure that the surgery and radiation would destroy all the mutant cells. The chemotherapy was an insurance against recurrence. Dr. Krantz assured her that he was not alone in his treatment recommendation. The cancer center had a board that reviewed each proposed treatment before its implementation. The other doctors on the board, respected professionals in the field of cancer research and treatment, all agreed with the plan. They had signed off on it; otherwise Dr. Krantz would not be allowed to proceed.

Then there was the depression. The hysterectomy alone would have been enough to cause depression but combined with the other treatments Belinda was to undergo; it was inevitable that she would suffer from the insidious disease. Dr. Krantz had prescribed medication for the illness but it didn't seem to be helping. He was concerned, Ed was concerned and Belinda just didn't care.

CHAPTER 41

Clare had just finished her first full night as at the Grille. It had not been as bad as she'd expected. Chef James had given her new instructions concerning the preparation of items for enchiladas and tacos, part of the night's special Mexican Combination Plate, and approved the use of her homemade salsa for accompaniment to the chips served as appetizers then left her on her own for the rest of the evening. The poor dishwasher wasn't as lucky – it seemed that Chef James was constantly yelling at Ralph to rewash some dish or clean up a spill. The poor boy was running to and fro all night. Clare actually felt sorry for the sometimes surly tween.

Too keyed up to sleep, Clare poured her a glass of Chardonnay from a chilled bottle James had brought her when he last visited. It had been in her frig for weeks and was cool and crisp if a little flat. Her eyes fell upon her journal as she eased into the corner recliner and she picked it up deciding on the spur of the moment to write about her new job. Maybe she'd relax enough to be able to sleep after drinking the wine and writing a little.

Friday, June 15, 2007

Wow, I have never done so much chopping, dicing, and slicing in my life! Tomatoes, onions, carrots, cucumbers and chili peppers, feel like a human Vega-Matic! I remember we had one of those when I was at home. We also had a thing to cut French fries but it wasn't anything like the one they have at the Grille. Their French fry cutter is a manual thing but it is so fast. At least I didn't have to peel the potatoes for fries – Chef James prefers to serve his fries with skins. Poor Ralph has to soak and scrub the potatoes though in addition to washing all the dishes, pots and pans! As for my job, it is hard work, but fun too. I'm really glad Chef James seems to be happy with what I am doing. He pretty much leaves me alone. Guess he's too busy yelling at Ralph! I felt sorry for the kid but he seemed to take it in stride.

Was hoping that Bill would come in but I didn't see him. He's not been at home much lately. Guess they are really cracking down on the border – at least the news hints at that. I'm not sure if I'm glad or not. I like him but sure don't want a relationship. I think of him more like an older brother. Don't really think he considers me "little sister" material! Lately I've been plagued by dreams of Steve. I wake up still feeling those kisses that are like bells ringing! I've not heard from him in several weeks either – wonder if he's found someone else? I think I'll call him tomorrow; won't take long to know if he's tired of waiting. I did want him to go on with his life but suddenly I'm not sure!

★ ★ ★ ★ ★ ★

Steve turned on a lamp beside his recliner and leaned back to enjoy the cool glass of wine he'd poured after getting home. He had recalled how he and Clare had felt guilty about sneaking a bottle of wine into her house shortly after they began dating. As he popped the cork on the bottle of fresh wine, he wondered if Clare still enjoyed a glass of wine in the evenings.

He had been working an inordinately lot of hours the last few weeks and was glad that he'd finally finished up his current project. His decision to authorize overtime for Julie, his secretary, had paid off as they'd managed to complete the program, print the graphics and assemble all the necessary written work to accompany his new project requirements and still have time for a leisurely dinner at a comfortable, if not pricey restaurant. He had been glad that Julie agreed to work. Her salary was good and he doubted she needed the time and a half offered, but he'd figured she'd jump at the opportunity to work with him alone on a weekend! She wasn't shy about her feelings for him and although he didn't return them, he figured she'd be glad to have a chance to work her considerable charm on him.

Julie was far from undesirable! Her long red hair, ready smile and throaty laugh augmented her perfect figure. She had told Steve often enough that she worked hard on her physical appearance. In a city overflowing with movie star wannabe's, she had to try to outdo the competition. Under no illusions as to her chances of breaking into movies or TV, Julie was happy to have a good job that allowed her sufficient time off to pursue her dream career and still provide a good living.

As they finished up their meal, Julie invited Steve to her apartment for a "night cap." Her tone of voice left no doubt exactly what she met by "night cap"!

"No, I'm tired and think I'll just go home and hit the hay."

"That's what I expected you to say but you can't blame a girl for trying, can you?"

"No, I can't. You are a very attractive girl – woman, actually – but I'm not in the market for a relationship. Let's not complicate our working relationship."

"Sure. I understand. Maybe you'll change your mind. If you do, you know where to find me!"

With that they parted ways, Julie to a local singles bar and Steve to the lonely apartment he still hoped to share someday with Clare. As he emptied his wineglass, he felt a twinge of guilt that he hadn't called Clare recently. Work on his project, the first big one he flown solo on, had kept his nose to the grindstone too long. There was a promise of a big bonus and movement up the rung of the corporate ladder if it was successful. He'd promised Julie that she'd see something worthwhile in her paycheck if all went well. He was glad that he could at least give her that much! Draining the last of the wine, he resolved to call Clare first thing in the morning and at least remove that one guilt trip from his back!

CHAPTER 42

James had completed the required paperwork for his planned trip to Arizona. What he hoped was that it was indeed his last trip! He had been assured by DEA that the information about the scheduled delivery had been passed to the Lordsburg agents and that appropriate security was being arranged for his mother, aunt and Clare. DEA acknowledged that the cartel had a history of retaliation when anyone crossed them. James wished he'd never started his association with either the DEA or Raphael D'Anda but...

His part was relatively simple from now on. He just had to pilot the plane to the proper airport. He wasn't involved with the loading, unloading or delivery of any goods to their destinations. He had a good reason to drive to Animas to see Clare; his mother had finally finished a handmade satin comforter intended for a birthday gift. The gift was long overdue since Clare's birthday was in April and here it was June! She wanted it hand carried to Clare along with apologies for being so late. For once, James was glad to have a good excuse to be in the area while the undercover activities went down. At least at Clare's he would be out of the line of fire, so to speak, and since he was with Clare, he felt comfortable about her security. Media reports were filled with news about murders every day in Cuidad Juarez and the drug activity along the border was steadily picking up. James wished Clare would give up her fool-brained idea of living alone in the small desert community of Animas. Maybe he could make up to her for his past indiscretions by being with her as often as possible. Having a man around her house would help deter any possible danger to her, he was sure of that at least. Isn't it strange how wrong a person can be in their assumptions?

★　★　★　★　★　★

Clare had settled into her new routine. She spent the morning hours on Monday, Tuesday and Wednesday working on her on-line college classes. There would be no problem with beginning her junior year college if she decided to return to Portland later in the summer. She had been seriously considering the move. Although she loved the desert and the peaceful community she'd chosen as her home, she was beginning to miss the companionship her family had given her. She figured her feelings of loneliness were signs that her mind and emotions were recovering from the shock of the *accident* just as her body had repaired itself. She spent time in the afternoons working on her cookbook and on Friday and Saturday nights she put in her time at the Grille.

Housework took only a little time and laundry was a snap. Living alone in a small mobile home had certain advantages!

The hours working at the Grille were the most enjoyable hours of her week as far as she was concerned. She had been able to forge a good relationship with Chef James and had learned from him. That was her reason for asking for the job in the first place. In return, Chef James was allowing Clare more and more freedom in his kitchen. The reputation of the Grille was spreading quickly among the residents of the valley and business was picking up every week. Tom was very happy. Chef James had received the raise he had felt necessary to keep him at the Grille and even Ralph had started receiving a decent salary!

"I really need to give you a salary," Tom had insisted again the week before, "it just isn't right that you work so hard and do it for nothing."

"I am getting paid in experience," Clare reiterated. "Just keep using the money you'd pay me to give Ralph a salary and to improve the Grille. That is as good as a salary to me – besides, it is job security!"

"Clare, I don't know what I'd have done without you. You have made a real contribution to our little place here. Chef James is happier than ever before, Ralph is in love with you, and I...."

Tom was at a loss for words, a very unusual condition for him. He had mixed feelings for Clare. Normally he was very suspicious of people but Clare had given him a look at someone very different from the people he'd worked with in the past. Her outgoing, undemanding attitude as she worked in the Grille had made him realize that not everyone was out to take advantage of a person. There was something unusual about her though; she had a way of keeping people out of her private life and that was puzzling. Whenever conversations got personal, she either changed the subject or just turned cold. It was strange and Tom wondered what she was hiding. He figured it couldn't be too serious since she was so young but it troubled him. The last thing he needed was to get involved with the law because one of his employees had a hidden past! There was enough scrutiny and suspicion by the border patrol whenever a new person showed their face in the valley. He didn't want to aggravate an already touchy situation.

Although Tom had strong feelings for Clare, they were not romantic in nature. He had a lovely wife and was devoted to her. His feelings for Clare were those one would have for a dear friend. That was a new feeling for Tom who had always been stingy with his friendship. That explained his discomfort that things were not as they seemed in her life.

Chef James agreed with him that Clare was definitely hiding something. "How can she afford to work here and not take a salary?" Tom asked after confiding to Chef James that she was working "to get experience," as she put it. "I mean, she obviously has some money from somewhere because she paid cash for that place and she drives a new SUV. I just can't help but wonder where it comes from. She's never given you any ideas?"

"None. The only thing I know is that she has a cousin or somebody who visits here sometimes. He flies his own plane, so maybe it is family money. She gives me the impression that she isn't really close to him but his mother and an aunt are dear to her. Other than that, she's never talked about her family or where she came from. I agree with you though, it is strange that someone so young would locate in this area unless they had a hidden agenda or something. I mean, I can see an older person … someone retired coming out here to get away from the hassle of city life but she's just beginning her life. To each his own, I say."

"Yeah, I guess so but it bugs me. There is just too much junk that goes on right under our noses sometimes. That is why I left Albuquerque and moved down here – to get away from that junk. I don't need someone working in my place who is involved in anything that's all I'm saying." The conversation ended with no questions answered but at least Tom felt he had a confidant who could keep his ears and eyes open for any hints to Clare's secrets!

* * * * * *

Belinda had come through her surgery in better condition than the doctors had expected. That she was young was in her favor as far as the recovery from the actual surgery went but not the radiation and chemotherapy. Radiation was done by implants and she had tolerated the procedure well but now was time to start the chemo, intravenous injections twice a week at the cancer treatment center in Silver City. These treatments would be a major blow to her already stressed body. She was not emotionally ready for the onslaught. Ed wasn't either but he swore to stand by her and support her through the ordeal. He would do anything for Belinda.

So on a rare rainy Monday morning, he set out for the hospital alone. The doctors had implanted the radiation devices on Thursday morning the previous week and kept Belinda in the hospital over the weekend to watch her reactions. This was the day of her first chemo treatment and he was going to be with her no matter what. Besides, she would be able to come home after the treatment. Ed was anxious to have his wife back in his house.

Just as he reached for the door, the phone rang. His first reaction was to let it go to the answering machine but then he thought *"what if something has happened?"* and picked it up.

"Hey bud," spoke the airy voice belonging to Al, "You ready to go to work?"

"Not right now, I'm on the way to Silver. Belinda has her first chemo treatment in a couple hours. I promised to be there."

"Not now, but on Saturday. The plane should get here about four and we can unload and deliver and be backing home in time to go to the Spur and knock back a few. You'll be ready for a break by then. I'll be at the hanger by four. Are you in?"

"Yeah, I'm in."

"You don't sound very enthusiastic about it. Not getting cold feet are you? I don't need anyone who is going to go soft on me. This is a big job this time. We're gonna take the stuff into the Chiricahua. There are some cabins there where we'll drop it. If you're not up to it, tell me now so I can line up someone else. Believe me there are plenty of guys I can get to do the job. This one will pay really well."

"No, no… I'm in. I'm just worried about Belinda. I'll be there. You can count on me."

"Well, don't let me down; it wouldn't be pretty if you did. I mean it. Meet you at the airport about four."

"Okay, I'll be there. I gotta go. See you then. I gotta run."

Hanging up the phone, Ed felt such heaviness come over him. What he was doing with Al wasn't smart and he knew it. He could get in big trouble; he felt it in every bone in his body. But he needed the extra money. Already the co-payments for her tests had put a big dent in their meager savings and by the time bills for the surgery and treatments started hitting the mailbox, it would be long gone. He no longer felt that he had any choice…

★ ★ ★ ★

Al shook his head as he closed his cell phone. He had real doubts about his old friend. Ed was just too honest to begin with and now, with the worries he had about his wife, Al didn't think he could trust him.

Everybody thought Al had it made – if only they knew! He was scared to death. He'd been talking with a counselor at a drug rehab center in Tucson and made tentative arrangements for self-admission in the near future. As soon as he finished up this job he planned to split and start his life over. He just prayed he could get into the facility without the cartel knowing where he was and trying to lure him back into their web or worse yet, removing him so they would never have to worry about him turning them in! He wanted to get clean and get an honest job. He wanted what Ed had.

— CHAPTER 43 —

Saturday was one of the busier days at the small airport that served the Lordsburg area. Farmers and ranchers often had weekend guests flying in or they flew out to spend a few hours with friends in the bigger cities of Albuquerque, Tucson, Phoenix and points even further. It was not unusual for Ed to work an extra-long day on Saturday so Belinda had no worries when he wasn't home for dinner; she just placed his plate in the oven to be warmed when he got home.

Ed had actually enjoyed a pretty uneventful day compared to some of the Saturday's he put in. The flight from Tucson was to be the last scheduled flight and Alvaro was already on site with his pickup anxious to unload the illicit cargo and take it to the destination deep in the Coronado National Forest where they would stow the boxes for pickup by members of the cartel sometime after dark.

The unloading was delayed by the apparent reluctance of the pilot to leave the airport. After checking out his plane, he paced the hanger watching Ed perform minor maintenance duties which he could have actually done by himself. His cursory oversight only served to make Ed edgy. He wished that the guy would get in the car parked outside and take off for wherever he usually went when flying into the little airport.

After what seemed an ungodly time, James did just that, leaving the two younger men to quickly unload the heavy boxes tucked into the cargo hold.

"My God, what is in these," asked Ed?

"I don't know and don't want to know," answered his partner in crime, "I suspect it is some kind of weapons or ammo by the weight. The cartels usually carry drugs into the States and carry munitions and arms out. I don't ask."

"Yeah, I remember the last time that the stuff weighed a ton too. You know, this is the last time I'm helping you with this stuff"?

"If all goes well, it will be the last time I do stuff like this. I've got plans to change my line of work."

"Really"? Ed couldn't keep the doubt from creeping into his voice. "You been making money like this for a long time, haven't you?"

"Too long," was the quick reply. The two men worked silently for the next few minutes while sweat poured off their bodies and soaked their shirts.

"Man, it is humid," mumbled Al. "I don't ever remember sweating like this before."

"Well, look at the sky," countered his friend. "If we don't get rain here it will be sure to be pouring in the forest. The monsoon is hitting a little early this year but we can always use the rain."

"Yeah," was the grunted reply as Al slammed the tailgate on his truck and headed to the cab. "Come on and let's get this over with so we can start a new phase of our lives!"

Leaving the dusty town behind, the two men entered Interstate 10 and headed for the turnoff to Hwy 80 and Rodeo. They neither one noticed the dark SUV following them and they were too far ahead of it to see that it also took the turnoff to Rodeo. Their minds were elsewhere; Al thinking of the treatment that was scheduled to begin on Monday to break his dependence on drugs and the plans for a new life, and Ed was thinking of Belinda and the way she didn't seem to be responding to the treatment for depression. The doctor's assurance that she would come around seemed to ring false to him. He couldn't help but compare the listlessness she demonstrated now to the vibrancy she had shown just a few short weeks ago.

Al turned at the proper road leading them to Portal and The Wonderland of Rocks. The roads were narrow but well maintained. Ed had been over them countless times in his life. His family had once spent weekends camping in the pine-covered mountains. It was a restful place; or had been before smugglers and coyotes had decided to use it as a crossing point for their trades. Now there were signs posted throughout the area warning of danger.

Al seemed to know exactly where he was going and turned onto a dirt road after getting a considerable distance into the park. "Our drop-off point is just up ahead. There are more caves around here than you can see at first glance and one in particular has fairly easy access. We'll unload and drop our stuff then be out of here."

Ed looked up at the spires surrounding the road, "Yeah, I would hate to have to climb up there to stash those boxes! Tell me we aren't going to have to climb."

"Nah, it is just off the path," said Al as he pulled to the side of the road. He got out of the car and quickly strode a short way into the scrub. Suddenly he pulled a creosote bush aside revealing a narrow path. "There is our path, grab a box and let's go."

The two young men labored fifty feet into the forest overgrowth with their loads. There were only a few shrubs grabbing at them and most of the larger rocks had been cleared away. It didn't take them long to get the last of the boxes safely stashed inside a small cave. Just as they finished stowing the final load, the thunder that had been rolling nearer and near to their site seemed to crash down upon their head! Both men jumped as they watched a lightning bolt strike a dead tree trunk uphill from where they stood.

"Let's get out of here," yelled Al over the roar of the continuous boom of the thunder and the roar of the blaze now encompassing the long-dead pine. "It's gonna catch everything and I don't want to be here."

He didn't have to speak twice; Ed was ahead of him down the narrow trail but came to a halt so suddenly that Al ran into him before he saw the two DEA agents standing beside his truck. They both had their guns drawn and pointed at the two men!

"Ah, to be caught on my last trip, what a bummer!" Al moaned as the agents recited the Miranda Act to him and placed the handcuffs tightly on his wrists.

"Don't suppose you'll believe me when I say I've never done this before," said Ed as the agent completed his obligatory spiel. His mind was churning; he could picture Belinda when she heard the news and he was sick at the mess he'd made of things as he, too, was placed in the maroon SUV that had followed them from Lordsburg. They passed the fire response vehicles speeding into the forest to fight the already growing blaze as they were being taken to the processing station at Wilcox.

CHAPTER 44

It had been a busy night at the Grille and Clare was glad that it was closing time. She was out-of-sorts because James had shown up just as she was leaving for work. She hadn't expected him, hadn't gotten her guest room prepared for company and it irritated her that he hadn't given her any advance notice.

"I don't even have anything fixed for you to eat" she told James as she handed him clean sheets. "You'll have to make up your own bed. I don't have time. I have to get to work."

"Work? Since when have you found it necessary to work?" he queried.

"I'm helping out at the Grille on weekends. It is a learning experience for me. I work with the chef, do whatever I can and learn as much as possible. I'm serious about a career in the culinary field, you know." She couldn't keep the irritation out of her voice and it made her even angrier that her frustration with James was obvious to him.

"Well, I guess that is a good way to learn the business – from the ground up, as they say. Don't worry, I can make a bed, and I'll drive over to the Grille later and eat so you won't have to fix anything. I'll just be here tonight, I'm sorry I didn't let you know I was coming. I actually forgot to call you – there was so much going on. I know it is a lame excuse."

"That's ok," Clare's voice was a little contrite as she spoke. "We'll manage but I've got to run."

Now, six hours later as she helped close down the kitchen and do the final chores associated with closing for the night, Clare was anxious to get home and get to bed. She felt one of her infrequent headaches trying to start up and her only desire in life was to take some medicine, and relax in the coolness that the "swamp cooler" that was installed on the roof of the mobile home, afforded her. Since the desert air was usually dry, the water coolers were more efficient and effective than air conditioners. Everyone seemed to have them perched on the roofs of their homes and occasionally in windows. Clare had heard stories about the days before car air conditioning became standard that people used small cylindrical units attached to their car windows to keep them cool while driving in the desert heat! She had never seen one but thought that piece of historical information interesting.

James had indeed appeared for a meal about an hour before closing. He seemed preoccupied but greeted Tomas and Chef James and ate his meal in silence. Clare noted that he didn't have his usual Jim Beam and coke or two before ordering but only water and coffee with his meal. As she prepared to leave, he met her at the door and walked her to her vehicle parked at the back of the grille. "I've got my own car so I'll just follow you home if that's okay."

"Sure. Whatever" she snapped. "I'm sorry; I'm getting a headache and just want to get home. I won't be much company tonight." Clare had just put her hand on the door handle when she felt a sharp jab in her back!

"Hold on a minute," spoke a heavily Mexican voice. "I think we can all go in the other car."

"What? Who are you?" Clare questioned as she tried to turn and see the face of the person who was now pulling her away from the car door and roughly shoving her toward the black SUV that James had driven to her home earlier in the day. She could see James had met with a man also and he was mechanically being herded toward the same vehicle which was parked just a short distance from her own.

"Just walk senorita, don't even try to look at me or you will seal your fate, and you don't want to do that," the man told her menacingly.

"Leave her alone," ordered James, "she isn't a part of this."

NEDRA J. BURCH

"Maybe yes, maybe no, I don't know. I just do what I'm told and I was told to take you to meet the boss. She's with you, so she goes too."

"No, she isn't with me! Let her go," James demanded as he struggled to overpower a second man who was trying corral him into the back of the vehicle. His hands were already securely tied behind his back with a large plastic tie so his attempt to overpower his captor was to no avail.

"Don't make us get rough, just get in and we'll work it all out when we get to the boss's place. Shut up and get in the car, both of you! Don't make no scene or try to attract attention. That could be bad for everyone!" There was no doubt from the tone of voice used by the man that every word he said was true.

Clare was scared; the plastic that had been used to quickly tie her hands behind her back was cutting into her flesh. She was cold. She'd only felt such fear once before in her life – when she faced Myra that night a year before. *Myra and the gun.* She didn't like the feeling but knew she could do nothing to change things. It was up to God and she once again silently called upon him to save her from what appeared to be certain death!

James leaned toward Clare and tried to apologize for the situation but their captors told them to "shut up" with such vehemence that James decided silence was the better part of valor!

The driver spun out of the parking area at the Grille leaving Clare's unlocked SUV in the lot, her keys lying unseen on the ground barely hidden under the vehicle. Nobody had even heard the keys hit as they fell to the gravel.

Heading toward the distant Arizona Mountains a heavy silence engulfed the dark vehicle. James, lost in thought, couldn't figure out what had gone wrong. DEA had assured him that his involvement in the proposed action to bring down D'Anda's cartel was a total secret. It was obvious that someone had spilled the beans. James had recognized his abductors as the two men he had seen in Portland when he and Myra had planned to kidnap Clare. They had failed in that task; it was no wonder that they would take no chances at failure again. Even as he placed the men, they also placed Clare.

"She's the one we were supposed to get last year, isn't she?" The question was directed at James.

"I don't know what you are talking about."

"Oh sure," sneered the shorter of the two men who was driving the SUV deeper into the Chiricahua National Forest. "You want to be innocent don't you? Well, I think your days of hiding your crimes are at an end. The boss isn't so forgiving to those who squeal to the Feds! This should be an interesting night; looks like we can wrap up two jobs tonight. You reckon we'll get paid for taking the right girl this time?"

James made no response as Clare, hunched into the corner of the seat, listened in shock. If she got the true gist of the thing, James was responsible for the kidnap attempt on Tina the year before in Portland. Maybe it really had been him that she'd seen speeding away after the near accident in the Pearl District! Everyone had assured her that it was her imagination but she'd known deep down that it was James. She'd allowed Myra and Alex to convince her otherwise but now that her suspicions had been confirmed she realized the root of the deep set feeling of distrust she'd harbored toward James. She'd never been able to dismiss her feeling that he knew more than he admitted about the events of the previous summer. And to think that she'd allowed him into her home, fed him, and sometimes even felt a kinship with him! She felt betrayed...again!

"James, what are they saying? Were you involved in that thing last year? I thought I saw you, but then Myra talked like it was her idea. How were you involved?"

James didn't want to answer her questions but knew that she deserved to know the truth. Taking a deep breath, he began his tale just as they turned off the paved road onto one of the many gravel trails into the high mountains. They turned off the main road onto a narrower side track but not before they saw the flashing lights of the forestry service trucks ahead. The lights didn't seem to faze their abductors at all.

"Looks like some lightening caused excitement up ahead," said the driver.

"That is good for us," replied the other man. "It'll keep them busy and we can do our job without worrying about them stumbling onto us."

"Yeah man," piped up one of their abductors, then to James, "you go ahead and tell her – they say "confession is good for the soul"! His deep laugh was not comforting!

"I was there, yes. I made contact with Myra quite by accident. She answered the phone one time when I was trying to call you. I guess she was upset because when I asked to speak with you, she began lambasting you. It didn't take much coaxing to get the story about how she wanted you out of the Goforth family. I told her that I, too, would like to see you disappear. Things just progressed from there. I got D'Anda to send a couple of his men to Portland. I really didn't know exactly what was going down, that was worked out between Myra and these two monkeys, but, yes, I was a party to it all."

"D'Anda? Who is this D'Anda"?

"He's our boss," piped up one of their captors. "You'll get to meet him soon enough. He has an eye for a pretty girl, so he will be muy interested in you!"

"After things turned out as they did, I was ashamed." James continued ignoring the interruption, "When I saw how my mother and Aunt Daisy reacted to your situation, I realized how much you really meant to them. It opened my eyes. You may find this hard to believe after I'd been such a scum, but I was ashamed of my participation. In fact, I have to say that it was a relief to me that Myra couldn't tell about my involvement. When they found your sister safe and sound, and you recovered it was like a new lease on life. I decided to change my ways but D'Anda figured I still owed him. This trip is the last one I planned to make for him."

Clare took in his story in a state of shock. Was this what Alex had intended to tell her when she had so rudely hung up on him? It was just like the nightmare she'd lived just a year before. She was physically ill and not just from the steadily worsening headache.

"You did it all for the money, didn't you? I can't believe it."

"Yeah, well, I'm not proud of that side of me. I hope I've changed.

Don't guess you'll ever believe me when I say that I'm sorry. I never intended that this stuff would involve you. In fact, I'm trying to do something right for a change, and it is turning out to be the worst mistake I've ever made. Go figure…"

"What do you mean? What are you involved in. Who are these men and what are they going to do with you…with us?

The questions were no more than out of Clare's mouth when the car came to a jerky stop.

"Okay, you turkeys, time to face the music. We'll have to walk from here on; this road won't take us to the cabin. Hope you've got on your hiking shoes."

The shorter of the two men opened the door and pulled Clare to her feet. She had on some good tennis shoes but as he jerked her out of the car, she twisted her ankle on a large rock!

"Ouch," she cried as her ankle gave way under her and she stumbled. Catching herself, she tried to regain balance only to experience excruciating pain!

"Oh, I … I have hurt myself. I can't walk; I've got to sit down. My ankle, oh my God, it hurts!" Tears came to her eyes as she thought that this was just what she needed on top of the headache and sickness that was overpowering her body and reason! She felt bile rise and thought she was going to vomit.

Her captor allowed her to sit back down on the edge of the seat and she put her head down into her lap. It was not a comfortable position at all. Her hands were tightly bound behind her but as some of the dizziness passed she gingerly tried to stand only to fall heavily back on the seat as pain shot up her leg. Between the pain in her ankle, her headache and inability to gain her balance with her hands tied she just wanted to lie down.

"What is wrong?" asked the taller of the two men. "We gotta get up the hill." He bent to feel Clare's ankle. The swelling was already evident and he knew that she'd never be able to climb up the steep rocky hill to the meeting site. Looking at her ankle by the dim interior light from the SUV, he realized that she'd have to be left behind. He immediately thought of the toilet located a short way up the road. It was a small metal building with a chemical toilet and was usually used by the rangers, forestry personnel and border agents on patrol in the area. It was always unlocked and available. He would have to find something to jam the door shut but it would be a safe place to leave her while they took James up the hill, then they could come back and get her or just leave her there if that was what the boss directed. Leaving her in the car would not be a good idea as she might manage to start honking the horn or something and alert rangers. They could hear vehicles making their way up to the site of the blaze already. The air was permeated with the smells of burning pine and the undergrowth. There was a breeze already and the combustion from the fire was bound to increase. The one thing in their favor was that the breeze was blowing away from the direction they planned to travel.

"We'll put her in el baño while we take him to the boss. He'll let us know what to do with her. If he says he doesn't want her, we will just leave her here, someone will find her in the morning and we'll be long gone."

"You can't just lock her up in a shed and leave her. Look at her, she's sick and cold, and God only knows what is inside there, remember we are in a desert region and there are snakes and spiders and …."

"We can, and we will," cut in his captor. "You got nothing to say about it. You would be smart to keep your mouth shut anyhow. Gonna need all your fancy words to explain to the boss why DEA and border patrol agents are trying to close in on his delivery boys! So, shut your trap!"

Turning to his partner, he gave directions for moving Clare from the car to the small toilet hidden among the brush. Quickly using another of the plastic ties they secured James to the door handle so he couldn't escape and sandwiching Clare between them headed toward the shed. They used a small mag-light to show the way to the building. The door, secured by a wooden peg inserted in a hasp, was quickly opened. One problem solved thought her captor. He could just lock the door again. Clare was unceremoniously shoved into the small space and the door shut. She could hear the peg as it slid into place in the hasp thus securing the door. It was dark in the building and smelled like sewage. The odor just added to her sick feeling. Her eyes had adjusted to the darkness and she could barely make out the stool in the center of the concrete floor, hobbling toward it she sat down on the closed lid. The small window high in one wall gave just enough light to see the outline of the door, a metal grate and another screened small window. Very little light penetrated through the dirty glass on the dark night.

Her eyes were becoming more used to the darkness but there was nothing to see. She was overwhelmed with a feeling that she had been here before and then she recalled the dream she'd had months before, *she was in a hot barren room,* the feeling of having lived this experience before was even more unsettling to Clare. She tried to remember more of the dream without success. She could only remember her fear and loneliness.

In the high desert, temperatures dropped quickly with the setting sun even in the summer. Being in the higher elevations of the National Forest, the temps were even lower and Clare's light sweater wasn't doing much good to protect her from the cold. In addition to the throbbing ankle, her headache was getting worse. She knew she had a sprain that would keep her off her feet for several days and the headache would get much worse without her medication. She had the pills that would bring her almost immediate relief at home, at least it would if she were ever able to escape her current situation and get back home!

Clare allowed thoughts of the home and family she'd left in Portland take over her mind. It would do no good for her to dwell on the current situation. She was filled with nostalgia for all she'd left behind. Not for the first time in recent days, she thought of returning to Portland and trying to pick up her life. Then she began to think about Steve. Was it too late for them?

CHAPTER 45

Bill drove past the Grille and saw Clare's vehicle still in the parking lot along with those belonging to Tom and Chef James. It was past closing time for the café but he knew the bar continued to serve drinks for an hour or two and decided to stop for a nightcap. It had been a long day.

He'd been assured that plans to take down the drug smugglers from Mexico had been finalized and that the action to stop the delivery from the US side was in process as he was driving home. He wasn't included in it simply to protect his cover as they still had to catch the big man involved from the patrol side. Bill had a good idea of who the culprit was but hated to admit it even to himself. He and Jamie had discussed the idea that Ron Hall could be the only person in the local office in a position to benefit from underhanded dealings with smugglers and the only one with access to the information needed to make the business profitable for both sides.

DEA had reason to believe that they were going to catch D'Anda this night! Rumor had it that he was actually taking part in this delivery! After they took D'Anda down, it would only be a short time before he'd spill the beans on his local accomplices in order to make a deal. Bill realized that his time in Hidalgo County was nearly ended.

It concerned Bill when he heard that D'Anda was expected to make an appearance at the exchange and he wondered if word had somehow leaked of the planned raid? He was glad that he wasn't involved in the night's activities. He'd had enough gun play to last him for the rest of his life the last time.

Parking next to Clare's white vehicle, he entered the almost empty Grille. Tom and James were sitting at the bar enjoying a Corona but there was no sign of Clare. He looked toward the kitchen and saw that it was dark and obviously empty.

"Is Clare not here?"

"No, she left about an hour ago," replied Tom. "Her cousin was here so I guess they are at her place."

"Well, that explains why her car is still outside. She probably rode home with him. Give me a Corona, will you?"

The sharp Mexican beer tasted good as it went down. Bill didn't engage either of the other men in conversation but sipped his beer and when finished left the bar quietly. It was chilly outside. It always surprised him that it got so cool after sunset.

It was just a mile to the turnoff to his home and he could normally see the lights from Clare's house when he turned off Hwy 9. Tonight, though, just the solar lamps on her front porch illuminated the night and that illumination wasn't visible until he was almost at his drive. He thought it strange that there were no lights shining from inside. Normally Clare was up till the wee morning hours watching TV, reading or working on the computer. In the darkness of the desert even the reflection from the television was bright and since neither he nor Clare had yard lights it was normally all he needed to know she was up and moving. As he turned into his drive, he looked again toward her house and could see no sign of a vehicle – any vehicle. Could she and her cousin have gone to Deming for some reason? It didn't seem likely. Especially not after a night's work but it wasn't his concern. He wasn't Clare's keeper although he had to admit that he'd like to be!

Bill went inside but couldn't shake the feeling that something wasn't right. He found himself outside staring across the road toward Clare's place and then, without even giving it a conscious thought, he was in his car and headed up her drive!

No sign of a car. Something just wasn't right. Bill couldn't put his finger on it, but his gut told him something had happened to Clare. Knowing that James was involved with D'Anda and that there was a deal going down just a few miles away added to his unease. He went to his car, pulled out his cell phone and punched in the number for his boss in Denver.

Their conversation was brief:

"Agents followed the two men transferring goods from the airport in Lordsburg to the National Forest. They've already taken them down, no fight there. They are just flunkies and can't even give us information that will help with finding the pickup men. The booty consisted of some semi-automatic weapons and ammo. The two are on their way from Wilcox to Tucson for booking into the FBI system as we talk. More agents are waiting to pick up the others when they come to gather the merchandise. We plan to take down the entire operation tonight. As far as I know, things are going as planned; there is no need for concern on your part. Unless there is a surprise, we don't think D'Anda is around. You know how these slime balls are, he'll sit at home where it is safe and have his peons do all the dirty work."

"That's where you are wrong," Bill told him. "I think more is going down."

"Why, what makes you say that," asked Mark his concern growing?

"I'm not sure, just a gut feeling. I've been playing this game for too long and I have a second sense about things. Give me a few minutes and I'll get back to you. I want to check something out."

After talking to his boss, Bill's concern accelerated! Jumping back into his own specially-equipped SUV, he sped toward the Grille where Clare's car sat alone. By now everyone had left and the people living in the small travel trailers parked behind the building were apparently asleep since no lights shown at their windows. Bill pulled up next to Clare's vehicle and got out. Shining his flashlight on the ground, he walked around his car. It wasn't hard to see the busy footprints near the driver's door and then in the brilliance from the light his eyes caught a gleam from some metal – a set of keys lying half buried in the dusty earth!

Bill grabbed the keys. He knew now why he'd felt so uneasy. It was obvious to him that Clare had met with some kind of foul play. He got back on the horn to his boss in Denver.

"Mark, I found Clare's keys in the dirt beside her SUV. There are signs of a struggle. I don't know how much of a head start they have on me, at least an hour and a half, I'd guess. I'm headed to the mountains. I need some backup! Where is this rendezvous supposed to take place?"

"You just keep out of this. I'll contact my agents and let them know what you suspect. They'll take it from there. There is no reason for Clare Smith to be involved in this, Bill; unless, of course, she *is* involved but all our info points to her not being."

"I don't care what your intel tells you, there is something wrong and she is in danger. I'm on my way. I suppose I'll find your guys in the forest, there can't be that many roads into the woods. Tell them I'm on the way."

"Bill, you stay out of it. We'll handle it…" but Bill had turned off the phone. He'd get no help from Denver or DEA now, he knew. He called the one person he knew he could trust to help him.

CHAPTER 46

It had taken Jaime a good hour to meet Bill at the entrance to the national forest. He didn't have the privilege of a patrol car and seeing that traffic was heavier than usual going south on Hwy 80, he stayed within the speed limit after exiting the interstate. Rumors had been flying all week that there was to be a big bust and he had been glad that he wasn't involved in it but when Bill's call came he couldn't refuse to help. It would probably mean his job if things didn't go well, or disciplinary action at the very least but he didn't care. Jaime liked Bill and trusted him. If his friend needed help, he would be there for him.

Spotting Bill's vehicle at the store near the entrance to the forest, Jaime jumped into the passenger seat and left his battered pickup parked on the side of the road.

"Okay boss, what is going on? You were vague on the phone."

"It's Clare. I think she got involved in this thing tonight. I found her car but not her, keys were in the dust. I'm sure someone has grabbed her and probably her cousin too. He was the mole on this deal. I think that D'Anda is expected to be here tonight. My bet is that he learned of the raid and is here to show Miller that he can't squeal on him. I don't much give a damn about Miller but Clare isn't involved in any of this. I don't want her to become collateral damage!"

"Gotchya. Have you been able to monitor any traffic on the radio?"

"No, they are going silent. But I know they are in the forest. I'll drive every road if I have to till I find them. I've already hit a couple of them near while waiting for you here with no luck. Traffic has gotten heavy the last hour. There is a fire somewhere up there and trucks have been going in to fight it before it gets out of hand. I talked to Denver and the guys who carried the stuff in have already been taken down; agents are waiting to close in on the pickup team. Have you got any ideas where they might meet up with their boss? It's a sure thing that he won't be piddling with a pickup if he's planning to do away with an informer. You know this area better than I do."

"Yeah, I've got an idea. There is one area where some cabins are just up the hill a ways. It isn't too far from here!"

"Okay, let's go!"

"Hang on a minute. I want to use my little snoop device before we get too deep into the trees."

"Snoop device? What are you talking about?"

"Well, a few of us guys decided that we needed to be able to keep in touch without the big shots knowing what we were doing. You see, you aren't the only one who thinks someone is crooked in our office. Some of the guys worked it out." Deftly Jaime tuned his hand-held device and, sure enough, picked up some clatter.

The two men listened for a bit but didn't gain any idea of the location of the agents. They heard the take down of the pickup men who had come to get the ammo and, then, shocking words spoken in a heavy Mexican accent.

"Ha, you gringos think you did good, huh? We are just small stuff," bragged one of the newly detained men. "The big man is up there. He's gonna put a bullet in your informant. That's the big deal tonight, not this stuff. This stuff isn't important."

"No, and neither are you," came a distant voice that Bill recognized as one of the other agents he'd worked with since coming to Lordsburg. "Be smart and tell us where your boss is so we can pick him up, too, and things might go a little easier with you later."

"You gotta be crazy, man. I'd rather spend time in one of your nice jails than cross D'Anda. He'd have my pelotas if I talked to you. Besides, I don't know where they are; only the boss knows where the pickup point is located."

Bill looked at Jaime. "So, they do have plans to get James. At least we know we are on the right track. Where should we start looking?"

"Yeah, I've got an idea. I've told the boss before about a cave near the Number 7 john/maintenance area. I've seen some disturbing signs around there; car tracks and a trail up the hill. He always ignored me and told me not to bother with investigating it, but since you have given me the idea that maybe the boss isn't as honest as he should be; it fits that he'd ignore my suggestion. You need to turn left at the second or third road ahead. I'll tell you when."

★ ★ ★ ★

Clare had tried to get more comfortable in her prison. Her ankle didn't seem to throb as badly, at least as long as she didn't move but her head was splitting. She thought she heard a vehicle engine then doors slam, but couldn't rouse herself enough to even shout. She was terribly cold. She didn't think she'd ever been so cold in her life. At the same time, she was sweaty! Clammy sweaty. She told herself it was shock but she really didn't know or care. She just wanted to get out of the shed. She had tried unsuccessfully to force the metal door open but it hadn't worked so she had given up. Now she was tired and just wanted to sleep. That was how the headaches affected her.

★ ★ ★ ★

After depositing Clare in the shed, James and the two thugs climbed quickly up the hillside. There were large rocks and small pebbles on the trail and James lost his footing more than once. The swords of the desert plants stabbed at him and the scrubby trees snagged his arms and slapped his face as they trudged upward. At last they reached a clearing and James saw a small cabin. They passed by the dark building. No sooner had they passed the building than he caught the light of a small fire. He had been aware of the odor of burning wood and assumed that the fire was the source of that smell. Three men sat around the fire on rocks. He recognized Raphael D'Anda immediately.

"Well, well, well, what do we have here?" asked the man as he rose majestically from his seat. "Is this the man who thought he'd betray me?"

"What are you talking about," asked James. He'd been trying to think of a story he could tell that would minimize his part in the actions that he knew were going down somewhere nearby but hadn't been able to think of anything convincing. He decided that truth was the only way he could go – truth in exchange for Clare's safe release.

"Like you don't know. I told you not to try to cross me or you'd be sorry. So what do you do, you spill the beans to the Feds. I've got friends, you should know that. My friends are as important as yours, maybe more. I don't know why you think you can turn on me. We had a good thing going, why you want to mess it up?" D'Anda's usually well controlled accent seemed to have a heavier, more hate filled than James had heard before.

"So, what are you going to do? Kill me. I don't care; just assure me that you'll let Clare go. She has nothing to do with this."

"What you talking about….?" D'Anda gave a hard look at the men who had hustled James up the hill.

"We brought his pretty little cousin along. They were together so we brought her too; only she twisted her ankle and we had to leave her down at the foot of the hill. She's locked up and can't get out though. You want us to go get her?"

"Oh, I'll have to think about that. Maybe we can use her. Make some kind of deal with the Feds." D'Anda cocked his head and thought briefly. "No, I don't think they'll deal. They don't even know where we are. They might pick up the delivery boys and take our ammo but no, they don't know where we are. We will be out of here before they find us. Maybe I could just take her with me as a play toy? What do you think about that?"

"Just leave her alone. She isn't involved in this," James pleaded.

"Or, I could just take her and get ransom from her father. He's that rich guy in Portland, isn't he? Yeah, that is a good idea. Leave him here and go get the girl, she'll come in handy; a good way for me to recoup my losses."

James was shoved to the ground and the two men scrambled down the hill toward the site where Clare was held captive! D'Anda walked over to where James was trying to get to his feet and quickly kicked him in the face. James felt his nose crunch as blood flowed freely.

Don't think you are gonna die quickly, gringo, it won't be that easy!" D'Anda almost chuckled as he kicked again and again. Blood spatters flecked the expensive ostrich boots the cartel chief wore!

$$* \quad * \quad * \quad * \quad * \quad *$$

Upon arrival at their destination, Bill and Jaime cautiously got out of their vehicle and began looking around. It didn't take much detective work to figure out that the trail led through the scrub up the mountain but in the dark it was difficult to pick up on what action might have occurred at the site. There was the black SUV that James drove and that was the only sign that anyone was in the area except for the scent of burning wood which Bill attributed to the fire he knew was blazing somewhere. Bill was about to start uphill when Jaime's hand on his arm stopped him. Shining his light on the path, tracks were faintly visible.

"Look, someone has gone down the hill too. That's where the john is. You never know. Let's check that area out first, wouldn't want someone coming up behind us." The two men began walking toward the small building but their movement was interrupted by sounds of someone coming downhill at a fast pace. They managed to get off the path and take cover in the shrub just as the two noise-making men came into view.

It didn't take long to realize that the two men, dressed in dark clothes, were headed to the same place that Bill and Jaime had been going to. Using their hands to signal caution, lights extinguished simultaneously as if reading each other's minds. As the two new comers passed them Bill and Jaime jumped from their hiding places and quickly and quietly pinned their arms to their sides, bringing them to their knees.

There wasn't much of a fight thanks to the surprise; a little tussle and the two desperados were disabled and sitting on the rough ground where Bill began a quick effective interrogation after Jaime, having disarmed his prey, used some of the plastic ties he always carried to secure their hands and feet.

Bill was more than grateful that he'd worked on improving his command of Spanish since arriving in the area as he felt comfortable speaking the language and knew he could understand anything the men said. He spoke unbroken Mexican, almost as rapidly as any native. "¿Donde está Clara? No te molestes en decir que no sabes ni te quedes callada porque no te lo creo." He knew the men could speak English and wanted them to know that he knew it! He didn't intend to take any guff from these low lives!

Neither of the captives spoke immediately. They looked at each other and then back at the two agents.

"No hay nada que decir las dos ya se pelaron. No ha nada que puedas hacer por ambas," lied one of the men.

"I don't believe you." Bill unthinkingly spoke in English and was answered in the same language.

"Well, man you'd better. You better get your butt out of here, now, while you can. The boss will be coming downhill pretty soon. He was right behind us. He just wanted to finish off the guy. He has people with him with lots more fire power than you have!"

Bill and Jaime looked at each other.

"We better lock these guys up and get out of sight." Jaime said and Bill nodded in apparent agreement. He planned to hit the trail uphill as soon as the captives were secured in the back of the specially built SUV. There would be no escaping from the border patrol equipped vehicle. They had completely forgotten the idea of investigating the path leading downhill. After hearing what the captives said, they were sure the people they were seeking were uphill and in immediate danger. Bill just hoped he wasn't too late.

* * * * * *

Clare, crouched in the cold, smelly john, had heard the commotion outside but, unable to speak more than simple greetings in Mexican couldn't make out any of the conversation. She didn't know if she should shout out for help or pray that the men had forgotten or didn't know that she was locked in the small john. She held her tongue and finally heard the voices move away from her location. Fear overwhelmed her once more. Clare had been thinking about the things that had happened the previous year when she had been in Myra's gun sights. The more she remembered, the more she was afraid that she was going to lose everything she had ever had and she'd come to realize how much she really valued all that she had voluntarily given up: her father, families, and the life she had been introduced to by them, and Steve! She found the phrase she'd prayed just before the attack running through her head: "Please, God, don't let me die."

CHAPTER 47

James groaned. He hurt worse than he had ever hurt in his life, worse than when he'd fallen out of the tree and hit the water pipes as a child, worse than when he'd fallen down the iron steps from his apartment to the parking lot after a night of wild drinking as a man. He didn't think there was a spot on his body, or in his body that didn't hurt! Why didn't D'Anda just shoot him? No, he knew that would be too easy. D'Anda wanted him to feel pain. D'Anda enjoyed causing pain and he was doing a good job of it. His head cleared slowly as he struggled to listen to the two talking by the fire.

"Where are those jerks?" voiced D'Anda. "It shouldn't take them this long to get that girl and get back here. We gotta be going. If we don't make our rendezvous on time we'll be up the creek. I sure don't want to have to hike out of here, especially with the Feds all around."

"Maybe they've run into some trouble. We should just go and leave them."

"Si, you are correct. I'd like to have the girl though," there was wistfulness in D'Anda's voice. "It would be fun to break her in and then sell her to Ortega. He always gets the most out of his girls and he pays well for one. Maybe I could make up some for the loss Miller has cost me this night. Or, maybe her father would pay more for her than Ortega? Either way, I'd have the use of some fresh meat for a while!"

James cringed as he heard the words. What had he done? He'd tried to make things right by working with the Feds but now Clare was in more danger than ever before! The things D'Anda was talking about were terrifying. He knew that white slavery continued south of the border. What if Clare became a victim of human trafficking? He was shattered by the thought of his cousin being abused by monsters. What could he do? He felt sure he had some broken ribs at the minimum and God alone knew what other internal injuries had been inflected on him. Based on the pain in his mid-section, he was sure there were some serious problems.

He heard a rustling in the shrubs below him; probably those two monkeys returning with Clare. His heart fell. He wished he could turn time back.

A voice broke the stillness of the night. "Hands up." Such a cliché! Out of the shadows stepped Bill Driver, his .45 pointed directly at D'Anda. Was he alone, the lone ranger come to the rescue? There was no way James could help him, he knew that; unless he could distract D'Anda and his buddy somehow.

He tried to wriggle and make some noise but he couldn't seem to move. When he tried his body was wracked by spasms of pain and he didn't actually make enough movement or noise to be heard. He felt blackness coming over him and although he wanted to help, he was grateful to know that he wouldn't be able to feel the pain that overwhelmed his body!

Surprised, D'Anda started to move from the firelight into the shadow. "Don't try it," Bill said. His voice was cold and hard. "I'm not alone, you are both covered. Your flunkies are locked up already. I'm sure they will enjoy the hospitality of the US Government for a long time. There is more help on the way too so you'd better just give up your firearms. Throw them over here," Bill indicated a spot near him, his voice bode no patience. James heard the words just as he fully blacked out and his last conscious thought was that Clare was safe!

The next several minutes were full of activity. James, out cold, didn't hear Bill, with the help of another man not only disarmed D'Anda and his crony but also tie them securely together with the handy nylon ties that were used extensively to secure people as well as materials. They had extinguished their flashlights and worked solely by the dim light from the dwindling campfire. When they had their prisoners secured Bill approached James' twisted but still body.

"Well, looks like we got here just in time." He nudged the man on the ground but there was no movement, only a low moan.

Bending over the bloody broken hunk of a man, Bill found a pulse, still strong in spite of the obvious beating that had been inflected. "I think he'll be alright," he informed Jaime as he came to his side. "Someone did a job on him though. How long till we can get a med-evac in here?"

"Don't think we ought to try to get anyone in here till we determine where they were headed; too much air noise will make the people who were supposed to pick these fellas up run. Besides, I doubt air-evac can land here; he'll have to be carried down to the road. I'll radio the guys and let them know what we have here and they can decide what to do. Guess it is time for us to make our presence known anyhow." With that fire in the area, people on the ground are going to be looking for strangers and since we are persona non grata as far as they know, we could be mistaken as arsonists!

"Yeah, there is a rendezvous somewhere near here from what they said and someone expects these two to appear soon. I overheard them talking about it."

"Me too. It won't take long for our reinforcements to get here, and then we can move James. In the meantime I'll give whatever first aid I can as soon as I make that call. Why don't you see if you can get any info out of those two as to where their cronies might be waiting and what they have done with the girl?"

As if on cue, James moaned and his eyes opened, or the slits that were left of his eyes opened. His face was swollen almost beyond recognition but his voice still worked. "Clare...do you have Clare?" he asked in a whisper.

"Clare, no, we figured she'd be up here. Have you any idea what they might have done with her?"

"They locked her in a building at the bottom of the hill. Two of D'Anda's men went back to get her but they haven't returned yet. They may still be out there somewhere..."

"No, we caught them. They were evidentially going to get her but we got to them first. I know where you mean. As soon as the other guys get here, I'll go back down and get her. She'll be okay, I promise. We've got help on the way. We'll get you out of here and to a doctor as soon as we can."

"Don't worry about me, just take care of Clare. I deserve what I've got but she is innocent. Always has been…." James' voice faded as he drifted off into the healing painless darkness again.

It seemed to take forever for the border patrol agents to arrive. Bill heard their 4-wheelers long before he saw them. Four more agents appeared ready to transport the injured man down the hillside where it would be easier to evaluate James' condition and arrange transport to medical facilities for him and to the lockup for the two captives. The Agent-In-Charge gave James a once over and decided the health of their informant was more important at this time than the risk of some kind of sneak attack by additional smugglers as he put in a call for a helicopter to meet the team on the main road..

"We've captured the delivery boys from our side, two young guys from Lordsburg, and the pickup men from their side. Now with the boss and his cronies we have a good haul. The others are probably already on their way back to Mexico but we'll get air on them right away. There are some copters trying to fly in some firefighters but the blaze isn't very big and it should be under control by morning. As fires in this forest go, this isn't much of one. It was started by lightning and there is a small stream running nearby that has blocked its progress. The forest got lucky this time. I don't imagine you've not gotten anything out of them," he said as he nodded toward the two tightly guarded men.

"No, D'Anda remained silent when questioned about the location of his exit site. His compatriot seemed willing to talk but a hard stare from his boss had silenced him quickly." Bill explained that there were two more men at the bottom of the hill and another call went out for a paddy wagon to meet agents at that area. Bill then scooted downhill to find and release Clare, hoping that she was indeed safe as he'd assured James.

Inside the stifling metal room, Clare still felt like she was going to vomit. The headache had become a full blown migraine. She hadn't had a headache so bad since she'd first woke up after the shooting a year before. She felt sure that if she could throw up, she'd feel better. How could she feel worse?

Above the buzzing in her head, she heard footsteps approaching, then the sound of the door clasp being opened. Cold fear surged through her.

"Clare, are you okay?"

Immediately recognizing Bill's voice, relief overwhelmed her as she began to cry. Within a split second, she was safely wrapped in Bill's arms, gone was the nausea and need to vomit as she stood basking in the warmth of his embrace and saying a prayer of thanks for her rescue.

Once in the fresh air, the headache also seemed to relent just as the nausea had vanished. She felt safe and secure once again.

"Oh, Bill, thank God you saved me. How did you know?"

"Long story." he said as he fought the urge to crush her to his body and shower her with kisses. He hadn't realized how scared he'd been for her until the moment he took her in his arms. "I found your car keys in the dust at the Grille. I knew something was wrong and figured it was tangled in the bust that I knew was happening tonight. Things just seemed to escalate after that. It's been an exciting night but don't worry it's over now; I'll get you home soon. Just have some mopping up to do, a few questions for you. We've got the thugs who kidnapped you in custody. They will be facing Federal kidnapping charges since they took you across state lines."

"They were the ones who took Belinda last year…"

"What?"

"Oh, you don't know about that. I've never told anyone here about what happened last year. It's a nasty story. I'm not up to telling it all now; maybe later. James had a part in it too. Where is he?"

"On the way to a hospital in Tucson; he was pretty badly beaten but we managed to get to him before they killed him. He told me where I could find you."

"Humph! He got me into this mess in the first place. He has been trying to eliminate me for over a year. I guess he'll be sorry he failed again."

"I do think we need to talk about this but you are right, now is neither the time nor the place! Right now, I just want to get you home,"

"I'll go for that," said Clare, tears of relief streaming down her dirty face.

CHAPTER 48

It was just a short walk from Clare's prison to the clearing where there had been several vehicles parked just a few minutes before. In the time it had taken Bill to release Clare, men had loaded James into one of the rescue cars, locked D'Anda and his friend in another and both vehicles had taken off down the road to meet the helicopter and transport truck. James' SUV was still parked to the side of the road and Bill's empty vehicle sat in the middle of the one-lane road. Jamie was nowhere in sight. Sounds of an approaching car could be heard coming down the hill.

"That's probably Jaime coming to be sure we are ok. It has been a long night for him too," said Bill as they headed towards his wheels.

Just as they reached the door of his SUV, the dark vehicle skidded to a stop next to it. It wasn't a Border Patrol vehicle, and it wasn't Jaime!

Fortunately Bill and Clare were on the passenger side of the car when the new comers slammed to a stop, and two men jumped out. They were dressed in black and carried heavy weapons. Bill knew immediately that this was not good news!

Pushing Clare down, he pulled his gun. Jaime, who had actually followed Bill down the hill, was sitting in the driver's seat of Bill's vehicle. The headlights of the new arrivals silhouetted his head and upper torso inside the vehicle. Suddenly he had a weapon pointed at him!

"Out," shouted the man, a burly Mexican with a heavy accent. "Don try nothing funny or I'll blow your brains out now! Where is the boss?"

Unable to do anything else, Jaime prepared to open the door. His mind was speedily making a plan. He figured he could use the lead lined door as a shield and take the man out before he would be able to get off a shot… if he moved fast enough. As he released his weapon from the holster preparing to get off the shot that would save them, he heard Bill's voice nearby. It made him feel good to know he was close. Bill's talking might just be the distraction needed to allow him to pull of his own intended action.

"Your *boss* is already on his way to jail. I guess you are his extraction team. You should've gone on to Mexico and saved yourselves, you can't help him. Now don't be stupid, throw your guns away and put your hands on top of the car," ordered Bill, still holding Clare down.

"Huh, you think I believe you? You crazy," stammered the surprised man. "I got your guy in my sights and I'm gonna blow his brains out!"

Just then, Jaime, threw open the door and catching his would-be killer with the heavy door, knocked him to the ground. A miscalculation on his part, as he hadn't realized the newly arrived man had moved up so close to the door. Still…quickly he jumped out of the vehicle and made a lunge for the gun held by his attacker. He had dropped his own weapon on the seat while getting out so as allowing him to use both his hands in the attempt to disarm his would-be-attacker. The two men fought over the gun, locked in a tight embrace and rolling over the rough ground; it was impossible to see who had control of the weapon!

A bullet exploded in night air. Jaime jerked but not before he had the gun in his hand and was pointing it at the other man on the ground. Bill was keeping his own gun on the second invader and it was time to disarm his also.

"Stay down," Bill told Clare as he went quickly around the front of his SUV and grabbed the compact sub-machine gun from the driver of the second car. Later, when Bill thought back on the night's events, he couldn't figure out why the man hadn't just opened fire. He could have killed everyone with just one spray of his weapon! Pressing his gun into the man's back, Bill ordered him to drop his weapon. The man did so.

It didn't take long to securely tie the two, once again using those handy nylon zip ties. Bill and Jaime hustled them into the back of the SUV so they could take them to the main road where they would join the earlier detained and accompany their friends to the border patrol wagon for transport to the Wilcox Border Patrol station. From there, they would probably be turned over to the FBI or DEA for formal charges on drug trafficking.

Bill had realized that Jaime was hurt in his scuffle with the gunman, but he didn't know how seriously the gunshot wound was until after the two men had been secured.

"It is nothing," Jaime assured him as Bill staunched the blood now flowing more heavily from Jaime's arm. "I'll be okay."

"Sure you will, pard," Bill agreed. "Just let me do a little doctoring here till we get somewhere for help. God, this has been a nasty night!" Placing a tight compress on the injury in Jaime's side, Bill hadn't liked the look of the wound. It appeared to have entered cleanly but there was no exit wound which meant that the bullet was still inside. Forcing Jaime to lie down, Bill explained that he feared too much movement might dislodge the bullet from wherever it had come to rest, and then it could do serious damage. How right could he be? He then changed his own plan of driving to the main road to deposit his charges and had Jaime call once again for help!

By the time the paddy wagon arrived, the two prisoners were loaded, and a second med-evac helicopter was called for Jaime, Clare was sleeping in the front seat of Bill's SUV. Once all the vehicles left, he sat beside Clare for a few minutes then proceeded to tell her the events of the evening in detail. The eastern skyline was beginning to lighten as Bill finished his tale of events of the night from his side. Clare had told him about the wily tricks that James had tried to play on her the year before. The story of Bettina's kidnapping and her subsequent shooting by her step-mother had been painful for Clare to tell but she knew it was time to let it all out. She was sobbing when she finished the tale and fell into Bills willing arms. His embrace was more than that of a friend.

"Clare, Clare," he said as he held her close. "You should have told me about this. I knew some of it, but not all the details…"

Clare jerked out of his arms and stared hard at Bill. "You knew? How did you know?"

"The DEA knew, they'd been investigating James for months and his connection with you led them to find out about your family and the things that happened last year."

"The DEA was spying on me! They thought I had something to do with drugs and ... stuff?"

"No, not really, they just uncovered your relationship with James in the course of checking him out. Then your father made some contacts with people in the area asking that we keep an eye on you. To be sure you were safe."

"Alex had people spying on me too!" Clare was incensed.

"You misunderstand, Clare. Not spying, just looking out to be sure you were safe. You don't seem to realize how much illegal activity goes down on the border. It really isn't safe for anyone to live here alone. You wanted to be left alone. It is only in the past few months that you've started to get out and associate with people. Your father wanted the assurance that you had someone watching out for you. His concern multiplied when he learned that James was involved in the events of last year..."

"He knew," Clare said with resignation. "That is what he was trying to tell me when he called after Myra died. I hung up on him. He wanted me to know that James wasn't my friend and I hung up on him." Clare began sobbing again and, again, Bill's arms comforted her.

"James said he was sorry, do you think he was being truthful?"

"Well, he put his neck on the line when he made a deal to help catch these crooks and he sure sounded concerned when he asked about you. I think it would be a good idea to give him the benefit of the doubt until we find out otherwise. He'll have to answer some questions about things that happened last year and who knows what can of worms that will open. He might end up doing time for that."

"Don't tell me I have to live through that nightmare again, please."

"Maybe not, I'm sure your family and the authorities realize that you've been through a lot. Everyone has been through a lot. They'll probably make a deal with him if he cooperates. Don't worry about that until it comes to pass."

Yeah, I guess you're right. Is he badly hurt" she asked as she regained control of herself.

"He seemed to have taken a good beating. No telling what kind of damage was done internally. His face was smashed up badly but he seemed to have all his senses. We'll just have to wait and see what the doc's say. I suspect he'll be fine, eventually. Now, let's get you home so you can clean up and rest."

Bill was reluctant to take Clare to her empty house, but he needed to get his own emotions under control and fast! He knew the things he was feeling and thinking as far as Clare was concerned they were taboo. Besides, he was going to have to face the music at work shortly and he knew the only way he'd get off the hot seat was by exposing Ron Hall as an informant to the cartel. He just hoped D'Anda would break and implicate the man. He started the SUV and headed down the mountain to the valley below. The sun was just breaking over the distant hills.

Thinking that the danger of the night was a thing of the past, Bill let his mind wander. There were so many things running around in his head. How was Jaime doing? The EMT who had treated him on site wasn't too happy with the injury. The bullet had entered nearer the spine than Bill had realized and appeared at first glance to have caused little injury but on closer examination the EMT was concerned.

"It has to be lodged near the spine. That could be bad. The slightest movement of the impacted bullet could cause serious damage to nerves." Of course, that was just the EMT's opinion. Only x-rays would confirm his worst suspicions. Bill was fearful for Jaime. It seemed that there were always people who suffered when he was involved in an action.

Then there was Clare. He had tried to keep his association with her on a strictly professional level but she had woven a spell over him. He liked being around her, liked looking at her. Hell, *like* wasn't nearly strong enough a word. When he saw her, he got tingly, like a little kid. He remembered his first girlfriend when he was in high school. Clare affected him the same way – he knew he more than liked her but she'd indicated that there was someone else…once anyway. Did he have any chance with her?

Knowing that the difference in their ages might have been considered a problem once, Bill felt that was an obstacle they didn't have to worry about now. In the modern world, marriage to a younger woman wasn't as frowned upon as in the past. Suddenly his mind hiccoughed – MARRIAGE! He wasn't sure that he was ready for that kind of commitment and he was sure that Clare wasn't!

His thoughts were interrupted when another black SUV pulled up close behind him. It didn't take much to ascertain that the new vehicle wasn't DEA, FBI or Border Patrol! He felt his adrenalin begin rushing. What now?

Through his rear view mirror, he saw that the occupants were wearing dark glasses and immediately knew that they met trouble for him.

"Clare, get down!" he ordered as she began to turn in her seat to look behind them.

"DON'T. Don't look back, just get down and stay down." Bill stepped on the accelerator and his SUV shot forward leaving his newly acquired tail in a cloud of dust.

"Damn, there is no way to hide out here. This dust leaves a trail for anyone to follow."

A quick phone call to alert others in the area of his tail and then some fancy driving on the narrow, dusty roads was all he had time for. As he straightened the wheels after one particularly sharp curve, he heard the burst of automatic weapon fire and the ping-ping of bullets. He was grateful for the lined body the government had supplied on some of the vehicles. It wasn't only soldiers in Afghanistan who needed armor plate. Thankfully none of the shells hit vital areas that would have disabled the machine! How long he could expect such luck to last was questionable!

Seeing a turnoff where he could spin his vehicle around, he skidded off the main track and made a 180 degree spin that would have made the best of trick drivers proud. Now, his vehicle facing his antagonist's, he prepared to exit. He gave Clare explicit instructions on what to do in order to assure that they both hit the ground safely.

"Wait till I'm clear of the car, then jump out, keep low and head to the rear of that rock building, don't bother shutting the car door," he ordered almost as an afterthought. Surveying his surroundings as best he could in the dawn light, he continued, "keep down and hide. Help will be here shortly. The others are close and will catch up before we are in any more trouble," he said hoping he sounded more confident than he felt! He was grateful for the tracking device implanted in his vehicle. It would be easy for the others to locate him. Strange, he thought, how things pop into your head at the craziest times!

Clare did as she was told and hit the ground on her belly. Ignoring the weeds that grabbed at her she ran behind a small storage building partially hidden by a large tree. Although she didn't consciously think about it, she was glad that she'd worn blue jeans to work. She usually wore slacks which would have snagged on the wild brambles and bushes that grew so abundantly in the hillsides of the forest. The blue jeans offered a little protection from the stickers and thorns that seemed to be on every desert plant. She hunkered down and began to pray again while picking the thorny stickers she'd picked up in her hands when she hit the ground.

Hearing the other car stop and doors slam, she waited for gunshots, shouts or something…anything. The silence was deafening. Where had Bill gone? Was he safe? Were these men looking for him? For her? Thoughts jumbled about in Clare's mind. Then she heard a burst of gunfire, then silence.

She didn't know how much time passed after the first burst of gunfire, but it was too quiet. She wanted to move, to see something, to hear something. The night animals had stopped making their scurrying sounds and the twitter of the early birds had stopped as soon the unfamiliar noise of gunfire had shattered the usual peaceful forest. She didn't know if it was just one weapon or several. She thought the sounds were different but she didn't know enough about firearms to discern differences in the types of weapons. Then she heard the arrival of more vehicles. She wanted to look, but was afraid to move. Hopefully the new arrivals were good guys but what if they weren't? What if they had shot Bill and were looking for her? The whole night had been filled with vehicles coming and going, good guys and bad guys. She just wanted it all to be over. And she wanted to be home, safe!

Suddenly, the silence was broken by the shouting of the new arrivals. She felt certain that they were the people that Bill had told her were on the way, but she wasn't confident enough to reveal her hiding place. Although she could hear talking, she couldn't understand what was being said on the other side of the building but she knew it was English and that gave her some comfort. Then she saw movement in the weeds nearby.

Thinking someone was crawling through the scrub, probably trying to escape, she tensed. Then she saw it – a snake! Headed directly toward her! She froze. Snakes were one thing that scared Clare beyond reason. She couldn't tell if this was a poisonous viper or not. What was it about the eyes, she struggled to remember? She was too scared to move or even scream. As she watched, the snake came nearer. Was she to have survived all that had happened this night just to get bitten by a snake and die of snakebite? She felt faint. If it touched her she'd die of fright even if it weren't poisonous!

A single shot broke the night air and she watched as the snake coiled into a ring and wriggled, headless, not two feet from her. Looking up, she saw Bill reaching, once again, for her.

She struggled to stand up but couldn't make herself move. Bill reached down and helped her to her feet. She sagged against him… again.

"Clare, it is alright now. We've got them. It was the group D'Anda was supposed to meet up with for his escape. The dummies came looking for him; looks like we got them all now. Come on, these guys can clean up here and we'll go home."

Nothing had ever sounded better to Clare Smith but there was just one more stop Bill planned to make.

CHAPTER 49

Pulling the once shinny SUV to the edge of the road Bill got out and walked to Clare's side of the vehicle just as the sun peaked over the hill and bathed the valley in golden light. He had to tell Clare something before the magic of the moment passed. They had crossed a barrier and he felt now was the time. Now, while there was no danger and nobody to interfere with them.

Without words, they walked to the rim of the overlook. This was one of the sights Bill had found while patrolling the forest with Jaime. It afforded a full view of the Animas Valley. As he walked with Clare to the edge of the road, there was no need for words, they each understood that they needed to breathe the clean fresh air and look upon the unspoiled beauty of the valley now bathed in early morning sunlight. Dirty and exhausted from the grueling night, they stood side by side for a moment quietly staring down at the valley. Grass, green and silky, waved in the early summer breeze. Already dust devils were swirling and twirling across the flats.

"Beautiful, isn't it?" Clare whispered. Her headache had disappeared as the last of the forest trees were blocked from sight by the mountain-high rocks of the Chiricahua National Forest.

"Yes, in a strange way, it is," Bill answered as he gently placed his arm around her shoulders. "Like you once told me. "It grows on you." "But to be honest, I've had enough of the desert."

"I think, maybe I have too," answered Clare.

The FBI, DEA and border patrol vehicles were no more than a dust trail in the distance, the whomp-whomp of helicopter rotors had faded in the sky leaving peace and quiet in their wake. The night of terror was over – not forgotten, but it seemed surreal in the light of day.

"There is something more I need to tell you about myself," Bill turned Clare to face him. "I am working undercover for the DEA; I'm not associated with the border patrol at all. I have been trying to find a leak in the Lordsburg office, and I think I have answers to that mystery. Soon there will be a shakeup in the office and my job will be finished."

Clare didn't seem to understand what he said. She had no reaction to the words he'd just spoken so Bill took another route.

"Clare, I'm going to be leaving here."

"Yes," she replied softly, "I know."

"I'd…"

"No, don't say it. I'm not ready. Not yet."

"But you know how I feel. It's never been like this before…"

"Please, don't say anything more. I value your friendship, but that is all it will ever be, a deep friendship. Remember what I told you?"

"About someone else? Yes, I remember."

Clare took a step nearer the cliff edge and gazed out over the rough terrain. She could see the dust devils develop as weak spirals, strengthen and form their tunnel spinning high in the air, then after dancing in the desert, disintegrating and melting back into the desert floor. She knew that as the heat of the day took control of the air, the devils would be larger and more violent.

She smiled at Bill, placed a tender kiss on his unshaven cheek, and said, "Let's go. There is nothing to talk about here. I need to get home and let my family know that I'm okay. I'll tell you the rest of the story."

"Sure, just like Paul Harvey," Bill smiled and hugged her close to him.

"Yeah," said Clare as she turned to go back to the waiting vehicle.

Bill nodded in assent and taking her hand walked toward the SUV now peppered with gunshots. It, too, had miraculously survived the night, although, like them, a little worse for wear!

CHAPTER 50

The ringing of the telephone broke the silence in the small cluttered office. Boxes holding books, photographs, and hurriedly packed mementos covered the desktop. Finally locating the phone that was hidden beneath a large drawing pad, the well-endowed redhead with a high reedy voice answered with a professional sounding "IBM, Mr. Burch's office." Then she called out loudly, "Steve, it's for you, someone named Clare."

Steve didn't even react to the unprofessional announcement by his secretary. He dropped the books he'd been packing into a box and grabbed the phone from the hand where highly polished nails gingerly released their hold. Normally he'd cringe at her unethical announcement, but he was too thrilled to hear from the love of his life. Clare had never called him at work before. In fact, he couldn't even recall giving her his office phone number. He was unsure if he should be excited or scared by the call.

"Clare," he answered in a cautious voice. "Are you alright?"

"Yes, I'm fine. Now at least. Alex told me you had called him, and he'd told you a little about my exciting experience. Steve, I don't want to talk about it right now, but trust me, I'm fine. Everything is fine and it is going to be even better. I'll tell you all about it sometime but not now so don't even ask."

"Sure, I understand," he said. He really didn't understand at all but he was basking in the warmth of Clare's voice.

"Steve, I need some help."

Immediately he tensed. She'd just said everything was alright, but then said she needed help! Was there more to her recent experience with the smugglers that he hadn't heard about?

"Sure, you know I'd do anything for you." He tried to keep the concern out of his voice.

"Relax, it isn't too bad," Clare assured him recognizing stress in his reply. "Fact is I've decided to relocate. I think I've had enough time alone. I want people around again."

"Clare, that's wonderful news! I'm sure Alex will be able to arrange the entire move and even put you up at the Mansion if you want."

"You don't understand, Steve, I don't plan to go back to Portland. I was thinking about L.A."

Steve was dumbfounded! Before he could say a word, Clare continued, "California Culinary Arts has a school in Pasadena and I can enroll in the next class. I just need to know I have somewhere to live. Will you help me?"

"Heck yeah, you can move in with me if you want. I... I mean I'll help you. I can probably get you an apartment where I'm living; in fact, unless you have a problem with that. I'm located not far from the Pasadena exit. It would be an easy drive for you."

"No problem at all. I do want to be near you. I need to talk to you about so much. I've really had my eyes opened lately and I know what I want to do with my future now. I want you to be a part of that future if you are still interested."

"Clare, you don't know how I've prayed to hear those words!"

Steve's secretary heard his words through the door and let out a big sigh, another dead end. She'd come to California hoping to break into movies but the only offer she'd gotten was as a Julia Roberts double. She'd turned that down knowing that there was only room for one Julia Roberts in movie town. Now she'd had her second dream snatched away. She might have had a chance with Steve Burch if she'd been able to erase the memory of his love from Portland, but from the sound of the one-sided phone conversation she was assured that it wouldn't happen. She shrugged her shoulders and began thinking. She'd need a new plan if she were ever to live the California dream.

EPILOGUE

CLARE SMITH is renovating a new apartment in Los Angles midway between her newly opened and tremendously successful bistro and Steve's job at IBM. They have their wedding rescheduled.

BILL DRIVER has retired from the DEA and now lives near the Pacific Ocean where he can bask in the sun and fish to his heart's content. His feelings for Clare Smith made him reevaluate what he desired out of the rest of his life and he has recently started dating a divorced woman with a teenage son. Their relationship is continuing to grow.

JAMES MILLER was able to work out a deal with the Portland district Attorney's office which included considerable public service, testimony against the two kidnappers of Bettina Goforth when the Federal Government if finished with them. Until then, he is still living in Orlando, managing his charter service (he can no longer pilot due to lasting problems from the beating he received at the hands of D'Anda) and taking care of his mother and aunt. He has stopped drinking and is seeing Michelle again. Their relationship is promising. He does not handle any shady business and allows no long-distance flights or flights out of US airspace by any of his pilots.

RAPHAEL D'ANDA is serving a reduced sentence for arms smuggling and attempted murder in exchange for information about other active drug cartels operating along the US/Mexican border and information about the leaks in the border patrol ranks. His own cartel has been disbanded and absorbed by his rivals.

EDUARDO GUERRERO is presently incarcerated in a Federal prison for his part in the smuggling operation but expects to be released early for good behavior. As a first offender, his sentence was light.

BELINDA GUERRERO is a survivor! Her cancer is in remission and she is anxiously waiting for her husband's release from prison.

ALVARO LOPEZ has just completed a drug rehabilitation program while an inmate of a Federal prison and is currently taking GED classes. He hopes to be released within three years.

ALEXANDER GOFORTH is still retired but more active than ever in his rose propagation experiments. His latest venture is to produce a "masculine" rose which he intends to name Myron after his grandson Alexander Myron Goforth. Little Alex lives near Chicago with his parents Aaron and Margaret who are thrilled at the thought of having a rose named for their firstborn.

BETTINA GOFORTH is in her last year at the university and looking forward to a European vacation before starting her new career as a crime scene investigator.

PANSY MILLER and DAISY SIMPSON continue to live in Orlando where they are both active in rehabilitation services for drug and alcohol addiction.

MARKIE MARKLAND continues to manage Clare's house in Portland. She has moved into the garage apartment and oversees the rental of the house to college students.

STEVEN BURCH is making plans for his honeymoon that will be spent in the Boot Heel of New Mexico where he and Clare plan to spend all of their vacation time as partners in a new fast-food place featuring pizza and Mexican food.

JAIME WELLS is adjusting to life as a medically retired border patrol officer. He raises horses on his property in New Mexico and travels around the state with his wife and his barbeque rig. He has earned quite a reputation as a BBQ Master!

BURRITOS BONITO

Burritos are a staple of Mexican cuisine. They are made from many different types of meat. This recipe is my version of the burrito we found in a small drive-up hole-in-the wall shop in El Paso in 1967.

I usually use either beef round or chuck steak but have been known to cut up a small roast or sirloin steak. You can make it with pork, goat, lamb or ground meat if you prefer. Necessity is the mother of invention and this recipe lends itself to personal inventive techniques as well as any I've ever seen! Instead of potatoes, you might want to try rice and/ or beans or a combination of all three!

1 - 1½ lbs meat (beef, pork, etc) cut in ¼ inch cubes (or ground)
1 – 2 medium to large potatoes cut into ¼ inch cubes (I prefer russets)
1 med onion, finely diced
2 cloves medium sized garlic cloves, finely diced
*1 – 2 jalapeño peppers, finely diced (optional) (you can use any kind
　　of hot pepper)
1 can green pepper/tomato's (with juice such as Ro-Tel) or ¾ cup store-
　　bought or homemade salsa
1 4-oz can tomato sauce
Salt, pepper, cumin, taco seasoning - to taste (optional)
Worchester sauce – to taste (optional)
Red pepper sauce – to taste (optional)
Grated cheddar cheese (optional)
Large flour tortillas

Place diced potatoes in salted water and boil until about half done.

While they cook, brown meat, when brown, removes meat and cook onion and garlic until transparent – do not overcook as garlic will be bitter. Return meat and all seasonings to pan. Add tomato & peppers or salsa and tomato sauce

Drain partially cooked potatoes and add to mixture in pan. Cook down to a nice thick mixture. Remember it will thicken further as it cools. Be sure the potatoes and fork-tender but not mushy!

When a nice thick consistency, allow to cool a little then place filling inside warmed tortilla (it rolls better if it is warm), sprinkle with grated cheese and roll into the traditional burrito shape or you can sprinkle cheese on after rolling and melt under the broiler.

Great for eating as is, or you can toast them on a grill, or even deep-fry for chimichangas.

I like to wrap them in plastic wrap and put in freezer bags. They store well and can be heated in the microwave or grilled as desired.